GAMBLING FEVER

"At the sixteenth Miss Lazy threw up her head like a swimmer going down and dropped back, and Tip-Top was on the King's shoulder. Fifty yards to the finish; twenty-five — then the King staggered as if he'd been hit between the ears, and Tip-Top jumped out to win by a neck.

"There was one big breath of silence in the grand stand — then a groan. I turned my head and saw the two wise guys looking at me with sick grins. Afterward I collected two thousand bucks from a sicker looking bookie."

Connor paused and smiled at the girl.

"That was the 11th of July. First real day of my life."

Books by Max Brand
from The Berkley Publishing Group

THE BIG TRAIL
BORDER GUNS
CHEYENNE GOLD
DAN BARRY'S DAUGHTER
DEVIL HORSE
DRIFTER'S VENGEANCE
THE FASTEST DRAW
FLAMING IRONS
FRONTIER FEUD
THE GALLOPING BRONCOS
THE GAMBLER
THE GARDEN OF EDEN
THE GENTLE GUNMAN
GOLDEN LIGHTNING
GUNMAN'S GOLD
THE GUNS OF DORKING HOLLOW
THE LONG CHASE
LOST WOLF
MIGHTY LOBO
MONTANA RIDES
MYSTERY RANCH
THE NIGHTHAWK TRAIL
ONE MAN POSSE
OUTLAW BREED
OUTLAW'S CODE
THE REVENGE OF BROKEN ARROW
RIDERS OF THE SILENCES
RUSTLERS OF BEACON CREEK
SILVERTIP
SILVERTIP'S CHASE
THE STRANGER
TAMER OF THE WILD
TENDERFOOT
TORTURE TRAIL
TRAILIN'
TRAIL PARTNERS
WAR PARTY

MAX BRAND

THE GARDEN OF EDEN

B

BERKLEY BOOKS, NEW YORK

This Berkley book contains the complete
text of the original edition.

THE GARDEN OF EDEN

A Berkley Book / published by arrangement with
G. P. Putnam's Sons

PRINTING HISTORY
Warner edition / January 1976
Berkley edition / April 1990

ISBN: 0-425-12056-2

A BERKLEY BOOK ® TM 757,375
Berkley Books are published by The Berkley Publishing Group,
200 Madison Avenue, New York, New York 10016.
The name "BERKLEY" and the "B" logo
are trademarks belonging to Berkley Publishing Corporation.

PRINTED IN THE UNITED STATES OF AMERICA

10 9 8 7 6 5 4 3 2

CHAPTER ONE

BY careful tailoring the broad shoulders of Ben Connor
were made to appear fashionably slender, and he disguised
the depth of his chest by a stoop whose model slouched
along Broadway somewhere between sunset and dawn.
He wore, moreover, the first or second pair of spats that
had ever stepped off the train at Lukin Junction, a glowing
Scotch tweed, and a Panama hat of the color and weave
of fine old linen. There was a skeleton at this Feast of
Fashion, however, for only tight gloves could make the
stubby fingers and broad palms of Connor presentable.
At ninety-five in the shade gloves were out of the question,
so he held a pair of yellow chamois in one hand and in
the other an amber-headed cane. This was the end of the
little spur-line, and while the train backed off down the
track, staggering across the switch, Ben Connor looked
after it, leaning upon his cane just forcibly enough to feel
the flection of the wood. This was one of his attitudes of
elegance, and when the train was out of sight, and only
the puffs of white vapor rolled around the shoulder of the
hill, he turned to look the town over, having already given
Lukin Junction ample time to look over Ben Connor.

The little crowd was not through with its survey, but the
eye of the imposing stranger abashed it. He had one of
those long somber faces which Scotchmen call "dour."
The complexion was sallow, heavy pouches of sleepless-
ness lay beneath his eyes, and there were ridges beside the
corners of his mouth which came from an habitual com-
pression of the lips. Looked at in profile he seemed to be
smiling broadly so that the gravity of the full face was
always surprising. It was this that made the townsfolk look
down. After a moment, they glanced back at him hastily.
Somewhere about the corners of his lips or his eyes there
was a glint of interest, a touch of amusement—they could

5

not tell which, but from that moment they were willing to forget the clothes and look at the man.

While Ben Connor was still enjoying the situation, a rotund fellow bore down on him.

"You're Mr. Connor, ain't you? You wired for a room in the hotel? Come on, then. My rig is over here. These your grips?"

He picked up the suit case and the soft leather traveling bag, and led the way to a buckboard at which stood two downheaded ponies.

"Can't we walk?" suggested Ben Connor, looking up and down the street at the dozen sprawling frame houses; but the fat man stared at him with calm pity. He was so fat and so good-natured that even Ben Connor did not impress him greatly.

"Maybe you think this is Lukin?" he asked.

When the other raised his heavy black eyebrows he explained: "This ain't nothing but Lukin Junction. Lukin is clear round the hill. Climb in, Mr. Connor."

Connor laid one hand on the back of the seat, and with surge of his strong shoulders leaped easily into his place; the fat man noted this with a roll of his little eyes, and then took his own place, the old wagon careening toward him as he mounted the step. He sat with his right foot dangling over the side of the buckboard, and a plump shoulder turned fairly upon his passenger so that when he spoke he had to throw his head and jerk out the words; but this was apparently his time-honored position in the wagon, and he did not care to vary it for the sake of conversation. A flap of the loose reins set the horses jog-trotting out of Lukin Junction down a gulch which aimed at the side of an enormous mountain, naked, with no sign of a village or even a single shack among its rocks. Other peaks crowded close on the right and left, with a loftier range behind, running up to scattered summits white with snow and blue with distance. The shadows of the late afternoon were thick as fog in the gulch, and all the lower mountains were already dim so that the snow-peaks in the distance seemed as detached, and high as clouds. Ben Connor sat with his cane between his knees and his hands draped over its amber head and watched those shining places until the fat man heaved his head over his shoulder.

6

"Most like somebody told you about Townsend's Hotel?"

His passenger moved his attention from the mountain to his companion. He was so leisurely about it that it seemed he had not heard.

"Yes," he said, "I was told of the place."

"Who?" said the other expectantly.

"A friend of mine."

The fat man grunted and worked his head around so far that a great wrinkle rolled up his neck close to his ear. He looked into the eye of the stranger.

"Me being Jack Townsend, I'm sort of interested to know things like that; the ones that like my place and them that don't."

Connor nodded, but since he showed no inclination to name his friend, Jack Townsend swung on a new tack to come to the windward of this uncommunicative guest. Lukin was a fairly inquisitive town, and the hotel proprietor usually contributed his due portion and more to the gossips.

"Some comes for one reason and some for another," went on Townsend, "which generally it's to hunt and fish. That ain't funny come to think of it, because outside of liars nobody ever hooked finer trout than what comes out of the Big Sandy. Some of 'em comes for the mining—they was a strike over to South Point last week—and some for the cows, but mostly it's the fishing and the hunting."

He paused, but having waited in vain he said directly: "I can show you the best holes in the Big Sandy."

There was another of those little waits with which, it seemed, the stranger met every remark; not a thoughtful pause, but rather as though he wondered if it were worth while to make any answer.

"I've come here for the silence," he said.

"Silence," repeated Townsend, nodding in the manner of one who does not understand.

Then he flipped the roan with the butt of his lines and squinted down the gulch, for he felt there might be a double meaning in the last remark. Filled with the gloomy conviction that he was bringing a silent man to his hotel, he gloomily surveyed the mountain sides. There was nothing about them to cheer him. The trees were lost in shadows and all the slopes seemed quite barren of

7

life. He vented a little burst of anger by yanking at the rein of the off horse, a dirty gray.

"Giddap, Kitty, damn your eyes!"

The mare jumped, struck a stone with a fore foot, and stumbled heavily. Townsend straightened her out again with an expert hand and cursed.

"Of all the no-good hosses I ever see," he said, inviting the stranger to share in his just wrath, "this Kitty is the outbeatingest, no good rascal. Git on, fool."

He clapped the reins along her back, and puffed his disgust.

"And yet she has points. Now, I ask you, did you ever see a truer Steeldust? Look at that high croup and that straight rump. Look at them hips, I say, and a chest to match 'em. But they ain't any heart in her. Take a hoss through and through," he went on oracularly, "they're pretty much like men, mostly, and if a man ain't got the heart inside, it don't make no difference how big around the chest he measures."

Ben Connor had leaned forward, studying the mare.

"Your horse would be all right in her place," he said. "Of course, she won't do up here in the mountains."

Like any true Westerner of the mountain-desert, Jack Townsend would far rather have been discovered with his hand in the pocket of another man than be observed registering surprise. He looked carefully ahead until his face was straight again. Then he turned.

"Where d'you make out her place to be?" he asked carelessly.

"Down below," said the other without hesitation, and he waved his arm. "Down in soft, sandy irrigation country she'd be a fine animal."

Jack Townsend blinked. "You know her?" he asked.

The other shook his head.

"Well damn my soul!" breathed the hotel proprietor. "This beats me. Maybe you read a hoss's mind, partner?"

Connor shrugged his shoulders, but Townsend no longer took offense at the taciturnity of his companion; he spoke now in a lower confiding voice which indicated an admission of equality.

"You're right. They said she was good, and she *was* good! I seen her run; I saddled her up and rode her thirty miles through sand that would of broke the heart

8

of anything but a Steeldust, and she come through without battin' an eye. But when I got her up here she didn't do no good. But"—he reverted suddenly to his original surprise—"how'd you know her? Recognize the brand, maybe?"

"By her trot," said the other, and he looked across the hills.

They had turned an angle of the gulch, and on a shelf of level ground, dishing out from the side of the mountain, stretched the town.

"Isn't it rather odd," said Connor, "for people to build a town over here when they could have it on the railroad?"

"Maybe it looks queer to some," nodded Townsend.

He closed his lips firmly, determined to imitate the terseness of his guest; but when he observed with a sideglance that Connor would not press the inquiry, talk suddenly overflowed. Indeed, Townsend was a running well of good nature, continually washing all bad temper over the brim.

"I'll show you how it was," he went on. "You see that shoulder of the mountain away off up there? If the light was clearer you'd be able to make out some old shacks up there, half standin' up and half fallin' down. That's where Lukin used to be. Well, the railroad come along and says: 'We're goin' to run a spur into the valley, here. You move down and build your town at the end of the track and we'll give you a hand bringing up new timber for the houses.' That's the way with railroads; they want to dictate; they're too used to handlin' folks back East that'll let capital walk right over their backs."

Here Townsend sent a glance at Connor to see if he stirred under the spur, but there was no sign of irritation.

"Out here we're different; nobody can't step in here and run us unless he's asked. See? We said, you build the railroad halfway and we'll come the other half, but we won't come clear down into the valley."

"Why?" asked Connor. "Isn't Lukin Junction a good place for a village?"

"Fine. None better. But it's the principle of the thing, you see? Them railroad magnates says to us: 'Come all the way.' 'Go to the devil,' says we. And so we come halfway to the new railroad and built our town;

9

It'd be a pile more agreeable to have Lukin over where the railroad ends—look at the way I have to drive back and forth for my trade? But just the same, we showed that railroad that it couldn't talk us down."

He struck his horses savagely with the lines; they sprang from the jog-trot into a canter, and the buckboard went bumping down the main street of Lukin.

CHAPTER TWO

BEN CONNOR sat in his room overlooking the crossing of the streets. It was by no means the ramshackle huddle of lean-to's that he had expected, for Lukin was built to withstand a siege of January snows and storm-winds which were scooped by the mountains into a funnel that focused straight on the village. Besides, Lukin was no accidental, crossroads town, but the bank, store, and amusement center of a big country. The timber was being swept from the Black Mountain; there were fairly prosperous mines in the vicinity; and cattlemen were ranging their cows over the plateaus more and more during the spring and summer. Therefore, Lukin boasted two parallel main streets, and a cross street, looking forward to the day when it should be incorporated and have a mayor of its own. At present it had a moving-picture house and a dance hall where a hundred and fifty couples could take the floor at once; above all, it had Jack Townsend's hotel. This was a stout, timber building of two stories, the lower portion of which was occupied by the restaurant, the drug store, the former saloon now transformed into an ice-cream parlor, and other public places.

It was dark, but the night winds had not yet commenced, and Lukin sweltered with a heat more unbearable than full noon.

It was nothing to Ben Connor, however, for he was fresh from the choking summer nights of Manhattan, and in Lukin, no matter how hot it became, the eye could always find a cool prospect. It had been unpleasant enough when the light was burning, for the room was done in a hot, orange-colored paper, but when he blew out the lamp and sat down before the window he forgot the room and let his glance go out among the mountains. A young moon drifted across the corner of his window, a sickle of light with a dim, phosphorescent line around the rest of the circle. It was bright enough to throw the peaks into strong relief, and dull enough to let the stars live.

His upward vision had as a rule been limited by the higher stories of some skyscraper, and now his eye wandered with a pleasant sense of freedom over the snow summits where he could imagine a cold wind blowing through reach after reach of the blue-gray sky. It pleased and troubled Ben Connor very much as one is pleased and troubled by the first study of a foreign language, with new prospects opening, strange turns of thought, and great unknown names like stars. But after a time Ben Connor relaxed. The first cool puff moved across his forehead and carried him halfway to a dreamless sleep.

Here a chorus of mirth burst up at him from the street, men's voices pitched high and wild, the almost hysterical laughter of people who are much alone. In Manhattan only drunken men laughed like this. Among the mountains it did not irritate Ben Connor; in tune with the rest it was full of freedom. He looked down to the street, and seeing half a dozen bearded fellows frolic in the shaft of light from a window, he decided that people kept their youth longer in Lukin.

All things seemed in order to Connor, this night. He rolled his sleeves higher to let all the air that stirred get at his bulky forearms, and then lighted a cigar. It was a dark, oily Havana—it had cost him a great deal in money and nerves to acquire that habit—and he breathed the scent deep while he waited for the steady wind which Jack Townsend had promised. There was just enough noise to give the silence that waiting quality which cannot be described; below him voices murmured, and lifted now and then, rhythmically. Ben Connor thought the sounds strangely musical, and he began to brim with the same good nature which puffed the cheeks of Jack Townsend.

11

There was a substantial basis for that content in the broiled trout which he had had for dinner. It was while his thoughts drifted back to those browned fish that the first wind struck him. Dust with an acrid scent whirled up from the street—then a steady stream of air swept his face and arms.

It was almost as if another personality had stepped into the room. The sounds from the street fell away, and there was the rustling of cloth somewhere, the cool lifting of hair from his forehead, and an odd sense of motion—as if the wind were blowing through him. But something else came with the breeze, and though he noted it at first with only a subconscious discontent, it beat gradually into his mind, a light ticking, very rapid, and faint, and sounding in an irregular rhythm. He wanted to straighten out that rhythm and make the flutter of tapping regular. Then it began to take on a meaning; it framed words.

"Philip Lord, jailed for embezzlement."

"Hell!" burst out Ben Connor. "The telegraph!"

He started up from his chair, feeling betrayed, for that light, irregular tapping was the voice of the world from which he had fled. A hard, cool mind worked behind the gray eyes of Ben Connor, but as he fingered the cigar his brain was fumbling at a large idea. Forty-Second and Broadway was calling him back.

When he looked out the window, now, the mountains were flat shapes against a flat sky, with no more meaning than a picture.

The sounder was chattering: "Kid Lane wins title in eighth round. Lucky punch dethrones lightweight champion." Ben Connor swallowed hard and found that his throat was dry. He was afraid of himself—afraid that he would go back. He was recalled from his ugly musing by the odor of the cigar, which had burned out and was filling the room with a rank smell; he tossed the crumbled remnants through the window, crushed his hat upon his head, and went down, collarless, coatless, to get on the street in the sound of men's voices. If he had been in Manhattan he would have called up a pal; they would have planned an evening together; but in Lukin—

At the door below he glared up and down the street. There was nothing to see but a light buggy which rolled noiselessly through the dust. A dog detached itself from

12

behind the vehicle and came to bark furiously at his feet. The kicking muscles in Connor's leg began to twitch, but a voice shouted and the mongrel trotted away, growling a challenge over its shoulders. The silence fell once more. He turned and strode back to the desk of the hotel, behind which Jack Townsend sat tilted back in his chair reading a newspaper.

"What's doing in this town of yours tonight?" he asked.

The proprietor moistened a fat thumb to turn the page and looked over his glasses at Connor.

"Appears to me there ain't much stirrin' about," he said. "Except for the movies down the street. You see, everybody's there."

"Movies," muttered Connor under his breath, and looked savagely around him.

What his eyes fell on was a picture of an old, old man on the wall, and the rusted stove which stood in the center of the room with a pipe zigzagging uncertainly toward the ceiling. Everything was out of order, broken down—like himself.

"Looks to me like you're kind of off your feet," said Jack Townsend, and he laid down his paper and looked wistfully at his guest. He made up his mind. "If you're kind of dry for a drink," he said, "I might rustle you a flask of red-eye—"

"Whisky?" echoed Connor, and moistened his lips. Then he shook his head. "Not that."

He went back to the door with steps so long and heavy that Jack Townsend rose from his chair, and spreading his hands on the desk, peered after the muscular figure.

"That gent is a bad hombre," pronounced Jack to himself. He sat down again with a sigh, and added: "Maybe."

At the door Connor was snarling: "Quiet? Sure; like a grave!"

The wind freshened, fell away, and the light, swift ticking sounded again more clearly. It mingled with the alkali scent of the dust—Manhattan and the desert together. He felt a sense of persecuted virtue. But one of his maxims was: "If anything bothers you, go and find out about it."

Ben Connor largely used maxims and epigrams; he met crises by remembering what some one else had said. The ticking of the sounder was making him homesick and

13

dangerously nervous, so he went to find the telegrapher and see the sounder which brought the voice of the world into Lukin.

A few steps carried him to a screen door through which he looked upon a long, narrow office.

In a corner, an electric fan swung back and forth through a hurried arc and fluttered papers here and there. Its whining almost drowned the ticking of the sounder, and Ben Connor wondered with dull irritation how a tapping which was hardly audible at the door of the office could carry to his room in the hotel. He opened the door and entered.

CHAPTER THREE

IT was a room not more than eight feet wide, very long, with the floor, walls, and ceiling of the same narrow, unpainted pine boards; the flooring was worn ragged and the ceiling warped into waves. Across the room a wide plank with a trapdoor at one end served as a counter, and now it was littered with yellow telegraph blanks, and others, crumpled up, were scattered about Connor's feet. No sooner had the screen door squeaked behind him and shut him fairly into the place than the staccato rattling of the sounder multiplied, and seemed to chatter from the wall behind him. It left an echoing in the ear of Ben Connor which formed into the words of his resolution, "I've made my stake and I'm going to beat it. I'm going to get away where I can forget the worries. To-day I beat 'em. To-morrow the worries will beat me."

That was why he was in Lukin—to forget. And here the world has sneaked up on him and whispered in his ear. Was it fair?

It was a woman who "jerked lightning" for Lukin. With that small finger on the key she took the pulse of the world.

"Belmont returns—" chattered the sounder.

14

Connor instinctively covered his ears. Then, feeling that he was acting like a silly child, he lowered his hands.

Another idea had come to him that this was fate—luck —his luck. Why not take another chance?

He wavered a moment, fighting the temptation and gloomily studying the back of the operator. The cheapness of her white cotton dress fairly shouted at him. Also her hair straggled somewhat about the nape of her neck. All this irritated Connor absurdly.

"Fifth race," said the sounder: "Lady Beck, first; Conqueror, second—"

Certainly this was fate tempting tune.

Connor snatched a telegraph blank and scribbled a message to Harry Slocum, his betting commissioner during this unhappy vacation.

"Send dope on Murray handicaps time—trials of Trickster and Caledonian. Hotel Townsend."

This done, having tapped sharply on the counter to call the operator's attention, he dropped his elbows on the plank and scowled downward in profound reverie. They were pouring out of Belmont Park, now, many a grim face and many a joyous face. Money had come easy and gone easy. Ah, the reckless bonhomie of that crowd, living for to-day only, because "to-morrow the ponies may have it!" A good day for the bookies if that old cripple, Lady Beck, had found her running legs. What a trimming they must have given the wise ones!

At this point another hand came into the circle of his vision and turned the telegram about. A pencil flicked across the words, checking them swiftly. Connor was fascinated by that hand, it was so cool, so slender and deft. He glanced up to her face and saw a resolute chin, a smiling mouth which was truly lovely, and direct eyes as dark as his own. She carried her head buoyantly, in a way that made Connor think, with a tingle, of some clean-blooded filly at the post.

The girl made his change, and shoving it across, she bent her head toward the sounder. The characters came through too swiftly for even Ben Connor's sharp ear, but the girl, listening, smiled slowly.

"Something about soft pine?" queried Connor.

She brightened at this unexpected meeting-point. Her eyes widened as she studied him and listened to the message at the same time, and she accomplished this double purpose with such calm that Connor felt a trifle abashed. Then the shadow of listening vanished, and she concentrated on Connor.

"Soft pine is up," she nodded. "I knew it would climb as soon as old Lucas bought in."

"Speculator in Lukin, is he?"

"No. California. The one whose yacht burned at Honolulu last year. Sold pine like wild fire two months ago; down goes the price. Then he bought a little while ago, and now the pine skyrockets. He can buy a new yacht with what he makes, I suppose!"

The shade of listening darkened her eyes again. "Listen!" She raised a hushing forefinger that seemed tremulous in rhythm with the ticking.

"Wide brims are in again," exclaimed the operator, "and wide hats are awful on me; isn't that the luck?"

She went back to her key with the message in her hand, and Connor, dropping his elbows on the counter, watched her send it with swift almost imperceptible flections of her wrist.

Then she sat again with her hands folded in her lap, listening. Connor turned his head and glanced through the door; by squinting he could look over the roof just across the street and see the shadowy mountains beyond; then he looked back again and watched the girl listening to the voice of the outer world. The shock of the contrast soothed. He began to forget about Ben Connor and think of her.

The girl turned in her chair and directly faced him, and he saw that she moved her whole body just as she moved her hand, swiftly, but without a jerk; she considered him gravely.

"Lonely?" she inquired. "Or worried?"

She spoke with such a commonplace intonation that one might have thought it her business to attend to loneliness and worries.

"As a matter of fact," answered Ben Connor, instinctively dodging the direct query, "I've been wondering how they happened to stick a number-one artist on this wire.

"I'm not kidding," he explained hastily. "You see, I used to jerk lightning myself."

16

For the first time she really smiled, and he discovered what a rare thing a smile may be. Up to that point he had thought she lacked something, just as the white dress lacked a touch of color.

"Oh," she nodded. "Been off the wire long?"

Ben Connor grinned. It began with his lips; last of all the dull gray eyes lighted.

"Ever since a hot day in July at Aqueduct. The Lorrimer Handicap on the 11th of July, to be exact. I tossed up my job the next day."

"I see," she said, becoming aware of him again. "You played Tip-Top Second."

"The deuce! Were you at Aqueduct that day?"

"I was here—on the wire." He restrained himself with an effort, for a series of questions was Connor's idea of a dull conversation. He merely rubbed his knuckles against his chin and looked at her wistfully.

"He nipped King Charles and Miss Lazy at the wire and squeezed home by a nose—paid a fat price, I remember," went on the girl. "I suppose you had something down on him?"

"Did a friend of yours play that race?"

"Oh, no; but I was new to the wire, then, and I used to cut in and listen to everything that came by."

"I know. It's like having some one whisper secrets in your ear, at first, isn't it? But you remember the Lorrimer, eh? That was a race!"

The sounder stopped chattering, and by an alternation in her eyes he knew that up to that moment she had been giving two-thirds of her attention to the voice of the wire and the other fraction to him; but now she centered upon him, and he wanted to talk. As if, mysteriously, he could share some of the burden of his unrest with the girl. Most of all he wished to talk because this office had lifted him back to the old days of "lightning jerking," when he worked for a weekly pay check. The same nervous eagerness which had been his in that time was now in this girl, and he responded to it like a call of blood to blood.

"A couple of wise ones took me out to Aqueduct that day: I had all that was coming to me for a month in my pocket, and I kept saying to myself: 'They think I'll fall for this game and drop my wad; here's where I fool 'em!'"

17

He chuckled as he remembered.

"Go on," said the girl. "You make me feel as if *I* were about to make a clean-up!"

"Really interested?"

She fixed an eager glance on him, as though she were judging how far she might let herself go. Suddenly she leaned closer to Connor.

"Interested? I've been taking the world off the wire for six years—and you've been where things happen."

"That's the way I felt at Aqueduct when I saw the ponies parade past the grand stand the first time," he nodded. "They came dancing on the bitt, and even I could see that they weren't made for use; legs that never pulled a wagon, and backs that couldn't weight. Just toys; speed machines; all heart and fire and springy muscles. It made my pulse jump to the fever point to watch them light-foot it along the rail with the groom in front on a clod of a horse. I felt that I'd lived the way that horse walked—downheaded, and I decided to change."

He stopped short and locked his stubby fingers together, frowning at her so that the lines beside his mouth deepened.

"I seem to be telling you the story of my life," he said. Then he saw that she was studying him, not with idle curiosity, but rather as one turns the pages of an absorbing book, never knowing what the next moment will reveal or where the characters will be taken.

"You want to talk; I want to hear you," she said gravely. "Go ahead. Besides—I don't chatter afterward. They paraded past the grand stand, then what?"

Ben Connor sighed.

"I watched four races. The wise guys with me were betting ten bucks on every race and losing on red-hot tips; and every time I picked out the horse that looked good to me, that horse ran in the money. Then they came out for the Lorrimer. One of my friends was betting on King Charles and the other on Miss Lazy. Both of them couldn't win, and the chance was that neither of them would. So I looked over the line as it went by the stand. King Charles was a little chestnut, one of those long fellows that stretch like rubber when they commence running; Miss Lazy was a gangling bay. Yes, they were both good horses, but I looked over the rest, and pretty soon

18

I saw a rangy chestnut with a white foreleg and a midget of a boy in the saddle. 'No. 7—Tip-Top Second,' said the wise guy on my right when I asked him; 'a lame one.' Come to look at him again, he was doing a catch step with his front feet, but I had an idea that when he got going he'd forget all about that catch and run like the wind. Understand?"

"Just a hunch," said the girl. "Yes!"

She stepped closer to the counter and leaned across it. Her eyes were bright. Connor knew that she was seeing that picture of the hot day, the crowd of straw hats stirring wildly, the murmur and cry that went up as the string of racers jogged past.

"They went to the post," said Connor, "and I got down my bet—a hundred dollars, my whole wad—on Tip-Top Second. The bookie looked just once at me, and I'll never forget how his eyebrows went together. I went back to my seat."

"You were shaking all over, I guess," suggested the girl, and her hands were quivering.

"I was not," said Ben Connor, "I was cold through and through, and never moved my eyes off Tip-Top Second. His jockey had a green jacket with two stripes through it, and the green was easy to watch. I saw the crowd go off, and I saw Tip-Top left flat-footed at the post."

The girl drew a breath. Connor smiled at her. The hot evening had flushed his face, but now a small spot of white appeared in either cheek, and his dull eyes had grown expressionless. She knew what he meant when he said that he was cold when he saw the string go to the post.

"It—it must have made you sick!" said the girl.

"Not a bit. I knew the green jacket was going to finish ahead of the rest as well as I knew that my name was Ben Connor. I said he was left at the post. Well, it wasn't exactly that, but when the bunch came streaking out of the shoot, he was half a dozen lengths behind. It was a mile and an eighth race. They went down the back stretch, eight horses all bunched together, and the green jacket drifting that half dozen lengths to the rear. The wise guys turned and grinned at me; then they forgot all about me and began to yell for King Charles and Miss Lazy.

"The bunch were going around the turn and the two favorites were fighting it out together. But I had an eye for the green jacket, and halfway around the turn I saw him move up."

The girl sighed.

"No," Connor continues, "he hadn't won the race yet. And he never should have won it at all, but King Charles was carrying a hundred and thirty-eight pounds, and Miss Lazy a hundred and thirty-three, while Tip-Top Second came in as a fly-weight eighty-seven pounds! No horse in the world could give that much to him when he was right, but who guessed that then?

"They swung around the turn and hit the stretch. Tip-Top took the curve like a cart horse. Then the bunch straightened out, with King Charles and Miss Lazy fighting each other in front and the rest streaking out behind like the tail of a flag. They did that first mile in 1.38, but they broke their hearts doing it, with that weight up.

"They had an eighth to go—one little measly furlong, with Tip-Top in the ruck, and the crowd screaming for King Charles and Miss Lazy; but just exactly at the mile post the leaders flattened. I didn't know it, but the man in front of me dropped his glasses and his head. 'Blown!' he said, and that was all. It seemed to me that the two in front were running as strongly as ever, but Tip-Top was running better. He came streaking, with the boy flattening out along his neck and the whip going up and down. But I didn't stir. I couldn't; my blood was turned to ice water.

"Tip-Top walked by the ruck and got his nose on the hip of King Charles. Somebody was yelling behind me in a squeaky voice: 'There is something wrong! There's something wrong!' There was, too, and it was the eighty-seven pounds that a fool handicapper had put on Tip-Top. At the sixteenth Miss Lazy threw up her head like a swimmer going down and dropped back, and Tip-Top was on the King's shoulder. Fifty yards to the finish; twenty-five—then the King staggered as if he'd been hit between the ears, and Tip-Top jumped out to win by a neck.

"There was one big breath of silence in the grand stand —then a groan. I turned my head and saw the two wise guys looking at me with sick grins. Afterward I collected two thousand bucks from a sicker looking bookie."

He paused and smiled at the girl.

"That was the 11th of July. First real day of my life."

She gathered her mind out of that scene.

20

"You stepped out of a telegraph office, with your finger on the key all day, every day, and you jumped into two thousand dollars?"

After she had stopped speaking her thoughts went on, written in her eyes.

"You'd like to try it, eh?" said Ben Connor.

"Haven't you had years of happiness out of it?"

He looked at her with a grimace.

"Happiness?" he echoed. "Happiness?"

She stepped back so that she put his deeply-marked face in a better light.

"You're a queer one for a winner."

"Sure, the turf is crowded with queer ones like me."

"Winners, all of 'em?"

His eye had been gradually brightening while he talked to her. He felt that the girl rang true, as men ring true, yet there was nothing masculine about her.

"You've heard racing called the sport of kings? That's because only kings can afford to follow the ponies. Kings and Wall Street. But a fellow can't squeeze in without capital. I've made a go of it for a while; pretty soon we all go smash. Sooner or later I'll do what everybody else does—put up my cash on a sure thing and see my money go up in smoke."

"Then why don't you pull out with what you have?"

"Why does the earth keep running around the sun? Because there's a pull. Once you've followed the ponies you'll keep on following 'em. No hope for it. Oh, I've seen the boys come up one after another, make their killings, hit a streak of bad luck, plunge, and then watch their sure-thing throw up its tail in the stretch and fade into the ruck."

He was growing excited as he talked; he was beginning to realize that he must make his break from the turf now or never. And he spoke more to himself than to the girl.

"We all hang on. We play the game till it breaks us and still we stay with it. Here I am, two thousand miles away from the tracks—and sending for dope to make a play! Can you beat that? Well, so-long."

He turned away gloomily.

"Good night, Mr. Connor."

He turned sharply.

21

"Where'd you get that name?" he asked with a trace of suspicion.

"Off the telegram."

He nodded, but said: "I've an idea I've been chattering too much."

"My name is Ruth Manning," answered the girl. "I don't think you've said too much."

He kept his eyes steadily on her while he shook hands.

"I'm glad I know some one in Lukin," said Connor. "Good night, again."

CHAPTER FOUR

WHEN Connor wakened the next morning, after his first impression of blinding light, he closed his eyes and waited for the sense of unhappy doom which usually comes to men of tense nerves and active life after sleep; but, with slow and unpleasant wonder, he realized that the old numbness of brain and fever of pulse was gone. Then he looked up and lazily watched the shadow of the vine at his window move across the ceiling, a dim-bordered shadow continually changing as the wind gathered the leaves in solid masses and shook them out again. He pored upon this for a time, and next he watched a spider spinning a web in the corner; she worked in a draft which repeatedly lifted her from her place before she had fastened her thread, and dropped her a foot or more into space. Connor sat up to admire the artisan's skill and courage. Compared to men and insects, the spider really worked over an abyss two hundred feet deep, suspended by a silken thread. Connor slipped out of bed and stood beneath the growing web while the main cross threads were being fastened. He had been there for some time when, turning away to rub the ache out of the back of his neck, he again met the contrast between the man of this morning and the man of other days.

This time it was his image in the mirror, meeting

him as he turned. That deep wrinkle in the middle of the forehead was half erased. The lips were neither compressed nor loose and shaking, and the eye was calm—it rested him to meet that glance in the mirror.

A mood of idle content always brings one to the window: Connor looked out on the street. A horseman hopped past like a day shadow, the hoofbeats muffled by thick sand, and the wind, moving at an exactly equal pace, carried a mist of dust just behind the horse's tail. Otherwise there was neither life nor color in the street of weatherbeaten, low buildings, and the eye of Connor went beyond the roofs and began to climb the mountains. Here was a bald bright cliff, there a drift of trees, and again a surface of raw clay from which the upper soil had recently slipped; but these were not stopping points—they were rather the steps which led the glance to a sky of pale and transparent blue, and Connor felt a great desire to have that sky over him in place of a ceiling.

He splashed through a hasty bath, dressed, and ran down the stairs, humming. Jack Townsend stood on a box in the corner of the room, probing at a spider web in the corner.

"Too late for breakfast?" asked Connor.

The fat shoulders of the proprietor quivered, but he did not turn.

"Too late," he snapped. "Breakfast over at nine. No favorites up here."

Connor waited for the wave of irritation to rise in him, but to his own surprise he found himself saying:

"All right; you can't throw a good horse off his feed by cutting out one meal."

Jack Townsend faced his guest, rubbing his many-folded chin.

"Don't take long for this mountain air to brace up a gent, does it?" he asked rather pointedly.

"I'll tell you what," said Connor. "It isn't the air so much; it's the people that do a fellow good."

"Well," admitted the proprietor modestly, "they may be something in that. Kind of heartier out here, ain't they? More than in the city, I guess. I'll tell you what," he added. "I'll go out and speak to the missus about a snack for you. It's late, but we like to be obligin'."

23

He climbed carefully down from the box and started away.

"That girl again," thought Connor, and snapped his fingers. His spirits continued to rise, if that were possible, during the breakfast of ham and eggs, and coffee of a taste so metallic that only a copious use of cream made it drinkable. Jack Townsend, recovering to the full his customary good nature, joined his guest in a huge piece of toast with a layer of ham on it—simply to keep a stranger from eating alone, he said—and while he ate he talked about the race. Connor had noticed that the lobby was almost empty.

"They're over lookin' at the hosses," said Townsend, "and gettin' their bets down."

Connor laid down knife and fork, and resumed them hastily, but thereafter his interest in his food was entirely perfunctory. From the corner of his eye a gleam kept steadily upon the face of Townsend, who continued:

"Speaking personal, Mr. Connor, I'd like to have you look over them hosses yourself."

Connor, on the verge of speech, checked himself with a quick effort.

"Because," continued Townsend, "if I had your advice I might get down a little stake on one of 'em. You see?"

Ben Connor paused with a morsel of ham halfway toward his lips.

"Who told you I know anything about horses?" he asked.

"You told me yourself," grinned the proprietor, "and I'd like to figure how you knew the mare come from Ballor Valley."

"From which?"

"From the Ballor Valley. You even named the irrigation and sand and all that. But you'd seen her brand before, I s'pose?"

"Hoofs like hers never came out of these mountains," smiled Ben Connor. "See the way she throws them and how flat they are."

"Well, that's true," nodded Jack Townsend. "It seems simple, now you say what it was, but it had me beat up to now. That is the way with most things. Take a fine hand with a rope. He daubs it on a cow so dead easy any fool thinks he can do the same. No, Mr. Connor, I'd

24

still like to have you come out and take a look at them hosses. Besides"—he lowered his voice—"you might pick up a bit of loose change yourself. They's a plenty rolling round today."

Connor laughed, but there was excitement behind his mirth.

"The fact is, Townsend," he said, "I'm not interested in racing now. I'm up here for the air."

"Sure—sure," said the hotel man. "I know all that. Well, if you're dead set it ain't hardly Christian to lure you into betting on a hoss race, I suppose."

He munched at his sandwich in savage silence, while Connor looked out the window and began to whistle.

"They race very often up here?" he asked carelessly.

"Once in a while."

"A pleasant sport," sighed Connor.

"Ain't it, now?" argued Townsend. "But these gents around here take it so serious that it don't last long."

"That so?"

"Yep. They bet every last dollar they can rake up, and about the second or third race in the year the money's all pooled in two or three pockets. Then the rest go gunnin' for trouble, and most generally find a plenty. Any six races that's got up around here is good for three shooting scrapes, and each shooting's equal to one corpse and half a dozen put away for repairs." He touched his forehead, marked with a white line. "I used to be considerable," he said.

"H-m," murmured Connor, grown absentminded again.

"Yes, sir," went on the other. "I've seen the boys come in from the mines with enough dust to choke a mule, and slap it all down on the hoss. I've seen twenty thousand cold bucks lost and won on a dinky little pinto that wasn't worth twenty dollars hardly. That's how crazy they get."

Connor wiped his forehead.

"Where do they race?" he asked.

"Right down Washington Avenue. That is the main street, y'see. Gives 'em about half a mile of runnin'."

A cigarette appeared with magic speed between the fingers of Connor, and he began to smoke, with deep inhalations, expelling his breath so strongly that the mist shot almost to the ceiling before it flattened into a leisurely spreading cloud. Townsend, fascinated, seemed to have forgotten all about the horse race, but there was in Connor a suggestion of new interest, a certain businesslike coldness.

"Suppose we step over and give the ponies a glance?" he queried.

"That's the talk!" exclaimed Townsend. "And I'll take any tip you have!"

This made Connor look at his host narrowly, but dismissing a suspicion from his mind, he shrugged his shoulders, and they went out together.

The conclave of riders and the betting public had gathered at the farther end of the street, and it included the majority of Lukin. Only the center of the street was left religiously clear, and in this space half a dozen men led horses up and down with ostentatious indifference, stopping often to look after cinches which they had already tested many times. As Connor came up he saw a group of boys place their wagers with a stakeholder—knives, watches, nickels and dimes. That was a fair token of the spirit of the crowd. Wherever Connor looked he saw hands raised, brandishing greenbacks, and for every raised hand there were half a dozen clamorous voices.

"Quite a bit of sporting blood in Lukin, eh?" suggested Townsend.

"Sure," sighed Connor. He looked at the brandished money. "A field of wheat," he murmured, "waiting for the reaper. That's me."

He turned to see his companion pull out a fat wallet.

"Which one?" gasped Townsend. "We ain't got hardly any time."

Connor observed him with a smile that tucked up the corners of his mouth.

"Wait a while, friend. Plenty of time to get stung where the ponies are concerned. We'll look them over."

Townsend began to chatter in his ear; "It's between Charlie Haig's roan and Cliff Jones's Lightning—You see that bay? Man, he can surely get across the ground. But the roan ain't so bad. Oh, no!"

"Sure they are."

The gambler frowned. "I was about to say that there was only one horse in the race, but—" He shook his head despairingly as he looked over the riders. He was hunting automatically for the fleshless face and angular body of a jockey; among them all Charlie Haig came the closest to this light ideal. He was a sun-dried fellow, but even Charlie must have weighed well over a hundred and forty pounds; the others made no pretensions toward small poundage; and Cliff Jones must have scaled two hundred.

"Which was the one hoss in your eyes?" asked the hotel man eagerly.

"The gray. But with that weight up the little fellow will be anchored."

He pointed to a gray gelding which nosed confidently at the back hip pockets of his master.

"Less than fifteen hands," continued Connor, "and a hundred and eighty pounds to break his back. It isn't a race, it's murder to enter a horse handicapped like that."

"The gray?" repeated Jack Townsend, and he glanced from the corner of his eyes at his companion, as though he suspected mockery. "I never seen the gray before," he went on. "Looks sort of underfed, eh?"

Connor apparently did not hear. He had raised his head and his nostrils trembled, so that Townsend did not know whether the queer fellow was about to break into laughter or a trade.

"Yet," muttered Connor, "he might carry it. God, what a horse!"

He still looked at the gelding, and Townsend rubbed his eyes and stared to make sure that he had not over-looked some possibilities in the gelding. But he saw again only a lean-ribbed pony with a long neck and a high croup. The horse wheeled, stepping as clumsily as a gangling yearling. Townsend's amazement changed to suspicion and then to indifference.

"Well," he said, smiling covertly, "are you going to bet on that?"

Connor made no answer. He stepped up to the owner of the gray, a swarthy man of Indian blood. His half sleepy, half sullen expression cleared when Connor shook hands and introduced himself as a lover of fast horseflesh.

He even congratulated the Indian on owning so fine a specimen, at which apparently subtle mockery Townsend, in the rear, set his teeth to keep from smiling; and the

27

big Indian also frowned, to see if there were any hidden insult. But Connor had stepped back and was looking at the forelegs of the gelding.

"There's bone for you," he said exultantly. "More than eight inches, eh—that Cannon?"

"Huh," grunted the owner, "I dunno."

But his last shred of suspicion disappeared as Connor, working his fingers along the shoulder muscles of the animal, smiled with pleasure and admiration.

"My name's Bert Sims," said the Indian, "and I'm glad to know you. Most of the boys in Lukin think my hoss ain't got a chance in this race."

"I think they're right," answered Connor without hesitation.

The eyes of the Indian flashed.

"I think you're putting fifty pounds too much weight on him," explained Connor.

"Yeh?"

"Can't another man ride your horse?"

"Anybody can ride him."

"Then let that fellow yonder—that youngster—have the mount. I'll back the gray to the bottom of my pocket if you do."

"I wouldn't feel hardly natural seeing another man on him," said the Indian. "If he's rode I'll do the riding. I've done it for fifteen years."

"What?"

"Fifteen years."

"Is that horse fifteen years old?" asked Connor, prepared to smile.

"He is eighteen," answered Bert Sims quietly.

The gambler cast a quick glance at Sims and a longer one at the gray. He parted the lips of the horse, and then cursed softly.

"You're right," said Connor. "He is eighteen."

He was frowning in deadly earnestness now.

"Accident, I suppose?"

The Indian merely stared at him.

"Is the horse a strain of blood or an accident? What's his breed?"

"He's an Eden gray."

"Are there more like him?"

28

"The valley's full of 'em, they say," answered Bert Sims.

"What valley?" snapped the gambler.

"I ain't been in it. If I was I wouldn't talk."

"Why not?"

In reply Sims rolled the yellow-stained whites of his eyes slowly toward his interlocutor. He did not turn his head, but a smile gradually began on his lips and spread to a sinister hint at mirth. It put a grim end to the conversation, and Connor turned reluctantly to Townsend. The latter was clamoring.

"They're getting ready for the start. Are you betting on that runt of a gray?"

CHAPTER FIVE

CONNOR shook his head almost sadly. "A horse that stands not a hair more than fourteen-three, eighteen years old, with a hundred and eighty pounds up—No, I'm not a fool."

"Which is it—the roan or the bay?" gasped Townsend. "Which d'you say? I'll tell you about the valley after the race. Which hoss, Mr. Connor?"

Thus appealed to, the gambler straightened and clasped his hands behind his back. He looked coldly at the horses.

"How old is that brown yonder—the one the boy is just mounting?"

"Three. But what's he got to do with the race?"

"He's a shade too young, or he'd win it. That's what he has to do with it. Back Haig's horse, then. The roan is the best bet."

"Have you had a good look at Lightnin'?"

"He won't last in this going with that weight up."

"You're right," panted Townsend. "And I'm going to risk a hundred on him. Hey, Joe, How d'you bet on Charlie Haig?"

"Two to one."

29

"Take you for a hundred. Joe, meet Mr. Connor."

"A hundred it is, Jack. Can I do anything for you, Mr. Connor?"

"I'll go a hundred on the roan, sir."

"Have I done it right?" asked Townsend fiercely, a little later. "I wonder do you know?"

"Ask that after the race is over," smiled Connor. "After all, you have only one horse to be afraid of."

"Sure; Lightnin'—but he's enough."

"Not Lightning, I tell you. The gray is the only horse to be afraid of though the brown stallion might do if he has enough seasoning."

For a moment panic brightened the eyes of Townsend, and then he shook the fear away.

"I've done it now," he said huskily, "and they's no use talking. Let's get down to the finish."

The crowd was streaming away from the start, and headed toward the finish half a mile down the street beyond the farther end of Lukin. Most of this distance Townsend kept his companion close to a run; then he suddenly appealed for a slower pace.

"It's my heart," he explained. "Nothin' else bothers it, but during a hoss race it sure stands on end. I get to thinkin' of what my wife will say if I lose; and that always plumb upsets me."

He was, in fact, spotted white and purple when they joined the mob which packed both sides of the street at the finish posts; already the choice positions were taken.

"We won't get a look," groaned Townsend.

But Connor chuckled: "You tie on to me and we'll get to the front in a squeeze." And he ejected himself into the mob. How it was done Townsend could never understand. They oozed through the thickest of the crowd, and when roughly pressed men ahead of them turned around, ready to fight, Connor was always looking back, apparently forced along by the pressure from the rear. He seemed, indeed, to be struggling to keep his footing, but in a few minutes Townsend found himself in the front rank. He mopped his brow and smiled up into the cool face of Connor, but there was no time for comments. Eight horses fretted in a ragged line far down the street, and as they frisked here and there the brims of the sombreros of the riders flapped up and down; only the Eden gray stood with downward head, dreaming.

"No heart," said Townsend, "in that gray hoss. Look at him!"

"Plenty of head though," replied Connor; "here they go!"

His voice was lost in a yell that went up wailing, shook into a roar, and then died off, as though a gust of wind had cut the sounds away. A murmur of voices followed, and then an almost womanish yell, for Lightning, the favorite, was out in front, and his rider leaned in the saddle with arm suspended and a quirt which never fell. The rest were a close group where whips worked ceaselessly, except that in the rear of all the rest the little gray horse ran without urge, smoothly, as if his rider had given up all hope of winning and merely allowed his horse to canter through.

"D'you see?" screamed Townsend. "Is that what you know about hosses, Mr. Connor? Look at Cliff Jones's Lightning! What do you—"

He cut his upbraidings short, for Connor's was a grisly face, white about the mouth and with gathered brows, as though, with intense effort, he strove to throw the influence of his will into that mass of horse-flesh. The hotel-keeper turned in time to see Lightning, already buckling under the strain, throw up his head.

The heavy burdens, the deep, soft going, and the fact that none of the horses were really trained to sprint, made the half-mile course a very real test, and now the big leader perceptibly weakened. Out of the pack shot a slender brown body, and came to the girth—to the neck of the bay.

"The stallion!" shouted Townsend. "By God, you do know hosses! Who'd of thought that skinny fellow had it in him?"

"He'll die," said Connor calmly.

The bay and the brown went back into the pack together, even as Connor spoke, though the riders were flogging hard, and now the roan drew to the front. It was plain to see that he had the foot of the rest, for he came away from the crowd with every leap.

"Look! Look! Look!" moaned Townsend. "Two for

one! Look!" He choked with pleasure and gripped Connor's arm in both his hands in token of gratitude.

Now the race bore swiftly down the finish, the horses looming bigger; their eyes could be seen, and their straining nostrils now, and the desperate face of each rider, trying to lift his horse into a great burst.

"He's got it," sobbed Townsend, hysterical. "Nothin' can catch him now."

But his companion, in place of answer, stiffened and pointed. His voice was a tone of horror, almost, as he said: "I knew, by God, I knew all the time and wouldn't believe my eyes."

For far from the left, rounding the pack, came a streak of gray. It caught the brown horse and passed him in two leaps; it shot by the laboring bay; and only the roan of Charlie Haig remained in front. That rider, confident of victory, had slipped his quirt over his wrist and was hand-riding his horse when a brief, deep yell of dismay from the crowd made him jerk a glance over his shoulder. He cut the quirt into the flank of the roan, but it was too late. Five lengths from the finish the little gray shoved his nose in front; and from that point, settling toward the earth, as he stretched into a longer and longer stride, every jump increased his margin. The nose of the roan was hardly on the rump of the gelding at the finish.

A bedlam roar came from the crowd. Townsend was cursing and beating time to his oaths with a fat fist. Townsend found so many companion losers that his feelings were readily salved, and he turned to Connor, smiling wryly.

"We can't win every day," he declared, "but I'll tell you this, partner; of all the men I ever seen, you get the medal for judgin' a hoss. You can pick my string any day."

"Eighteen years old," Connor was saying in the monotonous tone of one hypnotized.

"Hey, there," protested Townsend, perceiving that he was on the verge of being ignored.

"A hundred and eighty pounds," sighed the big man.

Townsend saw for the first time that a stop-watch was in the hand of his companion, and now, as Connor began to pace off the distance, the hotel proprietor tagged behind, curious. Twenty steps from the starting point the larger man stopped abruptly, shook his head, and then went on. When he came to the start he paused again, and Townsend found him staring with dull eyes at the face of the watch.

"What'd they make it in?" asked the little man.

The other did not hear.

"They ran from this line?" he queried in a husky voice.

"Sure. Line between them posts."

"Fifty-nine seconds!" he kept repeating. "Fifty-nine seconds! Fifty-nine!"

"What about the fifty-nine seconds?" asked Townsend, and receiving no answer he murmured to himself: "The heat has got to his head."

Connor asked quietly: "Know anything about these gray horses and where they came from?"

"Sure. As much as anybody. Come from yonder in the mountains. A Negro raises 'em. A deaf mute. Ain't ever been heard to say a word."

"And he raises horses like that?"

"Sure."

"And nobody's been up there to try to buy 'em?"

"Too far to go, you see? Long ride and a hard trail. Besides, they's plenty of good hoss-flesh right around Lukin, here."

"Of course," nodded Connor genially. "Of course there is."

"Besides, them grays is too small. Personally, I don't hanker after a runt of a hoss. I look like a fool on one of 'em."

The voice of Connor was full of hearty agreement.

"So do I. Yes, they're small, if they're all like that one. Too small. Much too small."

He looked narrowly at Townsend from the corner of his eyes to make sure that the hotel proprietor suspected nothing.

"This deaf-mute sells some, now and then?"

"Yep. He comes down once in a while and sells a hoss to the first gent he meets—and then walks back to the garden. Always geldings that he sells, I understand. Stand up under work pretty well, those little hosses. Harry Macklin has got one. Harry lives at Fort Andrew. There's a funny yarn about Harry—"

"What price does the mute ask?"

"Thinking of getting one of 'em?"

"Me? Of course not! What do I want with a runt of a horse like that? But I was wondering what they pay around here for little horses."

"I dunno."

"What's that story you were going to tell me about Harry Macklin?"

"You see, it was this way—"

And he poured forth the stale anecdote while they strolled back to the hotel. Connor smiled and nodded at appropriate places, but his absent eyes were seeing, once more, the low-running form of the little gray gelding coming away from the rest of the pack.

CHAPTER SIX

WHEN he arrived at the hotel Ben Connor found the following telegram awaiting him:

Lady Fay in with ninety-eight Trickster did mile and furlong in one fifty-four with one hundred twenty Caledonian stale mile in one thirty-nine Billy Jones looks good track fast.

HARRY SLOCUM.

That message blotted all other thoughts from the mind of Connor. From his traveling bag he brought out a portfolio full of wrinkled papers and pamphlets crowded with lists of names and figures; there followed a time of close work. Page after page of calculations scribbled with a soft pencil and in a large, sprawling hand, were torn from a pad, fluttered through the air and lay where they fell. When the hour was ended he pushed away the pamphlets of "dope" and picked up his notes. After that he sat in deep thought and drove puff after puff of cigarette-smoke at the ceiling.

As his brown study progressed, he began crumpling the slips in his moist fingers until only two remained. These he balanced on his finger-tips as though their weight might speak to his finely attuned nerves. At length, one hand closed slowly over the paper it held and crushed it to a ball. He flicked this away with his thumb and rose. On the remaining paper was written "Trickster." Connor had made his choice.

That done, his expression softened as men relax after a day of mental strain and he loitered down the stairs and into the street. Passing through the lobby he heard the voice of Jack Townsend raised obviously to attract his attention.

"There he goes now. And nothing but the weight kept him from bettin' on the gray."

Connor heard sounds, not words, for his mind was already far away in a club house, waiting for the "ponies" to file past. On the way to the telegraph office he saw neither street nor building nor face, until he had written on one of the yellow blanks, "A thousand on Trickster," and addressed it to Harry Slocum. Not until he shoved the telegram across the counter did he see Ruth Manning.

She was half-turned from the key, but her head was canted toward the chattering sound with a blank, inward look.

"Do you hear?" she cried happily. "Bjornsen is back!"

"Who?" asked Connor.

"Sveynrod Bjornsen. Lost three men out of eight, but he got within a hundred and fifty miles of the pole. Found new land, too."

"Lucky devil, eh?"

But the girl frowned at him.

"Lucky, nothing! Bjornsen is a fighter; he lost his father and his older brother up there three years ago and then he went back to make up for their deaths. Luck?"

Connor, wondering, nodding. "Slipped my mind, that story of Bjornsen. Any other news?"

She made a little gesture, palms up, as though she gathered something from the air.

"News? The old wire has been pouring it at me all morning. Henry Levateŭr went up thirty-two thousand feet yesterday and the Admiral Barr was launched."

Connor kept fairly abreast of the times, but now he was at sea.

"That's the new liner, isn't it?"

"Thirty thousand tons of liner at that. She took the water like a duck. Well, that's the stuff for Uncle Sam to give them; a few more like the Admiral Barr and we'll have the old colors in every port that calls itself a town. Europe will have to wake up."

She counted the telegram with a sweep of her pencil and flipped the change to Connor out of the coin-box. The rattle of the sounder meant new things to Connor; the edges of the world crowded close, for when the noise stopped, in the thick silence he watched her features relax and the light go out of her eyes. It enabled him to glance into her life in Lukin, with only the chattering wire for a companion. A moment before she had been radiant—now she was a tired girl with purple shadows beneath her eyes making them look ghostly large.

"Oh, Bobby," she called. A tall youth came out of an inner room. "Take the key, please; I'm going out for lunch."

"Come to the hotel with me," suggested Connor.

"Lunch at Townsend's?" She laughed with a touch of excitement. "That's a treat."

Already she gained color and her eyes brightened. She was like a motor, Connor decided, nothing in itself, but responding to every electric current.

"This lunch is on me, by the way," she added.

"Why is that?"

"Because I like to pay on my winning days. I cashed in on the Indian's horse this morning."

In Connor's own parlance—it brought him up standing.

"*You* bet on it? You know horse-flesh, then, I like the little fellow, but the weight stopped me."

He smiled at her with a new friendliness.

"Don't pin any flowers on me," she answered. "Oh, I know enough about horses to look at their hocks and see how they stand; and I don't suppose I'd buy in on a pony that points the toe of a fore-foot—but I'm no judge. I bet on the gray because I know the blood."

She had stopped at the door of the hotel and she did not see the change in Connor's face as they entered.

"Queer thing about horses," she continued. "They show their strain, though the finest man that ever stepped might have a son that's a quitter. Not that way with horses. Why, any scrubby pinto that has a drop of Eden Gray

36

blood in him will run till his heart breaks. You can bet on that."

Lunch at Townsend's, Connor saw, must be the fashionable thing in Lukin. The "masses" of those who came to town for the day ate at the lunch-counters in the old saloons while the select went to the hotel. Mrs. Townsend, billowing about the room in a dress of blue with white polka-dots, when she was not making hurried trips into the kitchen, cast one glance of approval at Ben Connor and another of surprise at the girl. Other glances followed, for the room was fairly well filled, and a whisper went trailing about them, before and behind.

It was easy to see that Ruth Manning was being accused of "scraping" acquaintance with the stranger, but she bore up beautifully, and Connor gauging her with an accurate eye, admired and wondered where she had learned. Yet when they found a table and he drew out a chair for her, he could tell from the manner in which she lowered herself into it that she was not used to being seated. That observation gave him a feeling of power over her.

"You liked the gray, too?" she was saying, as he took his place.

"I lost a hundred betting against him," said the gambler quietly. "I hope you made a killing."

He saw by the slight widening of her eyes that a hundred dollars was a good deal of money to her; and she flushed as she answered:

"I got down a bet with Jud Alison; it was only five dollars, but I had odds of ten to one. Fifty dollars looks pretty big to me," she added, and he liked her frankness.

"But does everybody know about these grays?"

"Not so many. They only come from one outfit, you see. Dad knew horses, and he told me an Eden Gray was worth any man's money. Poor Dad!"

Connor watched her eyes turn dark and dull, but he tossed sympathy aside and stepped forward in the business.

"I've been interested since I saw that little streak of gray shoot over the finish. Eighteen years old. Did you know that?"

"Really? Well, Dad said an Eden Gray was good to twenty-five."

"What else did he say?"

"He didn't know a great deal about them, after all, but he said that now and then a deaf and dumb Negro comes. He's a regular giant. Whenever he meets a man he gets off the horse and puts a paper into the hand of the other. On the paper it says: "Fifty dollars in gold coin! Always that.""

It was like a fairy tale to Connor.

"Jude Harper of Collinsville met him once. He had only ten dollars in gold, but he had three hundred in paper. He offered the whole three hundred and ten to the deaf-mute but he only shook his head."

"How often does he come out of the valley?"

"Once a year—once in two years—nobody knows how often. Of course it doesn't take him long to find a man who'll buy a horse like one of the grays for fifty dollars. The minute the horse is sold he turns around and starts walking back. Pete Ricks tried to follow him. He turned back on Pete, jumped on him from behind a rock, and jerked him off his horse. Then he got him by the hair and bent his head back. Pete says he expected to have his neck broken—he was like a child in the arms of that giant. But it seemed that the mute was only telling him in deaf-and-dumb talk that he mustn't follow. After he'd frightened the life out of Pete the big mute went away again, and Pete came home as fast as his horse could carry him."

Connor swallowed. "Where do they get the name Eden Gray?"

"I don't know. Dad said that three things were true about every gray. It's always a gelding; it's always one price, and it always has a flaw. I looked the one over that ran to-day and couldn't see anything wrong, though."

"Cow-hocked," said Connor, breathing hard. "Go on!"

"Dad made up his mind that the reason they didn't sell more horses was because the owner only sold to weed out his stock."

"Wait," said Connor, tapping on the table to make his point. "Do I gather that the only Eden Grays that are sold are the poorest of the lot?"

"That was Dad's idea."

"Go on," said Connor.

"You're excited?"

But he answered quickly: "Well, one of those grays beat me out of a hundred dollars. I can't help being interested.

He detached his watch-charm from its catch and began to finger it carelessly; it was the head of an ape carved in ivory yellowed with age.

The girl watched, fascinated, but she made no mention of it, for the jaw of the gambler was set in a hard line, and she felt, subconsciously, a widening distance between them.

"Does the deaf-mute own the horses?" he was asking.

"I suppose so."

"This sounds like a regular catechism, doesn't it?"

"I don't mind. Come to think of it, everything about the grays is queer. Well, I've never seen this man, but do you know what I think? That he lives off there in the mountains by himself because he's a sort of religious fanatic."

"Religion? Crazy, maybe."

"Maybe."

"What's his religion?"

"I don't know," said the girl coldly. "After you jerk lightning for a while, you aren't interested much in religion."

He nodded, not quite sure of her position, but now her face darkened and she went on, gathering interest in the subject.

"Oh, I've heard 'em rave about the Gód that made the earth and the stars and all that stuff; the mountains, too. I've heard 'em die asking for mercy and praising God. That's the way Dad went. It was drink that got him. But I'm for facts only. Far as I can see, when people come up against a thing they can't understand they just close their eyes and say, God! And when they're due to die, sometimes they're afraid and they say, God—because they think they're going out like a snuffed lantern and never will be lighted again."

The gambler sat with his chin buried in his palm, and from beneath a heavy frown he studied the girl.

"I don't hold malice more than the next one," said the girl, "but I saw Dad; and I've been sick of religion ever since. Besides, how do you explain the rotten things that happen in the world? Look at yesterday! The King of the Sea goes down with all on board. Were they all crooks?

39

Were they all ready to die? They can tell me about God, but I say, 'Give me the proofs!' "

She looked at Connor defiantly. "There's just one thing I believe in," she said, "that's luck!"

He did not stir, but still studied her, and she flushed under the scrutiny.

"Not that I've had enough luck to make me fond of it. I've been stuck up here on the edge of the world all my life. And how I've wanted to get away! How I've wanted it! I've begged for a chance—to cut out the work. If it doesn't make calluses on a girl's hands it will make them on her heart. I've been waiting all my life for a chance, and the chance has never come." Something flared in her.

"Sometimes I think," she whispered, "that I can't stand it! That I'd do anything! Anything—just to get away."

She stopped, as her passion ebbed she was afraid she had said too much.

"Shake," he said, stretching his hand across the table, "I'm with you. Luck! That's all there is running things!"

His fingers closed hard over hers and she winced, for he had forgotten to remove the ivory image from his hand, and the ape-head cut into her flesh.

CHAPTER SEVEN

THAT evening Ruth sent a boy over to the hotel with a telegram for Connor. It announced that Trickster, at six to one, came home a winner in the Murray. But Connor had time for only a grunt and a nod; he was too busy composing a letter to Harry Slocum, which read as follows:

DEAR HARRY:

I'm about to put my head in the lion's mouth; and in case you don't hear from me again, say within three months, this is to ask you to look for my bones. I'm starting out to nail a thousand-to-one shot. Working a hunch for the biggest clean-up we ever made. I'm going into

40

the mountains to find a deaf mute Negro who raises the finest horses I've ever seen. Do you get that? No white man has gone into that valley; at least, no one has come out talking. But I'm going to bring something with me. If I don't come out it'll be because I've been knocked on the head inside the valley. I'm not telling any one around here where I'm bound, but I've made inquiries, and this is what I gather: No one is interested in the mute's valley simply because it's so far away. The mute doesn't bother them and they won't bother him. That's the main reason for letting him alone. The other reasons are that he's suspected of being a bad actor.

But the distance is the chief thing that fences people away. The straight cut is bad going. The better way around is a slow journey. It leads west out of Lukin and down into the valley of the Girard River; then along the Girard to its headwaters. Then through the mountains again to the only entrance to the valley. I'm telling you all this so that you'll know what you may have ahead of you. If I'm mum for three months come straight for Lukin; go to a telegraph operator named Ruth Manning, and tell her that you've come to get track of me. She'll give you the names of the best dozen men in Lukin, and you start for the valley with the posse.

Around Lukin they have a sort of foggy fear of the valley, bad medicine, they call it.

I have a hard game ahead of me and I'm going to stack the cards. I've got to get into the Garden by a trick and get out again the same way. I start this afternoon.

I've got a horse and a pack mule, and I'm going to try my hand at camping out. If I come back it will be on something that will carry both the pack and me, I think, and it won't take long to make the trip. Our days of being rich for ten days and poor for thirty will be over.

Hold yourself ready; sharp at the end of ninety days, come West if I'm still silent.

As ever,

BEN.

Before the mail took that letter eastward, Ben Connor received his final advice from Jack Townsend. It was under the hotel man's supervision that he selected his outfit of soft felt hat, flannel shirts, heavy socks, and

Napatan boots; Townsend, too, went with him to pick out the pack mule and all the elements of the pack, from salt to canned tomatoes.

As for the horse, Townsend merely stood by to admire while Ben Connor went through a dozen possibilities and picked a solidly built chestnut with legs enough for speed in a pinch, and a flexible fetlock—joints that promised an easy gait.

"You won't have no trouble," said Townsend, as Connor sat the saddle, working the stirrups back and forth and frowning at the creaking new leather. "Wherever you go you'll find gents ready to give you a hand on your way."

"Why's that? Don't I look like an old hand at this game?"

"Not with that complexion; it talks city a mile off. If you'd tell me where you're bound for—"

"But I'm not bound anywhere," answered Connor. "I'm out to follow my nose."

"With that gun you ought to get some game."

Connor laid his hand on the butt of the rifle which was slung in a case under his leg. He had little experience with a gun, but he said nothing.

"All trim," continued Townsend, stepping back to look. "Not a flaw in the mule; no sign of ringbone or spavin, and when a mule ain't got them, he's got nothin' wrong. Don't treat him too well. When you feel like pattin' him, cuss him instead. It's mule nature to like a beatin' once in a while; they spoil without it, like kids. He'll hang back for two days, but the third day he'll walk all over your hoss; never was a hoss that could walk with a mule on a long trip. Well, Mr. Connor, I guess you're all fixed, but I'd like to send a boy along to see you get started right."

"Don't worry," smiled Connor. "I've written down all your suggestions."

"Here's what you want to tie on to special," said the fat man. "Don't move your camp on Fridays or the thirteenth: if you came nigh a town and a black cat crosses your trail, you camp right there and don't move on to that town till the next morning. And wait a minute—if you start out and find you've left something in camp, make a cross in the trail before you go back."

He frowned to collect his thoughts.

"Well, if you don't do none of them three things, you can't come out far wrong. S'long, and good luck, Mr. Connor."

Connor waved his hand, touched the chestnut with his heel and the horse broke into a trot, while the rope, coming taut, first stretched the neck of the mule and then tugged him into a dragging amble. In this manner Connor went out of Lukin. He smiled to himself, as he thought confidently of the far different fashion in which he would return.

The first day gave Connor a raw nose, a sunburned neck and wrists, and his supper was charred bacon and tasteless coffee; but the next morning he came out of the choppy mountains and went down a long, easy slope into the valley of the Girard. There was always water here, and fine grass for the horse and mule, with a cool wind off the snows coming down the ravine. By the third day he was broken into the routine of his work and knew the most vulnerable spot on the ribs of the mule, and had a pet name for the chestnut. Thereafter the camping trip was pleasant enough. It took him longer than he had expected, for he would not press the horse as the pitch of the ravine grew steeper; later he saw his wisdom in keeping the chestnut fresh for the final burst, for when he reached the head-spring of the Girard, he faced a confusion of difficult, naked mountains. He was daunted but determined, and the next morning he filled his canteens and struck into the last stage of his journey.

Luck gave him cool weather, with high moving clouds, which curtained the sun during the middle of the day, but even then it was hard work. He had not the vestige of a trail to follow; the mountain sides were bare rock. A scattering of shrubs and dwarfed trees found rooting in crevices, but on the whole Connor was journeying through a sea of stone, and sometimes, when the sun glinted on smooth surface, the reflection blinded him. By noon the chestnut was hobbling, and before nightfall even the mule showed signs of distress. And though Connor traveled now by compass, he was haunted by a continual fear that he might have mistaken his way, or that the directions he had picked up at Lukin might be entirely wrong. Evening was already coming over the mountains when he rounded a slope of black rock and found below him a picture that tallied in every detail with all he had heard of the valley.

The first look was like a glance into a deep well of stone with a flash of water in the bottom; afterward he sat on a boulder and arranged the details of that big vista. Nothing led up to the Garden from any direction; it was a freak of nature. Some convulsion of the earth, when these mountains were first rising, perhaps, had split the rocks, or as the surface strata rolled up, they parted over the central lift and left this ragged fissure. Through the valley ran a river, but water could never have cut those saw-tooth cliffs; and Connor noted this strange thing: that the valley came to abrupt ends both north and south. By the slant sunlight, and at that distance—for he judged the place to be some ten or fifteen miles in length—it seemed as if the cliff fronts to the north and south were as solid and lofty as a portion of the sides; yet this could not be unless the river actually disappeared under the face of the wall. Still, he could not make out details from the distance, only the main outline of the place, the sheen of growing things, whether trees or grass, and the glitter of the river which swelled toward the center of the valley into a lake. He could discover only one natural entrance; in the nearest cliff wall appeared a deep, narrow cleft, which ran to the very floor of the valley, and the only approach was through a difficult ravine. The sore-footed chestnut had caught the flash of green, and now he pricked his ears and whinnied as if he saw home. Connor started down the rocks toward the entrance, leading the horse, while the mule trailed wearily behind. As he turned, the wind blew to him out of the valley a faint rhythmical chiming. When he paused to listen the sound disappeared.

He dipped out of the brighter level into a premature night below; evening was gathering quickly, and with each step Connor felt the misty darkness closing above his head. He was stumbling over the boulders, downheaded, hardly able to see the ground at his feet, yet when he reached the bottom of the little ravine which ran toward the entrance, he looked up to a red sky, and the higher mountains rolled off in waves of light. Distances were magnified; he seemed to look from the bottom of the world to the top of it; he turned, a little dizzy, and between the edges of the cleft that rose straight as Doric pillars, he saw

44

a fire burning at the entrance to the Garden of Eden. The sunset was above them, but the fire sent a long ray through the night of the lower valley. Connor pointed it out to his horse, and the little cavalcade went slowly forward.

CHAPTER EIGHT

WITH every step that he took into the darkness the feeling of awe deepened upon Connor, until he went frowning toward the fire as though it were an eye that watched his coming. He was quite close when the chestnut threw up its head with a snort and stopped, listening; Connor listened as well, and he heard a music of men's voices singing together, faint with distance; the sound traveled so far that he caught the pulse of the rhythm and the fiber of the voices rather than the tune itself, yet the awe which had been growing in Connor gathered suddenly in his throat. He had to close his hands hard to keep from being afraid.

As though the chestnut felt the strangeness also, he neighed suddenly; the rock walls of the ravine caught up the sound and trumpeted it back. Connor recovering from the shock, buried his fingers in the nostrils of the horse and choked the sound away; but the echo still went faintly before them and behind. The alarm had been given. The fire winked once and went out. Connor was left without a light to guide him; he looked up and saw that the sunset flush had fallen away to a dead gray.

He looked ahead to where the fire had been. Just then the horse jerked his nose away and gasped in a new breath. Even that slight sound flurried Connor, for it might guide the unknown danger to him. Connor remembered that after all he was not a bandit stealing upon a peaceful town; he composed his mind again when he saw in the night just before him a deeper shade among the shadows. Peering, he discovered the dim outlines of a man.

Ben Connor was not a coward, but he was daunted by this apparition. His first impulse was to flee; his second was to leap at the other's throat. It spoke much for his steadiness in a crisis that he did neither, but called instead: "Who's there?"

Metal gritted on metal, and a shaft of light poured into Connor's face so unexpectedly that he shrank. The chestnut reared, and turning to control the horse, Connor saw his eyes and the eyes of the mule shining like phosphorus. When he had quieted the gelding he saw that it was a hooded lantern which had been uncovered. Not a ray fell on the bearer of the light.

"I saw a light down here," said Connor, after he had tried in vain to make out the features of the other. "It looked like a fire, and I started for it; I've lost my bearing in these mountains."

Without answering, the bearer of the lantern kept the shaft staring into Connor's face for another moment; then it was as suddenly hooded and welcome darkness covered the gambler. With a gesture which he barely could make out, the silent man waved him forward down the ravine. It angered Connor, this mummery of speechlessness, but with his anger was an odd feeling of helplessness as though the other had a loaded gun at his head.

The man walked behind him as they went forward, and presently the fire shone out at them from the entrance to the valley; thus Connor saw the blanket which had screened the fire removed, and caught a glimpse of a second form.

Even the zenith was dark now, and it was double night in the ravine. With the chestnut stumbling behind him, Connor entered the circle of the fire and was stopped by the raised hand of the second man.

"Why are you here?" said the guard.

The voice was thin, but the articulation thick and soft, and as the questioner stepped into the full glow of the fire, Connor saw a Negro whose head was covered by white curls. He was very old; it seemed as though time had faded his black pigment, and now his skin, a dark bronze, was puckered at the corners of his mouth, about his eyes, and in the center of his forehead, seeming to have dried in wrinkles like parchment. While he talked his expression never varied from the weary frown; yet years had not bowed him, for he stood straight as a youth, and though his neck was dried away until it was no thicker than a strong man's forearm, he kept his head high and looked at Connor.

The man who had gone out to stop Connor now answered for him, and turning to the voice the gambler saw that this fellow was a Negro likewise; as erect as the one by the fire, but hardly less ancient.

"He is lost in the mountains, and he saw the fire at the gate, Ephraim."

Ephraim considered Connor wistfully.

"This way is closed," he said; "you cannot pass through the gate."

The gambler looked up; a wall of rock on either side rose so high that the firelight failed to carry all the distance, and the darkness arched solidly above him. The calm dignity of the men stripped him of an advantage which he felt should be his, but he determined to appear at ease.

"Your best way," continued Ephraim, "is toward that largest mountain. You see where its top is still lighted in the west, while the rest of the range is black.

"Jacob can take you up from the ravine and show you the beginning of the way. But do not pass beyond the sight of the fire, Jacob."

"Good advice," nodded Connor, forcing himself to smile, "if it weren't that my horse is too sore-footed to carry me. Even the mule can hardly walk—you see."

He waved his hand and the chestnut threw up its head and took one or two halting steps to the side.

"In the meantime, I suppose you've no objection if I sit down here for a moment or two?"

Ephraim, bowing as though he ushered the other into an apartment of state, waved to a smooth-topped boulder comfortably near the fire.

"I wish to serve you," he went on, "in anything I can do without leaving the valley. We have a tank just inside the gate, and Jacob will fill your canteen and water the horse and mule as well."

"Kind of you," said Connor. "Cigarette?"

The proffered smoke brought a wrinkling of amazed delight into the face of Ephraim and his withered hand stretched tentatively forth. Jacob forestalled him with a

47

cry and snatched the cigarette from the open palm of Connor. He held it in both his cupped hands.

"Tobacco—again!" He turned to Ephraim. "I have not forgotten!"

Ephraim had folded his arms with dignity, and now he turned a reproving glance upon his companion.

"Is it permitted?" he asked coldly.

The joy went out of the face of Jacob.

"What harm?"

"Is it permitted?" insisted Ephraim.

"He will not ask," argued Jacob dubiously.

"He knows without asking."

At this, very slowly and unwillingly, Jacob put the cigarette back into the hand of Ben Connor. A dozen curious questions came into the mind of the gambler, but he decided wisely to change the subject.

"The boss gives you orders not to leave, eh?" he went on. "Not a step outside the gate? What's the idea?"

"This thing was true in the time of the old masters. Only Joseph can leave the valley," Ephraim answered.

"And you don't know why no one is allowed inside the valley?"

"I have never asked," said Ephraim.

Connor smoked fiercely, peering into the fire.

"Well," he said at length, "you see my troubles? I can't get into the valley to rest up. I have to turn around and try to cross those mountains."

"Yes," nodded Ephraim.

"But the horse and mule will never make it over the rocks. I'll have to leave them behind or stay and starve with them."

"That is true."

"Rather than do that," said Connor, fencing for an opening, "I'd leave the poor devils here to live in the valley."

"That cannot be. No animals are allowed to enter."

"What? You'd allow this pair to die at the gate of the valley?"

"No; I should lead them first into the mountains."

"This is incredible! But I tell you, this horse is my friend—I can't desert him!"

He fumbled in his coat pocket and then stretched out

his hand toward the chestnut; the horse hobbled a few steps nearer and nosed the palm of it expectantly.

"So!" muttered Ephraim, and shaded his eyes with his hand to look. He settled back and said in a different voice: "The horse loves you; it is said."

"I put the matter squarely up to you," said Connor. "You see how I stand. Give me your advice!"

Ephraim protested. "No, no! I cannot advise you. I know nothing of what goes on out yonder. Nevertheless—"

He broke off, for Connor was lighting another cigarette from the butt of the first one, and Ephraim paused to watch, nodding with a sort of vicarious pleasure as he saw Connor inhale deeply and then blow out a thin drift of smoke.

"You were about to say something else when I lighted this."

"Yes, I was about to say that I could not advise you, but I can send to Joseph. He is near us now."

"By all means send to Joseph."

"Jacob," ordered the keeper of the gate, "go to Joseph and tell him what has happened."

The other nodded, and then whistled a long note that drifted up the ravine. Afterward there was no answer, but Jacob remained facing expectantly toward the inside of the valley and presently Connor heard a sound that made his heart leap, the rhythmic hoof-beats of a galloping horse; and even in the darkness the long interval between impacts told him something of the animal's gait. Then into the circle of the firelight broke a gray horse with his tail high, his mane fluttering. He brought his gallop to a mincing trot and came straight toward Jacob, but a yard away he stopped and leaped catlike to one side; with head tossed high he stared at Connor.

Cold sweat stood on the forehead of the gambler, for it was like something he had seen, something he remembered; all his dreams of what a horse should be, come true.

Ephraim was saying sternly:

"In my household the colts are taught better manners, Jacob."

And Jacob answered, greatly perturbed: "There is a wild spirit in all the sons of Harith."

"It is Cassim, is it not?" asked Ephraim.

"Peace, fool!" said Jacob to the stallion, and the horse came and stood behind him, still watching the stranger over the shoulder of his master.

"Years dim your eyes, Ephraim," he continued. "This is not Cassim and he is not the height of Cassim by an inch. No, it is Abra, the son of Hira, who was the daughter of Harith."

He smiled complacently upon Ephraim, nodding his ancient head, and Ephraim frowned.

"It is true that my eyes are not as young as yours, Jacob; but the horses of my household are taught to stand when they are spoken to and not dance like foolish children."

This last reproof was called forth by the continual weaving back and forth of the stallion as he looked at Connor, first from one side of Jacob and then from the other. The old man now turned with a raised hand.

"Stand!" he ordered.

The stallion jerked up his head and became rigid.

"A sharp temper makes a horse without heart," said the oracular Ephraim.

Jacob scowled, and rolling his eyes angrily, searched for a reply; but he found none. Ephraim clapsed one knee tightly in both hands, and weaving his head a little from side to side, delighted in his triumph.

"And the hand which is raised," went on the tormentor, "should always fall."

He was apparently quoting from an authority against which there was no appeal; now he concluded:

"Threats are for children, and yearlings; but a grown horse is above them."

"The spirit of Harith has returned in Abra," said Jacob gloomily. "From that month of April when he was foaled he has been a trial and a burden; yes, if even a cloud blows over the moon he comes to my window and calls me. There was never such a horse since Harith. However, he shall make amends. Abra!"

The stallion stepped nearer and halted, alert.

"Go to him, fool. Go to the stranger and give him your head. Quick!"

The gray horse turned, hesitated, and then came straight to Connor, very slowly; there he bowed his head and dropped his muzzle on the knee of the white man, but all the while his eyes flared at the strange face in terror.

Jacob turned a proud smile upon Ephraim, and the latter nodded.

"It is a good colt," he admitted. "His heart is right, and in time he may grow to some worth."

Once more Connor fumbled in his pocket.

"Steady," he said, looking squarely into the great, bright eyes. "Steady, boy."

He put his hand under the nose of the stallion.

"It's a new smell, but little different."

Abra snorted softly, but though he shook he dared not move. The gambler, with a side glance, saw the two men watching intently.

"Ah," said Connor, "you have pulled against a head-stall here, eh?"

He touched an old scar on the cheek of the horse, and Abra closed his eyes, but opened them again when he discovered that no harm was done to him by the tips of those gentle fingers.

"You may let him have his head again," said Connor. "He will not leave me now until he is ordered."

"So?" exclaimed Jacob. "We shall see! Enough Abra!"

The gray tossed up his head at that word, but after he had taken one step he returned and touched the back of the white man's hand, snuffed at his shoulder and at his hat and then stood with pricking ears. A soft exclamation came in unison from Jacob and Ephraim.

"I have never seen it before," muttered Jacob. "To see it, one would say he was a son of Julanda."

"It is my teaching and not the blood of Julanda that gives my horses manners," corrected Ephraim. "However, if I might look in the hand of the stranger—"

"There is nothing in it," answered Connor, smiling, and he held out both empty palms. "All horses are like this with me."

"Is it true?" they murmured together.

"Yes; I don't know why. But you were going to bring Joseph."

"Ah," said Ephraim, shaking his head. "I had almost forgotten. Hurry, Jacob; but if you will take my advice in the matter you will teach your colts fewer tricks and more sound sense."

The other grunted, and putting his head on the withers of Abra, he leaped to the back with the lightness of a strong youth. A motion of his hand sent the gray into a gallop that shot them through the gate into darkness.

CHAPTER NINE

THAT faint and rhythmic chiming which Connor had heard from the mountain when he first saw the valley now came again through the gate, more clearly. There was something familiar about the sound—yet Connor could not place it.

"Did you mark?" said Ephraim, shaking his head. "Did you see the colt shy at the white rock as he ran? In my household that could never happen; and yet Jacob does well enough, for the blood of Harith is as stubborn as old oak and wild as a wolf. But your gift, sir"—and here he turned with much respect toward Connor—"is a great one. I have never seen Harith's sons come to a man as Abra came to you."

He was surprised to see the stranger staring toward the gate as if he watched a ghost.

"He did not gallop," said Connor presently, and his voice faltered. "He flowed. He poured himself through the air."

He swept a hand across his forehead and with great effort calmed the muscles of his face.

"Are there more horses like that in the valley?"

Ephraim hesitated, for there was such a glittering hunger in the eyes of this stranger that it abashed him. Vanity, however, brushed scruple away.

"More like Abra in the valley? So!"

He seemed to hunt for superlatives with which to overwhelm his questioner.

"The worst in my household is Tabari, the daughter of Numan, and she was foaled lame in the left foreleg. But if ten like Abra were placed in one corral and Tabari in the other, a wise man would give the ten and take the

52

one and render thanks that such good fortune had come his way."

"Is it possible?" exclaimed Connor in that same, small, choked voice.

"I speak calmly," said Ephraim gravely. He added with some hesitation: "But if I must tell the whole truth, I shall admit that my household is not like the household of the blood of Rustir. Just as she was the queen of horses, so those of her blood are above other horses as the master is above me. Yet, if ten like Tabari were placed in one corral and the stallion Glani were placed in another, I suppose that a wise man would give the ten for the one."

He added with a sigh: "But I should not have such wisdom."

"And at that rate it would require a hundred like Abra to buy Glani?" he asked.

"A thousand," said the old man instantly, "and then the full price would not be paid. I have already asked the master to cross him with Hira. He will answer me soon; one touch of Glani's blood will lift the strain in my household. My colts are good mettle—but the fire, the soul of Glani!"

He bowed his head.

"Ah, they are coming, Jacob and Joseph."

His keen ear heard a sound which was not audible to Connor for several moments; then two gray horses swept into the circle of the firelight, and from the mare which led Abra by several yards, a huge Negro dismounted.

"If you are Joseph," the gambler said, "I suppose Jacob has already told you about me. My name is Connor. I've been hunting up the Girard River, struck across the mountains yonder, and here I've brought up with a lame mule and a lamer horse. The point is that I want to rest up in your valley until my animals can go on. Is it possible?"

While he spoke the giant watched him with eyes which squinted in their intensity, but when he ended Joseph answered not a word. Connor remembered now what he had heard of the deaf mute who alone went back and forth from the Garden of Eden and his heart fell. It was talking to a face of stone.

In the meantime Joseph continued to examine the stranger. From head to foot the little bright eyes moved, leisurely, and Connor grew hot as he endured it. When the survey was completed to his own satisfaction, Joseph went first to the mule and next to the horse, lifting their feet one by one, then running his hands over their legs. After this he turned to Jacob and his great fingers glided through the characters of the language of the mute, bunching, knotting, darting out in a fluid swiftness.

"Joseph says," translated Ephraim, "that your horse is lame, but that he can climb the hills if you go on foot; the mule is not lame at all, but is pretending, because he is tired."

An oath rose up in the throat of Connor, but he checked it against his teeth and smiled at Joseph. The big man hissed through his teeth and his mare sprang to his side. She was not more than fourteen two, and slenderly made compared with Abra, yet she had borne the great bulk of Joseph with ease before, and now she was apparently ready to carry him again. He dropped his hand upon her withers, and facing Connor, swept his arm out in a broad gesture of dismissal. Vaguely the gambler noticed this, but his real interest centered on the form of the mare. He was seeing her not with that unwieldly bulk crushing her back, but with a flyweight jockey mounted on a racing pad riding her past the grand stand. He was hearing the odds which the bookies offered; he was watching those odds drop by leaps and bounds as he hammered away at them, betting in lumps of hundreds and five hundreds, staking his fortune on his first "sure thing." Even as she stood passive, tossing her nose, he knew her speed, and it took his breath. Abra himself would walk away from ordinary company, but this gray mare—slowly Connor looked back to the face of Joseph and saw that the giant was waiting to see his command obeyed. For the first time he noted the cartridge belt strung across the fellow's gaunt middle and the holster in which pulled the weight of a forty-five. In case of doubt, here was a cogent reason to hurry a loiterer. To persuade the giant would never have been easy, but to persuade him through an interpreter made the affair impossible. Struggling for a loophole of escape, he absentmindedly unsnapped from his watch chain the little ivory talisman, the ape head, and commenced to finger it. It had been his constant companion for years and in a measure he connected his luck with it.

"My friend," said Connor to Ephraim, "you see my position? But if I can't do better is there any objection to my using this fire of yours for cooking? The fire, at least, is outside the valley."

Even this question Ephraim apparently did not feel qualified to answer. He turned first to the gigantic mute and conversed with him at some length; his own fluent signals were answered by single movements on the part of Joseph, and Connor recognized the signs of dissent.

"I have told him everything," said Ephraim, turning again to Connor and shaking his head in sympathy. "And how Abra came to you, but though the horse trusted you, Joseph does not wish you to stay. I am sorry."

Connor looked through the gate into the darkness of the Garden of Eden; at the entrance to his promised land he was to be turned back. In his despair he opened his palm and looked down absently at the little grinning ape head of ivory. Even while he was deep in thought he felt the silence which settled over the three men, and when he looked up he saw the glittering eyes of Joseph fixed upon the trinket. That instant new hope came to Connor; he closed his hand over the ape head, and turning to Ephraim he said:

"Very well. If there's nothing else for me to do, I'll take the chance of getting through the mountains with my lame nags."

As he spoke he threw the reins over the neck of the chestnut; but before he could put his foot in the stirrup Joseph was beside him and touched his shoulder.

"Wait!" said he, and the gambler paused with astonishment. The mask of the mute which he had hitherto kept on his face now fell from it.

"Let me see," the giant was saying, and held out his hand for the ivory image.

The pulse of Connor doubled its beat—but with his fingers still closed he said:

"The ivory head is an old companion of mine and has brought me a great deal of luck."

The torchlight changed in the eyes of Joseph as the sun glints and glimmers on watered silk.

"I would not hurt it," he said, and made a gingerly motion to show how light and deft his fingers could be.

"Very well," said Connor, "but I rarely let it out of my hand."

He stepped closer to the firelight and exposed the little carving again. It was a curious bit of work, with every detail nicely executed; pinpoint emeralds were inset for eyes, the lips grinned back from tiny fangs of gold, and the swelling neck suggested the powerful ape body of the model. In the firelight the teeth and eyes flashed.

Joseph grinned in sympathy. Ephraim and Jacob also had drawn close, and the white man saw in the three faces one expression: they had become children before a master, and when Connor placed the trinket in the great paw of Joseph the other two flashed at him glances of envy. As for the big man, he was transformed.

"Speak truth," he said suddenly. "Why do you wish to enter the Garden?"

"I've already told you, I think," said Connor. "It's to rest up until the horse and the mule are well again."

The glance of the huge man, which had hitherto wandered from the trinket to Connor's face, now steadied brightly upon the latter.

"There must be another reason."

Connor felt himself pressed to the wall.

"Look at the thing you have in your hand, Joseph. You are asking yourself: 'What is it? Who made it? See how the firelight glitters on it—perhaps there is life in it!' "

"Ah!" sighed the three in one breath.

"Perhaps there is power in it. I have used it well and it has brought me a great deal of good luck. But you would like to know all those things, Joseph. Now look at the gate to the Garden!"

He waved to the lofty and dark cleft before them.

"It is like a face to me. People live behind it. Who are they? Who is the master? What does he do? What is his power? That is another reason why I wish to go in; and why should you fear me? I am alone; I am unarmed."

It seems that Joseph learned more from Connor's expression than from his words.

"The law is the will of David."

The Garden became to Connor as the forbidden room to Bluebeard's wife; it tempted him as a high cliff tempts the climber toward a fall. He mustered a calm air and voice.

"That is a matter I can arrange with your master. He

may have laws to keep out thieves, but certainly he has nothing against honest men."

Joseph shrugged his big shoulders, but Ephraim answered: "The will of David never changes. I am no longer young, but since I have been old enough to remember, I have never seen a man either come into the valley or leave it except Joseph."

The solemnity of the old man staggered Connor. He felt his resolution to enter at any cost waver, and then Abra, the young stallion, came to his side, and looked in his face.

It was the decisive touch. The life which the devotee would risk for his God, or the patriot for his country, the gambler was willing to venture for the sake of a "sure thing."

"Let us exchange gifts," said Connor; "I give you the ivory head. It may bring you good luck. You give me the right to enter the valley and I accept any good or evil that comes to me."

The huge fingers of Joseph curled softly over the image.

"Beware of the law!" cried Ephraim. "And the hand of the master!"

The giant shrank, but he looked at Ephraim with sullen defiance.

"Come," he said to Connor. "This is on your own head."

CHAPTER TEN

"IT is a long ride to the house of David," said Jacob. "Your horse is footsore; take Abra."

But Ephraim broke in: "If you care for speed and wise feet beneath you, Tabari herself is there."

"Those of my household answer when they are called," continued the old man proudly. "Listen!"

A soft whinny out of the darkness, and Tabari galloped into the firelight, and stopped at the side of her master motionless.

"Choose," said Ephraim.

He smiled at Jacob, who in return was darkly silent.

The mare tugged at the heartstrings of Connor, but he answered, slipping carefully into the formal language which apparently was approved most in the valley.

"She is worthy of a king, but Abra was offered to me first. But will he carry a saddle?"

"He will carry anything but a whip," said Jacob, casting a glance of triumph at Ephraim. "You will see!" He was already busy at the knot under the flap of Connor's saddle, and presently he slipped the saddle from the back of the chestnut. "Come!" he called.

Abra came, but he came like a fighter into the ring, dancing, ready for trouble.

"Fool!" shouted Jacob, stamping. "Fool, and grandson of a fool, stand!"

The ears of Abra flickered back along his neck and he trembled as the saddle was swung over him. Under its impact he crouched and shuddered, but the outbreak of bucking for which Connor waited did not come. The jerk on the cinch brought a snort from him, but that was all.

"We may not put iron in his mouth," said Jacob, as Connor came up with the bridle, "but a touch on this will turn him or stop him, as you wish."

As he spoke he picked up a small rope, which he knotted around the neck of Abra close to the ears, and handed the end to Connor.

"Look!" he said to the horse, pointing to Connor. "This is your master to-night. Bear him as you would bear me, Abra, without leaping or stumbling, smoothly, as son of Khalissa should do. And hark," he added in the ear of the young stallion; "if the mare of Joseph outruns you, you are no horse of my household, but a mongrel, a bloodless knave."

Joseph was already trotting through the gate and growing dim beyond, so Connor put his foot in the stirrup and swung into the saddle. He landed as upon springs, all Connor felt a quivering power beneath him like the lithe body of the stallion giving under the shock; and vibration of a racing motor. Abra's eyes glinted as he threw his head high to take stock of the new master.

"Go," commanded Jacob; "and remember your speed, for the honor of him who trained you!"

The last words were whipped away from the ear of Connor and trailed into a murmur behind him, for without a preliminary step Abra sprang from a stand into a full gallop. That forward lurch swayed Connor far back; he lost touch with his stirrups, but, clinging desperately with his knees, he was presently able to right himself. There was hard gravel beneath them, but the gait was as soft as if Abra ran in deep sand without labor; there was no more wrench and shock than the ghost of a man riding a ghost of a horse.

A column of black shot by-on either hand; Connor was through the gate to the Garden of Eden and rushing down the slope beyond. He knew this dimly, but chiefly he was aware only of the whipping of the wind. Something Ephraim had said came into his memory: "If there were ten like Abra in one corral, and one like Tabari in another, a wise man—" But, no doubt, Ephraim had jested.

For, glancing up, he saw the tops of tall trees rushing past him against the sky, and for the first time he knew the speed of that gallop. In his exultation he threw up his hands, and his shout rang before him and behind. That taught him a lesson he would never forget when he sat the saddle on an Eden Gray; for Abra lurched into a run with a suddenness that swayed Connor against the cantle again.

He steadied himself quickly and called to Abra; the first word cut down that racing gait to the long, free stride, but the brief rush had taken the breath of the rider, and now he looked about him.

He had been in California years before, and now he recognized the peculiar, clean perfume of the trees which lined the road; they were the eucalyptus, and they fenced the way with a gigantic hedge several rows deep. It was a winding road that they followed, dipping over a rolling ground and swinging leisurely from side to side to avoid high places, so that the vista of the trees was continually in motion, twisting back and forth; or when he looked straight up he saw the slender tree-points brushing past the stars. So he galloped into a long, straight stretch with a pale gleam of water beyond it; and between he saw Joseph.

It was strange that in spite of the speed of Abra, Joseph's mare had not been overtaken; for no matter what

59

quality the mare might have, she carried in the gigantic Negro an impost of some two hundred and fifty pounds. A suspicion of discourtesy on his part must have come to Joseph, for now he brought his horse back to a canter that allowed Connor to come close; so close indeed that he saw Joseph laughing in a horrible soundless way and beckoning him on, very much as though he challenged Abra. Surely the fellow must know that no horse could concede such weight to Abra, but Connor waved his arm to signify that he accepted the challenge, and called on Abra.

There followed the breathless lunge forward, the sinking of the body as the stride lengthened, the whir of wind against his face; Connor sat the saddle erect, smiling, and waited for Joseph to come back to him.

But Joseph did not come, and as the mare reached the river and her hoofs rang on the bridge Connor saw with unspeakable wonder that he had actually lost ground. Once more he called on Abra, and as they struck the bridge in turn the young stallion was fully extended, while Connor swung forward in the saddle to throw more weight on the withers and take the strain from the long back muscles. Leaning close to the neck of Abra, with the mane whipping his face, he squinted down the road at Joseph, and growled with savage satisfaction as he saw the mare drift back to him. If he could reach her with a sprint she was beaten, for she bore the extra burden. Once more he called on Abra, and heard a slight grunt as the stallion gave the last burst of his strength; the hoofs of the two roared on the hard road, and Joseph came back hand over hand. Connor, laughing exultantly, squinted into the wind.

"Good boy!" he muttered. "Good old Abra! If he had Salvator under him we'd get him at this rate. We're on his hip—Now!"

He was indeed in touch with the flying mare, and looking through the dimness, he marveled at her long, free swing, the level drive of the croup, and—he saw with astonishment—her pricking ears! Not as if she were racing, but merely galloping. He flattened himself along the neck of Abra and called on him again, slapped his shoulder with the flat of his hand, flicked him along the flank with the butt of the rope; but the mare held him invincibly; he could not gain the breadth of a hair, and by the pounding of Abra's forefeet he knew that the stallion was running himself out. At that moment, to crown his bewilderment, Joseph turned, laughing again in that soundless way. Only for a moment; then he turned, and, leaning over the withers of his mount, the mare lengthened, it seemed to Connor, and moved away.

Her hips went past him, then her tail, flying out straight behind, a streak of silver; and last of all, there was the hiss of derision from Joseph whistling back to him.

Connor threw himself back into the saddle and brought the stallion down to a moderate pace. One hand was clutched at his throat, for it seemed to him that his heart was beating there. Before him raced a vision of Ben Connor, king of the racetracks of the world, with horses no handicapper could measure.

CHAPTER ELEVEN

A SECOND thought made him lean a little, listening closely, and then he discovered that after this terrific trial Abra was breathing deep and free. Connor sat straight again and smiled. They must be close to the lake he had seen from the mountain, for among the trees to his left was a faint gleam of water. A moment later this glimmer went out, and the hoofbeats of Abra were muffled on turf. They had left the road and headed for a scattering of lights. Joseph had drawn the mare back to a hand-gallop, and Abra followed the example; at this rocking gait they swept through the grove between two long, low buildings, always climbing, and came suddenly upon a larger house. On three sides Connor looked down upon water; the building was behind him. Not a light showed in it, but he made out the low, single story, the sense of weight, and crude arches of the Mission style. Through an opening in the center of the façade he looked into darkness which he knew must be the patio.

Following the example of Joseph, he dismounted, and

while the big man, with his waddling, difficult walk, disappeared into the court, Connor stepped back and looked over Abra. Starlight was enough to see him by, for he glimmered with running sweat even in the semi-darkness, but it was plain from his high head and inquisitive muzzle that he was neither winded nor down-hearted. He followed Connor like a dog when the gambler went in turn to the mare. She turned about nervously to watch the newcomer. Not until Abra had touched noses with her and perhaps spoken to her the dumb horse-talk would she allow Connor to come close, and even then he could not see her as clearly as the stallion. By running his fingertips over her he discovered the reason—only on the flanks and across the breast was she wet with perspiration, and barely moist on the thighs and belly. The race had winded her no more than a six-furlong canter.

He was still marveling at this discovery when Joseph appeared under the arch carrying a lantern and beckoned him in, leading the way to a large patio, surrounded by a continuous arcade. In the center a fountain was alternately silver and shadow in the swinging lantern light. The floor of the patio was close-shaven turf.

Joseph hung the lantern on the inside of one of the arches and turned to Connor, apparently to invite him to take one of the chairs under the arcade. Instead, he raised his hand to impose silence. Connor heard, from some distance, a harsh sound of breathing of inconceivable strength. For though it was plainly not close to them, he could mark each intake and expulsion of breath. And the noise created for him the picture of a monster.

"Let us go to the master," said Joseph, and turned straight across the patio in the direction of that sonorous breathing.

Connor followed, by no means at ease. From the withered old men to huge Joseph had been a long step. How far would be the reach between Joseph himself and the omnipotent master?

He passed in the track of Joseph toward the rear of the patio. Presently the big man halted, removed his hat, and faced a door beneath the arcade. It was only a momentary interruption. He went on again at once, replacing his hat, but the thrill of apprehension was still tingling in the blood of the gambler. Now they went under the arcade, through an open door, and issued in the rear of the house, Connor's imaginary "monster" dissolved.

For they stood in front of a blacksmith shop, the side toward them being entirely open so that Connor could see the whole interior. Two sooty lanterns hung from the rafters, the light tangling among wreaths of smoke above and showing below a man whose back was turned toward them as he worked a great snoring bellows with one hand.

That bellows was the source of the mysterious breathing. Connor chuckled; all mysteries dissolved as this had done the moment one confronted them. He left off chuckling to admire the ease with which the blacksmith handled the bellows. A massive angle of iron was buried in the forge, the white flames spurting around it as the bellows blew, casting the smith into high relief at every pulse of the fire. Sometimes it ran on the great muscles of the arm that kept the bellows in play; sometimes it ran a dazzling outline around his entire body, showing the leather apron and the black hair which flooded down about his shoulders.

"Who—" began Connor.

"Hush," cautioned Joseph in a whisper. "David speaks when he chooses—not sooner."

Here the smith laid hold on the iron with long pincers, and, raising it from the coals, at once the shop burst with white light as David placed the iron on the anvil and caught up a short-handled sledge. He whirled it and brought it down with a clangor. The sparks spurted into the night, dropping to the ground and turning red at the very feet of Connor. Slowly David turned the iron, the steady shower of blows bending it, changing it, molding it under the eye of the gambler. This was that clangor which had floated through the clear mountain air to him when he first gazed down on the valley; this was the bell-like murmur which had washed down to him through the gates of the valley.

At least it was easy to understand why the servants feared him. A full fourteen pounds was in the head of that sledge, Connor guessed, yet David whirled it with a light and deft precision. Only the shuddering of the anvil told the weight of those blows. Meantime, with every leap of the spark-showers the gambler studied the face of the master. They were features of strength rather than beauty from the frowning forehead to the craggy jaw. A sort of fierce happiness lived in that face now, the thought of the craftsman and the joy of the laborer in his strength.

As the white heat passed from the iron and it no longer flowed into a shape so readily under the hammer of the smith, a change came in him. Connor knew nothing of ironcraft, but he guessed shrewdly that another man would have softened the metal with fire again at this point. Instead, David chose to soften it with strength. The steady patter of blows increased to a thundering rain as the iron turned a dark and darker red.

The rhythm of the worker grew swifter, did not break, and Connor watched with a keen eye of appreciation. Just as a great thoroughbred makes its supreme effort in the stretch by a lengthening and slight quickening of stride, but never a dropping into the choppy pace of unskilled labor at speed, so the man at the anvil was now rocking steadily back and forth from heel to toe, the knees unflexing a little as he struck and stiffening as he swung up the hammer. The greater effort was told only by the greater ring of the hammer face on the hardening iron—by that and by the shudder of the arm of the smith as the fourteen pounds went clanging home to the stroke.

And now the iron was quite dark—the smith stood with the ponderous sledge poised above his head and turned the bar swiftly, with study, to see that the angle was exactly what he wished. The hammer did not descend again on the iron; the smith was content, and plunging the big angle iron into the tempering tub, his burly shoulders were obscured for a moment by a rising cloud of steam.

He stepped out of this and came directly to them. Now the lantern was behind him, he was silhouetted in black, a mighty figure. He was panting from his labor, and the heavy sound of his breathing disturbed the gambler. He had expected to find a wise and simple old man in David. Instead, he was face to face with a Hercules.

His attention was directed entirely to Joseph.

"I come from my work unclean," he said. "Joseph, take the stranger within and wait."

Joseph led back into the patio to a plain wooden table beside which Connor, at the gesture of invitation, sat down. Here Joseph left him hurriedly, and the gambler looked about. The arcade was lightened by a flagging of crystalline white stone, and the ceiling was inlaid with the same material. But the arches and the wall of the building were of common dobe, massive, but roughly built.

Beyond the fountain nodded like a ghost in the patio, and now and then, when the lantern was swayed by the wind, the pool glinted and was black again. The silence was beginning to make him feel more than ever like an unwelcome guest when another old Negro came, and Connor noted with growing wonder the third of these ancients. Each of them must have been in youth a fine specimen of manhood. Even in white-headed age they retained some of that noble countenance which remains to those who have once been strong. This fellow bore a tray upon his arm, and in the free hand carried a large yellow cloth of a coarse weave.

He placed on the table a wooden trencher with a great loaf of white bread, a cone of clear honey, and an earthen pitcher of milk. Next he put a wooden bowl on a chair beside Connor, and when the latter obediently extended his hands, the old man poured warm water over them and dried them with a napkin.

There was a ceremony about this that fitted perfectly with the surroundings, and Connor became thoughtful. He was to tempt the master with the wealth of the world, but what could he give the man to replace his Homeric comfort?

In the midst of these reflections soft steps approached him, and he saw the brown-faced David coming in a shapeless blouse and trousers of rough cloth, with moccasins on his feet. Rising to meet his host, he was surprised to find that David had no advantage in height and a small one in breadth of shoulder; in the blacksmith shop he had seemed a giant. The brown man stopped beside the table. He seemed to be around thirty, but because of the unwrinkled forehead Connor decided that he was probably five years older.

"I am David," he said, without offering his hand.

"I," said the gambler, "am Benjamin."

There was a flash that might have been either pleasure or suspicion in the face of David.

"Joseph has told me what has passed between you," he said.

"I hope he's broken no law by letting me come in."

"My will is the law; in disregarding me he has broken a law."

He made a sign above his shoulder that brought Joseph hurrying out of the gloom, his keen eyes fastened upon the face of the master with intolerable anxiety. There was another sign from David and Joseph, without a glance at Connor, snatched the ivory head out of his pocket, thrust it upon the table, and stood back, watching the brown man with fascination.

"You see," went on David, "that he returns to you the price which you paid him. Therefore you have no longer a right to remain in the Garden of Eden."

Connor flushed. "If this were a price," he answered, clinging as closely as he could to language as simple and direct as that of David, "it could be returned to me. But it is not a price. It is a gift, and gifts cannot be returned."

He held out the ape-head, and when Joseph could see nothing save the face of David, he pushed the trinket back toward the huge man.

"Then," said the brown man, "the fault which was small before is now grown large."

He looked calmly upon Joseph and the giant quailed. By the table hung a gong on which the master tapped; one of the ancient servants appeared instantly.

"Go to my room," said David, "and bring me the largest nugget from the chest."

The old man disappeared, and while they waited for his return the little bright eyes of Joseph went to and fro on the face of the master; but David was staring into the darkness of the patio. The servant brought a nugget of gold, as large as the doubled fist of a child, and the master rolled it across the table to Connor.

A tenseness about his mouth told the gambler that

much was staked on this acceptance. He turned the nugget in his hand, noting the discoloration of the ore from which it had been taken.

"It is a fine specimen," he said.

"You will see," said David, "both its size and weight."

And Connor knew; it was an exchange for the ivory head. He laid the nugget carelessly back upon the table, thankful that the gift had been offered with such suspicious bluntness.

"It is a fine specimen," he repeated, "but I am not collecting."

There was a heavy cloud on the face of David as he took up the nugget and passed it into the hand of the waiting servant; but his glance was for Joseph, not Connor.

Joseph burst into speech for the first time, and the words tumbled out.

"I do not want it. I shall not keep it. See, David; I give it up to him!" He made a gesture with both hands as though he would push away the ape-head forever.

The master looked earnestly at Connor.

The latter shrugged his shoulders, saying: "I've never taken back a gift, and I can't begin now."

Connor's heart was beating rapidly, from the excitement of the strange interview and the sense of his narrow escape from banishment. Because he had made the gift to Joseph he had an inalienable right, it seemed, to expect some return from Joseph's master—even permission to stay in the valley, if he insisted.

There was another of those uncomfortable pauses, with the master looking sternly into the night.

"Zacharias," he said.

The servant stepped beside him.

"Bring the whip—and the cup."

The eyes of Zacharias rolled once toward Joseph and then he was gone, running; he returned almost instantly with a seven foot blacksnake, oiled until it glistened. He put it in the hand of David, but only when Joseph stepped back, shuddering, and then turned and kneeled before David, the significance of that whip came home to Connor, sickening him. The whites of Joseph's eyes rolled at him and Connor stepped between Joseph and the whip.

"Do you mean this?" he gasped. "Do you mean to say

that you are going to flog that poor fellow because he took a gift from me?"

"From you it was a gift," answered the master, perfectly calm, "but to him it was a price. And to me it is a great trouble."

"God!" murmured Connor.

"Do you call on him?" asked the brown man severely. "He is only here in so far as I am the agent of his justice. Yet I trust it is not more His will than it is the will of David. Also, the heart of Joseph is stubborn and must be humbled. Tears are the sign of contrition, and the whip shall not cease to fall until Joseph weeps."

His glance pushed Connor back; the gambler saw the lash whirled, he turned his back sharply before it fell. Even so, the impact of the lash on flesh cut into Connor, for he had only to take back the gift to end the flogging. He set his teeth. Could he give up his only hold on David and the Eden Grays? By the whizzing of the lash he knew that it was laid on with the full strength of that muscular arm. Now a horrible murmur from the throat of Joseph forced him to turn against his will.

The face of David was filled, not with anger, but with cruel disdain; under his flying lash the welts leaped up on the back of Joseph, but he, with his eyes shut and his head strained far back, endured. Only through his teeth, each time he drew breath, came that stifled moan, and he shuddered at each impact of the whip. Now his eyes opened, and through the mist of pain a brutal hatred glimmered at Connor. That flare of rage seemed to sap the last of his strength, for now his face convulsed, tears flooded down, and his head dropped. Instantly the hand of David paused.

Something had snapped in Connor at the same time that the head of Joseph fell, and while he wiped the wet from his face he only vaguely saw Joseph hurry down the corridor, with Zacharias carrying the whip behind.

But the master? There was neither cruelty nor anger in his face as he turned to the table and filled with milk the wooden cup which Zacharias had brought.

"This is my prayer," he said quietly, "that in the justice of David there may never be the poison of David's wrath."

He drained the cup, broke a morsel of bread from the

loaf and ate it. Next he filled the second cup and handed it to the gambler.

"Drink."

Automatically Connor obeyed.

"Eat."

In turn he tasted the bread.

"And now," said the master, in the deep, calm voice, "you have drunk with David in his house, and he has broken bread with you. Hereafter may there be peace and good will between us. You have given a free gift to one of my people, and he who gives clothes to David's people keeps David from the shame of nakedness; and he who puts bread in the mouths of David's servants feeds David himself. Stay with me, therefore, Benjamin, until you find in the Garden the thing you desire, then take it and go your way. But until that time, what is David's is Benjamin's; your will be my will, and my way be your way."

He paused.

"And now, Benjamin, you are weary?"

"Very tired."

"Follow me."

It seemed well to Connor to remove himself from the eye of the master as soon as possible. Not that the host showed signs of anger, but just as one looks at a clear sky and forebodes hard weather because of misty horizons, so the gambler guessed the frown behind David's eyes. He was glad to turn into the door which was opened for him. But even though he guessed the danger, Connor could not refrain from tempting Providence with a speech of double meaning.

"You are very kind," he said. "Good night, David."

"May God keep you until the morning, Benjamin."

CHAPTER TWELVE

FROM the house of David, Joseph skulked down the terraces until he came to the two long buildings and entered the smaller of these. He crossed a patio, smaller than the court of David's house; but there, too, was the fountain in the center and the cool flooring of turf. Across this, and running under the dimly lighted arcade, Joseph reached a door which he tore open, slammed behind him again, and with his great head fallen upon his chest, stared at a little withered Negro who sat on a stool opposite the door. It was rather a low bench of wood than a stool; for it stood not more than six inches above the level of the floor. His shoes off, and his bare feet tucked under his legs, he sat tailorwise and peered up at the giant. The sudden opening of the door had set his loose blouse fluttering about the old man's skeleton body. The sleeves fell back from bony forearms with puckered skin. He was less a man than a receptacle of time. His temples sank in like the temples of a very old horse; his toothless mouth was crushed together by the pressure of the long bony jaw, below which the skin hung in a flap. But the fire still glimmered in the hollows of his eyes. A cheerful spirit lived in the grasshopper body. He was knitting with a pair of slender needles, never looking at his work, nor during the interview with Joseph did he once slacken his pace. The needles clicked with such swift precision that the work grew perceptibly, flowing slowly under his hands.

Meanwhile this death's head looked at the giant so steadily that Joseph seemed to regret his unceremonious entrance. He stood back against the door, fumbling its knob for a moment, but then his rage mastered him once more, and he burst into the tale of Connor's coming and the ivory head. He brought his story to an end by depositing the trinket before the ancient man and then stood back, his face still working, and waited with every show of confident curiosity.

As for the antique, his knitting needles continued to fly, but to view the little carving more closely he craned his skinny neck. At that moment, with his fallen features, his fleshless nose, he was a grinning mummy head. He remained gloating over the little image so long that Joseph stirred uneasily; but finally the grotesque lifted his head. It at once fell back, the neck muscles apparently unable to support its weight. He looked more at the ceiling than at Joseph. His speech was a writhing of the lips and the voice a hollow murmur.

"This," he said, "is the face of a great suhman. It is the face of the great suhman, Haneemar. It was many years ago that I knew him. It was before your birth and the birth of your father. It was when I lived in a green country where the air is thick and sweet and the sun burns. There I knew Haneemar. He is a strong suhman. You see, his eyes are green; that is because he has the strength of the great snake that ties its tail around a branch and hangs down with its head as high as the breast of a man. Those snakes kill an antelope and eat it at a mouthful. Their eyes are green and so are the eyes of Haneemar. And you see that Haneemar has golden teeth. That is because he has eaten wisdom. He knows the meat of all things like a nut he can crack between his teeth. He is as strong as the snake which eats monkeys, and he is as wise as the monkeys that run from the snake and throw sticks from the tops of the trees. That is Haneemar.

"There is no luck for the man who carries the face of Haneemar with him. That is why David uses the whip. He knew Haneemar. Also, in the other days I remember that when a child was sick in the village they tied a goat in the forest and Haneemar came and ate the goat. If he ate the goat like a lion and left tooth marks on the bones then the child got well and lived. If he ate the goat like a panther and left the guts the child died. But if the goat was not eaten for one day then Haneemar came and ate the child instead. I remember this. There will be no luck for you while you carry Haneemar."

The big man heard this speech with eyes that grew rounder and rounder. Now he caught up the little image and raised his arm to throw it through the window. But the old man hissed, and Joseph turned with a shudder.

"You cannot throw Haneemar away," said the other. "Only when some one takes him freely will you be rid of him."

"It is true," answered Joseph. "I remember the visitor would not take him back."

"Then," said the old sage, "if the stranger will not take him back, bad luck has come into the Garden, for only the stranger would carry Haneemar out again. But do not give Haneemar to one of our friends, for then he will stay with us all. If you dig a deep hole and bury him in it, Haneemar may not be able to get out."

Joseph was beginning to swell with wrath.

"The stranger has put a curse on me," he said. "Abraham, what shall I do to him? Teach me a curse to put on him!"

"Hush!" answered Abraham. "Those who pray to evil spirits are the slaves of the powers they pray to."

"Then I shall take this Benjamin in my hands!"

He made a gesture as though he were snapping a stick of dry wood.

"You are the greater fool. Is not this Benjamin, this stranger, a guest of the master?"

"I shall steal him away by night in such a manner that he shall not make the noise of a mouse when the cat breaks its back. I shall steal him away and David will never know."

The loose eyelids of the old man puckered and his glance became a ray of light.

"The curse already works; Hannemar already is in your mind, Joseph. David will not know? Child, there is nothing that he does not know. He uses us. We are his tools. My mind is to him as my hand is to me. He comes inside my eyes; he knows what I think. And if old Abraham is nothing before David, what is Joseph? Hush! Let not a whisper go out! Do not even dare to think it. You have felt the whip of David, but you have not felt his hand when he is in anger. A wounded mountain lion is not so terrible as the rage of David; he would be to you as an ax at the root of a sapling. These things have happened before. I remember. Did not Boram once anger John? And was not Boram as great as Joseph? And did not John take Boram in his hands and conquer him and break him? Yes, and David is a greater body and a stronger hand than John. Also, his anger is as free as the running of an untaught colt. Remember, my son!"

Joseph stretched out his enormous arms and his voice was a broken wail.

"Oh, Abraham, Abraham, what shall I do?"

"Wait," said the old man quietly. "For waiting makes the spirit strong. Look at Abraham! His body has been dead these twenty years, but still his spirit lives."

"But the curse of Haneemar, Abraham?"

"Haneemar is patient. Let Joseph be patient also."

CHAPTER THIRTEEN

CONNOR wakened in the gray hour of the morning, but beyond the window the world was much brighter than his room. The pale terraces went down to scattered trees, and beyond the trees was the water of the lake. Farther still the mountains rolled up into a brighter morning. A horse neighed out of the dawn; the sound came ringing to Connor, and he was suddenly eager to be outside.

In the patio the fountain was still playing. As for the house, he found it far less imposing than it had been when lantern light picked out details here and there. The walls and the clumsy arches were the disagreeable color of dried mud and all under the arcade was dismal shadow. But the lawn was already a faintly shining green, and the fountain went up above the ground shadow in a column of light. He passed on. The outside wall had that squat, crumbling appearance which every one knows who has been in Mexico—and through an avenue of trees he saw the two buildings between which he had ridden the night before. From the longer a man was leading one of the gray horses. This, then, was the stable; the building opposite it was a duplicate on a smaller scale of the house of David, and must be the servants' quarters.

Connor went on toward a hilltop which alone topped

the site of the master's house; the crest was naked of trees, and over the tops of the surrounding ones Connor found that he commanded a complete view of the valley. The day before, looking from the far-off mountaintop, it had seemed to be a straight line very nearly, from the north to the south; now he saw that from the center both ends swung westward. The valley might be twelve miles long, and two or three wide, fenced by an unbroken wall of cliffs. Over the northern barrier poured a white line of water, which ran on through the valley in a river that widened above David's house into a spacious lake three or four miles long. The river began again from the end of the lake and continued straight to the base of the southern cliffs. Roads followed the swing of the river closely on each side, and the stream was bridged at each end of the lake. His angle of vision was so small that both extremities of the valley seemed a solid forest, but in the central portion he made out broad meadow lands and plowed fields checkering the groves. The house, as he had guessed the evening before, stood into the lake on a slender peninsula. And due west a narrow slit of light told of the gate into the Garden. It gave him a curiously confused emotion, as of a prisoner and spy in one.

He had walked back almost to the edge of the clearing when David, from the other side went up to the crest of the hill. Connor was already among the trees and he watched unobserved. The master of the Garden, at the top of the hill, paused and turned toward Connor. The gambler flushed; he was about to step out and hail his host when a second thought assured him that he could not have been noticed behind that screen of shrubbery and trunks; moreover the glance of David Eden passed high above him. It might have been the cry of a hawk that made him turn so sharply; but through several minutes he remained without moving either hand or head, and as though he were waiting. Even in the distance Connor marked the smile of happy expectation. If it had been another place and another man Connor would have thought it a lover waiting for his mistress.

But, above all, he was glad of the opportunity to see David and remain unseen. He realized that the evening before it had been difficult to look directly into David's

74

face. He had carried away little more than impressions; of strength, dignity, a surface calm and strong passions under it; but now he was able to see the face. It was full of contradiction; a profile irregular and deeply cut, but the full face had a touch of nobility that made it almost handsome.

As he watched, Connor thought he detected a growing excitement in David—his head was raised, his smile had deepened. Perhaps he came here to rejoice in his possessions; but a moment later Connor realized that this could not be the case, for the gaze of the other must be fixed as high as the mountain peaks.

At that instant came the revelation; there was a stiffening of the whole body of David; his breast filled and he swayed forward and raised almost on tiptoe. Connor, by sympathy, grew tense—and then the miracle happened. Over the face of David fell a sudden radiance. His hair, dull black the moment before, now glistened with light, and the swarthy skin became a shining bronze; his lips parted as though he drank in strength and happiness out of that miraculous light.

The hard-headed Connor was staggered. Back on his mind rushed a score of details, the background of this picture. He remembered the almost superhuman strength of Joseph; he saw again the old servants withering with many years, but still bright-eyed, straight and agile. Perhaps they, too, knew how to stand here and drink in a mysterious light which filled their outworn bodies with youth of the spirit, at least. And David? Was not this the reason that he scorned the world? Here was his treasure past reckoning, this fountain of youth. Here was the explanation, too, of that intolerable brightness of his eye. The gambler bowed his head.

When he looked up again his soul had traveled higher and lower in one instant than it had ever moved before; he was staring like a child. Above all, he wanted to see the face of David again, to examine that mysterious change, but the master was already walking down the hill and had almost reached the circle of the trees on the opposite side of the slope. But now Connor noted a difference everywhere surrounding him. The air was warmer; the wind seemed to have changed its fiber; and then he saw that the treetops opposite him were shaking and glistening in a glory of light. Connor went limp and leaned against a tree, laughing weakly, silently.

"Hell," he said at length, recovering himself. "It was only the sunrise! And me—I thought—"

He began to laugh again, aloud, and the sound was caught up by the hillside and thrown back at him in a sharp echo. Connor went thoughtfully back to the house. In the patio he found the table near the fountain laid with a cloth, the wood scrubbed white, and on it the heavy earthenware. David Eden came in with the calm, the same eye, difficult to meet. Indeed, then and thereafter when he was with David, he found himself continually looking away, and resorting to little maneuvers to divert the glance of his host.

"Good morrow," said David.

"I have kept you waiting?" asked Connor.

The master paused to make sure that he had understood the speech, then replied:

"If I had been hungry I should have eaten."

There was no rebuff in that quiet statement, but it opened another door to Connor's understanding.

"Take this chair," said David, moving it from the end of the table to the side. "Sitting here you can look through the gate of the patio and down to the lake. It is not pleasant to have four walls about one; but that is a thing which Isaac cannot understand."

The gambler nodded, and to show that he could be as unceremonious as his host, sat down without further words. He broke a morsel from the loaf of bread, which was yet the only food on the table, and turned to the East with a solemn face.

"Out of His hands from whom I take this food," said the master—"into His hands I give myself."

He sat down in turn, and Isaac came instantly with the breakfast. It was an astonishing menu to one accustomed to toast and coffee for the morning meal. On a great wooden platter which occupied half the surface of the table, Isaac put down two chickens, roasted brown. A horn-handled hunting knife, razor sharp, was the only implement at each place, and fingers must serve as forks. To David that was a small impediment. Under the deft edge of his knife the breast of one chicken divided rapidly; he ate the white slices like bread. Indeed, the example

76

was easy to follow; the mountain air had given him a vigorous appetite, and when Connor next looked up it was at the sound of glass tinkling. He saw Isaac holding toward the master a bucket of water in which a bottle was immersed almost to the cork; David tried the temperature of the water with his fingers with a critical air, and then nodded to Isaac, who instantly drew the cork. A moment later red wine was trickling into Connor's cup. He viewed it with grateful astonishment, but David, poising his cup, looked across at his guest with a puzzled air.

"In the old days," he said gravely, "when my masters drank they spoke to one another in a kindly fashion. It is now five years since a man has sat at my table, and I am moved to say this to you, Benjamin: it is pleasant to speak to another not as a master who must be obeyed, but as an equal who may be answered, and this is my wish, that if I have doubts of Benjamin, and unfriendly thoughts, they may disappear with the wine we drink."

"Thank you," said Connor, and a thrill went through him as he met the eye of David. "That wish is my wish also—and long life to you, David."

There was a glint of pleasure in the face of David, and they drank together.

"By Heaven," cried Connor, putting down the cup, "it is Médoc! It is Château Lafite, upon my life!"

He tasted it again.

"And the vintage of '96! Is that true?"

David shook his head.

"I have never heard of Médoc or Château Lafite."

"At least," said Connor, raising his cup and breathing the delicate bouquet, "this wine is Bordeaux you imported from France? The grapes which made this never grew outside of the Gironde!"

But David smiled.

"In the north of the Garden," he said, "there are some low rolling hills, Benjamin; and there the grapes grow from which we make this wine."

Connor tasted the claret again. His respect for David had suddenly mounted; the hermit seemed nearer to him.

"You grew these grapes in your valley?" he repeated softly.

"This very bottle we are drinking," said David, warming to the talk. "I remember when the grapes of this vintage were picked; I was a boy, then."

"I believe it," answered Connor solemnly, and he raised the cup with a reverent hand, so that the sun filtered into the red and filled the liquid with dancing points of light.

"It is a full twenty years old."

"It is twenty-five years old," said David calmly, "and this is the best vintage in ten years." He sighed. "It is now in its perfect prime and next year it will not be the same. You shall help me finish the stock, Benjamin."

"You need not urge me," smiled Connor.

He shook his head again.

"But that is one wine I could have vowed I knew—Médoc. At least, I can tell you the soil it grows in."

The brows of the host raised; he began to listen intently.

"It is a mixture of gravel, quartz and sand," continued Connor.

"True!" exclaimed David and looked at his guest with new eyes.

"And two feet underneath there is a stone for subsoil which is a sort of sand or fine gravel cemented together."

David struck his hands together, frankly delighted.

"This is marvelous," he said, "I would say you have seen the hills."

"I paid a price for what I know," said Connor rather gloomily. "But north of Bordeaux in France there is a strip of land called the Médoc—the finest wine soil in the world, and there I learned what claret may be—there I tasted Château Lafite and Château Datour. They are both grown in the commune of Pauillac."

"France?" echoed David, with the misty eyes of one who speaks of a lost world. "Ah, you have traveled?"

"Wherever fine horses race," said Connor, and turned back to the chicken.

"Think," said David suddenly, "for five years I have lived in silence. There have been voices about me, but never mind; and now you here, and already you have taken me at a step half-way around the world.

"Ah, Benjamin, it is possible for an emptiness to be in a manlike hunger, you understand, and yet different—and nothing but a human voice can fill the space."

"Have you no wish to leave your valley for a little

while and see the world?" said Connor, carelessly.

He watched gloomily, while an expression of strong distaste grew on the face of David. He was still frowning when he answered:

"We will not speak of it again."

He jerked his head up and cleared away his frown with an effort.

"To speak with one man in the Garden—that is one thing," he went on, "but to hear the voices of two jabbering and gibbering together—grinning like mindless creatures—throwing their hands out to help their words, as poor Joseph does—bah, it is like drinking new wine; it makes one sick. It made me so five times."

"Five times?" said Connor. "You have traveled a good deal, then?"

"Too much," sighed David. "And each time I returned from Parkin Crossing I have cared less for what lies outside the valley."

"Parkin Crossing?"

"I have been told that there are five hundred people in the city," said David, pronouncing the number slowly. "But when I was there, I was never able to count more than fifty, I believe."

Connor found it necessary to cough.

"And each time you have left the valley you have gone no farther than Parkin Crossing?" he asked mildly, his spirits rising.

"And is not that far enough?" replied the master, frowning. "It is a ride between dawn and dark."

"What is that in miles?"

"A hundred and thirty miles," said David, "or thereabout."

Connor closed his eyes twice and then: "You rode that distance between dawn and dark?"

"Yes."

"Over these mountains most of the way?" he continued gently.

"About half the distance," answered David.

"And how long"—queried Connor hoarsely—"how long before your horse was able to make the trip back after you had ridden a hundred and thirty miles in twelve hours?"

"The next day," said David, "I always return."

"In the same time?"

"In the same time," said David.

To doubt that simple voice was impossible. But Connor knew horses, and his credence was strained to the breaking point.

"I should like very much," he said, "to see a horse that had covered two hundred and sixty miles within forty-eight hours." ·

"Thirty-six," corrected David.

Connor swallowed.

"Thirty-six," he murmured faintly.

"I shall send for him," said the master, and struck the little gong which stood on one side of the table. Isaac came hurrying with that light step which made Connor forget his age.

"Bring Glani," said David.

Isaac hurried across the patio, and David continued talking to his guest.

"Glani is not friendly; but you can see him from a distance."

"And yet," said Connor, "the other horses in the Garden seem as friendly as pet dogs. Is Glani naturally vicious?"

"His is of other blood," replied David. "He is the blood of the great mare Rustir, and all in her line are meant for one man only. He is more proud than all the rest."

He leaned back in his chair and his face, naturally stern, grew tender.

"Since he was foaled no hand has touched him except mine; no other has ridden him, groomed him, fed him."

"I'll be glad to see him," said Connor quietly. "For I have never yet found a horse which would not come to my hand."

As he spoke, he looked straight into the eyes of David, with an effort, and at the same time took from the pocket of his coat a little bulbous root which was always with him. A Viennese who came from a life half spent in the Orient had given him a small box of those herbs as a priceless present. For the secret was that when the root was rubbed over the hands it left a faint odor on the skin, like freshly cut apples; and to a horse that perfume was irresistible. They seemed to find in it a picture of sweet clover, blossoming, and clean oats finely headed; yet to

80

the nostrils of a man the scent was barely perceptible. Under cover of the table the gambler rubbed his hands swiftly with the little root and dropped it back into his pocket. That was the secret of the power over Abra which had astonished the two old men at the gate. A hundred times, in stable and paddock, Connor had gone up to the most intractable race horses and looked them over at close hand, at his leisure. The master seemed in nowise disturbed by the last remark of Connor.

"That is true of old Abraham, also," he said. "There was never a colt foaled in the valley which Abraham had not been able to call away from its mother; he can read the souls of them all with a touch of his withered hands. Yes, I have seen that twenty times. But with Glani it is different. He is as proud as a man; he is fierce as a wolf; and Abraham himself cannot touch the neck of my horse. Look!"

CHAPTER FOURTEEN

UNDER the arch of the entrance Connor saw a gray stallion, naked of halter or rope, with his head raised. From the shadow he came shining into the sunlight; the wind raised his mane and tail in ripples of silver. Ben Connor rose slowly from his chair. Horses were religion to him; he felt now that he had stepped into the inner shrine.

When he was able to speak he turned slowly toward David. "Sir," he said hoarsely, "that is the greatest horse ever bred."

It was far more than a word of praise; it was a confession of faith which surrounded the moment and the stallion with solemnity, and David flushed like a proud boy.

"There he stands," he said. "Now make him come to your hand."

It recalled Connor to his senses, that challenge, and

feeling that his mind had been snatched away from him for a moment, almost that he had been betrayed, he looked at David with a pale face.

"He is too far away," he said. "Bring him closer."

There was one of those pauses which often come before crises, and Connor knew that by the outcome of this test he would be judged either a man or a cheap boaster.

"I shall do this thing," said the master of the Garden of Eden. "If you bring Glani to your hand I shall give him to you to ride while you stay in the valley. Listen! No other man had so much as laid a hand on the withers of Glani, but if you can make him come to you of his own free will—"

"No," said Connor calmly. "I shall make him come because my will is stronger than his."

"Impossible!" burst out David.

He controlled himself and looked at Connor with an almost wistful defiance.

"I hold to this," he said. "If you can bring Glani to your hand, he is yours while you stay in the Garden—for my part, I shall find another mount."

Connor slipped his right hand into his pocket and crushed the little root against the palm.

"Come hither, Glani," commanded the master. The stallion came up behind David's chair, looking fearlessly at the stranger.

"Now," said David with scorn. "This is your time."

"I accept it," replied Connor.

He drew his hand from his pocket, and leaning over the table, he looked straight into the eye of the stallion. But in reality, it was only to bring that right hand closer; the wind was stirring behind him, and he knew that it wafted the scent of the mysterious root straight to Glani.

"That is impossible," said David, following the glance of Connor with a frown. "A horse has no reasoning brain. Silence cannot make him come to you."

"However," said Connor carelessly, "I shall not speak."

The master set his teeth over unuttered words, and glancing up to reassure himself, his face altered swiftly, and he whispered:

"Now, you four dead masters, bear witness to this marvel! Glani feels the influence!"

For the head of Glani had raised as he scented the wind. Then he circled the table and came straight toward Connor. Within a pace, the scent of strange humanity must have drowned the perfume of the root; he sprang away, catlike and snorted his suspicion.

David heaved a great sigh of relief.

"You fail!" he cried, and snatching up a bottle of wine he poured out a cup. "Brave Glani! I drink this in your honor!"

Every muscle in David's strong body was quivering, as though he were throwing all the effort of his will on the side of the stallion.

"You think I have failed?" asked Connor softly.

"Admit it," said David.

His flush was gone and he was paler than Connor now; he seemed to desire with all his might that the test should end; there was a fiber of entreaty in his voice.

"Admit it, Benjamin, as I admit your strange power."

"I have hardly begun. Give me quiet."

David flung himself into his chair, his attention jerking from Glani to Connor and back. It was at this critical moment that a faint breeze puffed across the patio, carrying the imperceptible fragrance of the root straight to Glani. Connor watched the stallion prick up his ears, and he blessed the quaint old Viennese with all his heart.

The first approach of Glani had been in the nature of a feint, but now that he was sure, he went with all the directness of unspoiled courage straight to the stranger. He lowered the beautiful head and thrust out his nose until it touched the hand of Connor. The gambler saw David shudder.

"You have conquered," he said, forcing out the words. "Take Glani; to me he is now a small thing. He is yours while you stay in the Garden. Afterward I shall give him to one of my servants."

Connor stood up, and though at his rising Glani started back, he came to Connor again, following that elusive scent. To David it seemed the last struggle of the horse before completely submitting to the rule of a new master. He rose in turn, trembling with shame and anger, while Connor stood still, for about this stranger drifted a perfume of broad green fields with flowering tufts of grass, the heads well-seeded and sweet. And when a hand touched his withers, the stallion merely turned his head and nuzzled the shoulder of Connor inquisitively.

With his hand on the back of the horse, the gambler realized for the first time Glani's full stature. He stood at least fifteen-three, though his perfect proportions made him seem smaller at a distance. No doubt he was a giant among the Eden Grays, Connor thought to himself. The gallop on Abra the night before had been a great moment, but a ride on Glani was a prospect that took his breath. He paused. Perhaps it was the influence of a forgotten Puritan ancestor, casting a shade on every hope of happiness. With his weight poised for the leap to the back of the stallion, Connor looked at David. The master was in a silent agony, and the hand of Connor fell away from the horse. He was afraid.

"I can't do it," he said frankly.

"Jump on his back," urged David bitterly. "He's no more to you than a yearling to the hands of Abraham."

Connor realized now how far he had gone; he set about retracing the wrong steps.

"It may appear that way, but I can't trust myself on his back. You understand?"

He stepped back with a gesture that sent Glani bounding away.

"You see," went on Connor, "I never could really understand him."

The master seized with eagerness upon this gratifying suggestion.

"It is true," he said, "that you are a little afraid of Glani. That is why none of the rest can handle him."

He stopped in the midst of his self-congratulation and directed at Connor one of those glances which the gambler could never learn to meet.

"Also," said David, "you made me happy. If you had sat on his back I should have felt your weight on my own shoulders and spirit."

He laid a hand on Connor's shoulder, but the gambler had won and lost too often with an impenetrable face to quail now. He even manged to smile.

"Hearken," said David. "My masters taught me many things, and everything they taught me must be true, for they were only voices of a mind out of another world. Yet, in spite of them," he went on kindly, "I begin to feel a kinship with you, Benjamin. Come, we will walk and talk together in the cool of the morning. Glani!"

The gray had wandered off to nibble at the turf; he whirled and came like a thrown lance.

"Glani," said David, "is usually the only living thing that walks with me in the morning; but now, my friend, we are three."

CHAPTER FIFTEEN

IN the mid-afternoon of that day Connor rested in his room, and David rested in the lake, floating with only his nose and lips out of water. Toward the center of the lake even the surface held the chill of the snows, but David floated in the warm shallows and looked up to the sky through a film of water. The tiny ripples became immense air waves that rushed from mountain to mountain, dashed the clouds up and down, and then left the heavens placid and windless.

He grew weary of this placidity, and as he turned upon one side he heard a prolonged hiss from the shore. David rolled with the speed of a water moccasin and headed in with his arm flashing in a powerful stroke that presently brought him to the edge of the beach. He rose in front of old Abraham.

A painter should have seen them together—the time-dried body of the old man and the exuberant youth of the master. He looked on the servant with a stern kindness.

"What are you doing here without a covering for your head while the sun is hot? Did they let you come of their own accord, Abraham?"

"I slipped away," chuckled Abraham. "Isaac was in the patio, but I went by him like a hawk-shadow. Then I ran among the trees. Hat? Well, no more have you a hat, David."

The master frowned, but his displeasure passed quickly and he led the way to the lowest terrace. They sat on the soft thick grass, with their feet in the hot sand of the beach, and as the wind stirred the tree above them a mottling of shadow moved across them.

"You have come to speak privately with me," said David. "What is it?"

But Abraham embraced his skinny knees and smiled at the lake, his jaw falling.

"It's not what it was," he said, and wagged his head. "It's a sad lake compared to what it was."

David controlled his impatience.

"Tell me how it is changed."

"The color," said the old man. "Why, once, with a gallon of that blue you could have painted the whole sky." He shaded his face to look up, but so doing his glance ventured through the branches and close to the white-hot circle of the sun. His head dropped and he leaned on one arm.

"Look at the green of the grass," suggested David. "It will rest your eyes."

"Do you think my eyes are weak? No, I dropped my head to think how the world has fallen off in the last fifty years. It was all different in the days of John. But that was before you came to the valley."

"The sky was not the same?" queried the master.

"And men, also," said Abraham instantly. "Ho, yes! John was a man; you will not see his like in these days."

David flushed, but he held back his first answer. "Perhaps."

"There is no 'perhaps.'"

Abraham spoke with a decision that brought his jaw close up under his nose.

"He is my master," insisted Abraham, and, smiling suddenly, he whispered: "Mah ol' Marse Johnnie Cracken!"

"What's that?" called David.

Abraham stared at him with unseeing eyes. A mist of years drifted between them, and now the old man came slowly out of the past and found himself seated on the lawn of the valley with great, naked mountains piled around it.

"What did you say?" repeated David.

Abraham hastily changed the subject.

"In those days if a stranger came to the Garden of Eden he did not stay. Aye, and in those days Abraham could have taken the strongest by the neck and pitched his through the gates. I remember when the men came over the mountains—long before you were born. Ten men at the gate, I remember, and they had guns. But when my master told them to go away they looked at him and they looked at each other, but after a while they went away."

Abraham rocked in an ecstasy.

"No man could face my master. I remember how he sat on his horse that day."

"It was Rustir?" asked David eagerly.

"She was the queen of horses," replied the old man indirectly, "and he was the king of men; there are no more men like my master, and there are no more horses like Rustir."

"John was a good man and a strong man," he said, looking down at his own brown hands. "And Rustir was a fine mare, but it is foolish to call her the best."

"There was never a horse like Rustir," said the old man monotonously.

"Bah! What of Glani?"

"Yes, that is a good colt."

"A good colt! Come, Abraham! Have you ever opened your dim eyes and really looked at him? Name one fault."

"I have said Glani is a good colt," repeated Abraham, worried.

"Come, come! You have said Rustir was better."

"Glani is a good colt, but too heavy in the forehand. Far too heavy there."

The restraint of David snapped.

"It is false! Ephraim, Jacob, they all say that Glani is the greatest."

"They change like the masters," grumbled Abraham. "The servants change. They flatter and the master believes. But my master had an eye—he looked through a man like an eagle through mist. When I stood before my master my soul was naked; a wind blew through me. But I say John was one man; and there are no other horses like his mare Rustir. My master is silent; other men have words as heavy as their hands."

"Peace, Abraham, peace. You shame me. The Lord was far from me, and I spoke in anger, and I retract it."

"A word is a bullet that strikes men down, David. Let

87

the wind blow on your face when your heart is hot."

"I confess my sin," said David, but his jaw was set.

"Confess your sins in silence."

"It is true."

He looked at Abraham as if he would be rid of him.

"You are angry to-day, Abraham."

"The law of the Garden has been broken."

"By whom?"

"David has unbarred the gate."

"Yes, to one man."

"It is enough."

"Peace, Abraham. You are old and look awry. This one man is no danger. I could break him in my hands—so!"

"A strong man may be hopeless against words," said the oracular old man. "With a word he may set you on fire."

"Do you think me a tinder and dry grass? Set me on fire with a word?"

"An old man who looks awry had done it with a word. And see—again!"

There was a silence filled only by the sound of David's breathing and the slow curling of the ripples on the beach.

"You try me sorely, Abraham."

"Good steel will bend, but not break."

"Say no more of this man. He is harmless."

"Is that a command, David?"

"No—but at least be brief."

"Then I say to you, David, that he has brought evil into the valley."

The master burst into sudden laughter that carried away his anger.

"He brought no evil, Abraham. He brought only the clothes on his back."

"The serpent brought into the first Garden only his skin and his forked tongue."

"There was a devil in that serpent."

"Aye, and what of Benjamin?"

"Tell me your proofs, and let them be good ones, Abraham.

"I am old," said Abraham sadly, "but I am not afraid."

"I wait."

"Benjamin brought an evil image with him. It is the face of a great suhman, and he tempted Joseph with it, and Joseph fell."

"The trinket of carved bone?" asked David.

"The face of a devil! Who was unhappy among us until Benjamin came? But with his charm he bought Joseph, and now Joseph walks alone and thinks unholy thoughts, and when he is spoken to he looks up first with a snake's eye before he answers. Is not this the work of Benjamin?"

"What would you have me do? Joseph has already paid for his fault with the pain of the whip."

"Cast out the stranger, David."

David mused. At last he spoke. "Look at me, Abraham!"

The other raised his head and peered into the face of David, but presently his glance wavered and turned away.

"See," said David. "After Matthew died there was no one in the Garden who could meet my glance. But Benjamin meets my eye and I feel his thoughts before he speaks them. He is pleasant to me, Abraham."

"The voice of the serpent was pleasant to Eve," said Abraham.

The nostrils of David quivered.

"What is it that you call the trinket?"

"A great suhman. My people feared and worshiped him in the old days. A strong devil!"

"An idol!" said David. "What! Abraham, do you still worship sticks and stones? Have you been taught no more than that? Do you put a mind in the handiwork of a man?"

The head of Abraham fell.

"I am weak before you, David," he said. "I have no power to speak except the words of my master, which I remember. Now I feel you rise against me, and I am dust under your feet. Think of Abraham, then, as a voice in the wind, but hear that voice. I know, but I know not why I know, or how I know, there is evil in the valley, David. Cast it out!"

"I have broken bread and drunk milk with Benjamin. How can I drive him out of the valley?"

"Let him stay in the valley if you can keep him out

of your mind. He is in your thoughts. He is with you like a shadow."

"He is not stronger than I," said the master.

"Evil is stronger than the greatest."

"It is cowardly to shrink from him before I know him."

"Have no fear of him—but of yourself. A wise man trembleth at his own strength."

"Tell me, Abraham—does the seed of Rustir know men? Do they know good and evil?"

"Yes, for Rustir knew my master."

"And has Glani ever bowed his head for any man saving for me?"

"He is a stubborn colt. Aye, he troubled me!"

"But I tell you, Abraham, he came to the hand of Benjamin!"

The old man blinked at the master.

"Then there was something in that hand," he said at last.

"There was nothing," said David in triumph. "I saw the bare palm.

"You are wrong. Admit it."

"It is strange."

"I must think, David."

"Yes," said the master kindly. "Here is my hand. Rise, and come with me to your house."

They went slowly, slowly up the terrace, Abraham clinging to the arm of the master.

"Also," said David, "he has come for only a little time. He will soon be gone. Speak no more of Benjamin."

"I have already spoken almost enough," said Abraham. "You will not forget."

CHAPTER SIXTEEN

ALTHOUGH David was smiling when he left Abraham, he was serious when he turned from the door of the old man. He went to Connor's room, it was empty. He summoned Zacharias.

"The men beyond the mountains are weak," said David, "and when I left him a little time since Benjamin was sighing and sleepy. But now he is not in his room. Where is he, Zacharias?"

"Shakra came into the patio and neighed," Zacharias answered, "and at that Benjamin came out, rubbing his eyes. 'My friend,' said he to me, and his voice was smooth —not like those voices—"

"Peace, Zacharias," said David. "Leave this talk of his voice and tell me where he is gone."

"Away from the house," said the old man sullenly.

The master knitted his brows.

"You old men," he said, "are like yearlings who feel the sap running in their legs in the spring. You talk as they run—around and around. Continue."

Zacharias sulked as if he were on the verge of not speaking at all. But presently his eye lighted with his story.

"Benjamin," he went on, "said to me, 'My friend, that is a noble mare.'

" 'She is a good filly,' said I.

" 'With a hundred and ten up,' said Benjamin, 'she would make a fast track talk.' "

"What?" said David.

"I do not know the meaning of his words," said the old servant, "but I have told them as he said them."

"He is full of strange terms," murmured David. "Continue."

"He went first to one side of Shakra and then to the other. He put his hand into his coat and seemed to think. Presently he stretched out his hand and called her. She came to him slowly."

"Wonderful!"

"That was my thought," nodded Zacharias.

"Why do you stop?" cried David.

"Because I am talking around and around, like a running yearling," said Zacharias ironically. "However, he stood back at length and combed the forelock of Shakra with his fingers. 'Tell me, Zacharias,' he said, 'if this is not the sister of Glani?' "

"He guessed so much? It is strange!"

"Then he looked in her mouth and said that she was four years old."

"He is wise in horses, indeed."

"When he turned away Shakra followed him; he went to his room and came out again, carrying the saddle with which he rode Abra. He put this on her back and a rope around her neck. 'Will the master be angry if I ride her?' he asked.

"I told him that she was first ridden only three months before to-day, and that she must not be ridden more than fifty miles now in a day.

"He looked a long time at me, then said he would not ride farther than that. Then he went galloping down the road to the south."

"Good!" said the master, and sent a long whistle from the patio; it was pitched as shrill and small as the scream of a hawk when the hawk itself cannot be seen in the sky.

Zacharias ran into the house, and when he came out again bringing a pad Glani was already in the patio.

David took the pad and cinched it on the back of the stallion.

"And when Shakra began to gallop," said Zacharias, "Benjamin cried out."

"What did he say?"

"Nothing."

"Zacharias, men do not cry out without speaking."

"Nevertheless," said Zacharias, "it was like the cry of a wolf when they hunt along the cliffs in winter and see the young horses and the cattle in the Garden below them. It was a cry, and there was no spoken word in it."

The master bit his lip.

"Abraham has been talking folly to you," he said; and, springing on the back of the stallion, he raced out of the patio and on to the south road with his long, black hair whipping straight out behind his head.

At length the southern wall rose slowly over the trees, and a deep murmur which had begun about them as soon as they left the house, light as the humming of bees, increasing as they went down the valley, now became a great rushing noise. It was like a great wind in sound; one expected the push of a gale, coming out from the trees, but there was only the river which ran straight at the cliff, split solid rock, and shot out of sunlight into a black cavern. Beside this gaping mouth of rock stood Connor with Shakra beside him. Twice the master called, but Connor could not hear.

The tumbling river would have drowned a volley of musketry. Only when David touched his shoulder did Connor turn a gloomy face. They took their horses across the bridge which passed over the river a little distance from the cliff, and rode down the farther side of the valley until the roar sank behind them. A few barriers of trees reduced it to the humming which on windless days was picked up by echoes and reached the house of David with a solemn murmur.

"I thought you would rest," and David, when they were come to a place of quiet, and the horses cantered lightly over the road with that peculiar stride, at once soft and reaching, which Connor was beginning to see as the chief characteristic of the Eden Gray.

"I have rested more in two minutes on the back of Shakra than I could rest in two hours on my bed."

It was like disarming a father by praise of his son.

"She has a gentle gait," smiled David.

"I tell you, man, she's a knockout!"

"A knockout?"

The gambler added hastily: "Next to Glani the best horse I have seen."

"You are right. Next to Glani the best in the valley."

"In the world," said Connor, and then gave a cry of wonder.

They had come through an avenue of the eucalyptus trees, and now they reached an open meadow, beyond which aspens trembled and flashed silver under a shock from the wind. Half the meadow was black, half green; for one of the old men was plowing. He turned a rich furrow behind him, and the blackbirds followed in chattering swarms in their hunt for worms. The plow team was a span of slender-limbed Eden Grays. They walked lightly with plow, shaking their heads at the blackbirds, and sometimes they touched noses in that cheery, dumb conversation of horses. The plow turned down the field with the sod curling swiftly behind. The blackbirds followed. There were soldier-wings among them making flashes of red, and all the swarm scolded.

"David," said Connor when he could speak, "you might as well harness lightning to your plow. Why in the name of God, man, don't you get mules for this work?"

The master looked to the ground, for he was angered.

"It is not against His will that I work them at the plow," he answered. "He has not warned me against it."

"Who hasn't?"

"Our Father whose name you spoke. Look! They are not unhappy, Jurith and Rajima, of the blood of Aliriz."

He whistled, whereat the off mare tossed her head and whinnied.

"By Heaven, she knows you at this distance!" gasped Connor.

"Which is only to say that she is not a fool. Did I not sit with her three days and three nights when she was first foaled? That was twenty-five years ago; I was a child then."

Connor, staring after the high, proud head of Jurith, sighed. The horses started on at a walk which was the least excellent gait in the Eden Grays. Their high croups and comparatively low withers, their long hindlegs and the shorter forelegs, gave them a waddling motion with the hind quarters apparently huddling the forehand along.

Indeed, they seemed designed in every particular for the gallop alone. But Glani was an exception. Just as in size he appeared a freak among the others, so in his gaits all things were perfectly proportioned. Connor, with a deep, quiet delight, watched the big stallion stepping freely. Shakra had to break into a soft trot now and then to catch up.

"Let us walk," said David. "The run is for when a man feels with the hawk in the sky; the gallop is for idle pleasure; the trot is an ugly gait, for distance only; but a walk is the gait when two men speak together. In this manner Matthew and I went up and down the valley roads. Alas, it is five years since I have walked my horse! Is it not, Glani, my king? And now, Benjamin, tell me your trouble."

"There is no trouble," said Connor.

But David smiled, saying: "We are brothers in Glani, Benjamin. To us alone he has given his head. Therefore speak freely."

"Look back," said Connor, feeling that the crisis had

94

come and that he must now put his fortune to the touch.

David turned on the stallion. "What do you see?"

"I see old Elijah. He drives the two mares, and the furrow follows them—the blackbirds also."

"Do you see nothing else?"

"I see the green meadow and the sky with a cloud in it; I see the river yonder and the aspens flash as the wind strikes them."

"And do you hear nothing?"

"I hear the falling of the Jordan and the cry of the birds. Also, Elijah has just spoken to Rajima. Ah, she is lazy for a daughter of Aliriz!"

"Do you wish to know what I see and hear, David?"

"If it is your pleasure, brother."

"I see a blue sky like this, with the wind and the clouds in it and all that stuff—"

"All of what?"

"And I see also," continued Connor, resolving to watch his tongue, "thousands of people, acres of men and women."

David was breathless with interest. He had a way of opening his eyes and his mind like a child.

"We are among them; they jostle us; we can scarcely breathe. There is a green lawn below us; we cannot see the green, it is so thickly covered with men. They have pulled out their wallets and they have money in their hands."

"What is it?" muttered David. "For my thoughts swim in those waves of faces."

"I see," went on Connor, "a great oval road fenced on each side, with colored posts at intervals. I see horses in a line, dancing up and down, turning about—"

"Ah, horses!"

"Kicking at each other."

"So? Are there such bad manners among them?"

"But what each man is trembling for, and what each man has risked his money upon, is this question: Which of all those is the fastest horse? Think! The horses which fret in that line are the finest money can buy. Their blood lines are longer than the blood lines of kings. They are all fine muscles and hair-trigger nerves. They are poised for the start. And now—"

"Benjamin, is there such love of horses over the mountains? Listen! Fifty thousand men and women breathe with those racers."

"I know." There was a glint in the eyes of David. "When two horses match their speed—"

"Some men have wagered all their money. They have borrowed, they have stolen, to get what they bet. But these are two men only who bet on one of the horses. You, David, and I!"

"Ha? But money is hard to come by."

"We ask them the odds," continued Connor. "For one dollar we shall take a hundred if our horse wins—odds of a hundred to one! And we wager. We wager the value of all we have. We wager the value of the Garden of Eden itself!"

"It is madness, Benjamin!"

"Look closer! See them at the post. There's the Admiral. There's Fidgety—that tall chestnut. There's Glorious Polly—the little bay. The greatest stake horses in the country. The race of the year. But the horse we bet on, David, is a horse which none of the rest in that crowd knows. It is a horse whose pedigree is not published. It is a small horse, not more than fourteen-three. It stands perfectly still in the midst of that crowd of nervous racers. On its back is an old man."

"But can the horse win? And who is the old man?"

"On the other horses are boys who have starved until they are wisps with only hands for the reins of a horse and knees to keep on his back. They have stirrups so short that they seem to be floating above the racers. But on the back of the horse on which we are betting there is only an old, old man, sitting heavily."

"His name! His name!" David cried.

"Elijah! And the horse is Jurith!"

"No, no! Withdraw the bets! She is old."

"They are off! The gray mare is not trained for the start. She is left standing far behind.

"Ah!" David groaned.

"Fifty thousand people laughing at the old gray mare left at the post!"

"I see it! I hear it!"

"She's too short in front; too high behind. She's a joke horse. And see the picture horses! Down the back stretch! The fifty thousand have forgotten the gray, even to laugh

96

at her. The pack drives into the home stretch. There's a straight road to the finish. They straighten out. They get their feet. They're off for the wire!"

The voice of Connor had risen to a shrill cry. "But look! Look! There's a streak of gray coming around the turn. It's the mare! It's old Jurith!"

"Jurith!"

"No awkwardness now! She spreads herself out and the posts disappear beside her. She stretches down low and the rest come back to her. Fine horses; they run well. But Jurith is a racing machine. She's on the hip of the pack! Look at the old man all the thousand were laughing at. He sits easily in the saddle. He has no whip. His reins are loose. And then he uses the post ahead of him. He leans over and speaks one word in the ear of the gray mare.

"By the Lord, she was walking before; she was cantering! Now she runs! Now she runs! And the fifty thousand are dumb, white. A solid wall of faces covered with whitewash! D'you see? They're sick! And then all at once they know they're seeing a miracle. They have been standing up ever since the horses entered the home-stretch. Now they climb on one another's shoulders. They forget all about thousands—the hundreds of thousands of dollars which they are going to lose. They only know that they are seeing a great horse. And they love that new, great horse. They scream as they see her come. Women break into tears as the old man shoots past the grand stand. Men shriek and hug each other. They dance.

"The gray streak shoots on. She is past the others. She is rushing for the finish wire as no horse ever ran before. She is away. One length, two lengths, six lengths of daylight show between her and the rest. She gallops past the finish posts with Elijah looking back at the others!

"She has won! You have won, David. I have won. We are rich. Happy. The world's before us. David, do you see?"

"Is it possible? But no, Benjamin, not Jurith. Some other, perhaps. Shakra—Glani—"

"No, we would take Jurith—twenty-five years old!"

Connor's last words trailed off into hysterical laughter.

CHAPTER SEVENTEEN

DAVID was still flushed with the excitement of the tale, and he was perplexed and troubled when Connor's strange, high laughter brought to an abrupt end the picture they had both lived in.

The gambler saw the frown on David's brow, and with an effort he made himself suddenly grave, though he was still pale and shaking.

"David, this is the reason Jurith can win. Somewhere in the past there was a freak gray horse. There are other kinds of freaks; oranges had seeds in 'em; all at once up pops a tree that has seedless fruit. People plant shoots from it. There you have the naval orange, all out of one tree. It's the same way with that gray horse. It was a freak; had a high croup and muscles as stretchy as India-rubber, and strong—like the difference between the muscles of a mule and the muscles of most horses. That's what that first horse was. He was bred and the get came into this valley. They kept improving—and the result is Glani! The Eden Gray, David, is the finest horse in the world because it's a *different* and a better horse!"

The master paused for some time, and Connor knew he was deep in thought. Finally he spoke:

"But if we know the speed of the Eden Grays, why should we go out into the world and take the money of other men because they do not know how fast our horses run?"

Connor made sure the master was serious and nerved himself for the second effort.

"What do you wish, David?"

"In what measure, Benjamin?"

"The sky's the limit! I say, what do you wish? The last wish that was in your head."

"Shakra stumbled a little while ago; I wished for a smoother road."

"David, with the money we win on the tracks we'll tear up these roads, cut trenches, fill 'em with solid blocks of rock, lay 'em over with asphalt, make 'em as smooth as glass! What else?"

"You jest, Benjamin. That is a labor for a thousand men."

"I say, it's nothing to what we'll do. What else do you want? Turn your mind loose—open up your eyes and see something that's hard to get."

"Every wish is a regret, and why should I fail of gratitude to God by making my wishes? Yet, I have been weak, I confess. I have sometimes loathed the crumbling walls of my house. I have wished for a tall chamber—on the floor a covering which makes no sound, colors about me—crystal vases for my flowers—music when I come—"

"Stop there! You see that big white cliff? I'll have that stone cut in chunks as big as you and your horse put together. I'll have 'em piled on a foundation as strong as the bottom of those hills. You see the way those mountain-tops walk into the sky? That's how the stairways will step up to the front of your house and put you out on a big terrace with columns scooting up fifty feet, and when you walk across the terrace a couple of great big doors weighing about a ton apiece will drift open and make a whisper when you mosey in. And when you get inside you'll start looking up and up, but you'll get dizzy before your eyes hit the ceiling; and up there you'll see a lighting stunt that looks like a million icicles with the sun behind 'em."

He paused an instant for breath and saw David smiling in a hazy pleasure.

"I follow you," he said softly. "Go on!" And his hand stretched out as though to open a door.

"What I've told you is only a beginning. Turn yourself loose; dream, and I'll turn your dream into stone and color, and fill up your windows with green and gold and red glass till you'll think a rainbow has got all tangled up there! I'll give you music that'll make you forget to think, and when you think I'll give you a room so big that you'll have silence with an echo to it."

"All this for my horses?"

"Send one of the grays—just one, and let me place the wagers. You don't even have to risk your own money. I've made a slough of it betting on things that weren't lead pipe cinches like this. I made on Fidgety Midget at fifty to one. I made on Gosham at eight to one. Nobody told me how to bet on 'em. I know a horse—that's all! You stay in the Garden; I take one of the grays; I bring her back in six months with more coin than she can pack, and we split it fifty-fifty. You furnish the horse. I furnish the jack. Is it a go?"

A bird stopped above them, whistled and dipped away over the tree-tops. David turned his head to follow the trailing song, and Connor realized with a sick heart that he had failed to sweep his man off his feet.

"Would you have me take charity?" asked David at length.

It seemed to Connor that there was a smile behind this. He himself burst into a roar of laughter.

"Sure, it sounds like charity. They'll be making you a gift right enough. There isn't a horse on the turf that has a chance with one of the grays! But they'll bet their money like fools."

"Would it not be a sin, then?"

"What sin?" asked Connor roughly. "Don't they grab the coin of other people? Does the bookie ask you how much coin you have and if you can afford to lose it? No, he's out to get all that he can grab. And we'll go out and do some grabbing in turn. Oh, they'll squeal when we turn the screw, but they'll kick through with the jack. No fear, Davie!"

"Whatever sins may be theirs, Benjamin, those sins need not be mine."

Connor was dumb.

"Because they are foolish," said David, "should I take advantage of their folly? A new man comes into the valley. He sees Jurith, and notices that she runs well in spite of her years. He says to me: 'This mare will run faster than your stallion. I have money and this ring upon my finger which I will risk against one dollar of your money; If the mare beats Glani I take your dollar. If Glani beats the mare, you take my purse and my ring; I have no other wealth. It will ruin me, but I am willing to be ruined if Jurith is not faster than Glani.

"Suppose such foolish man were to come to me, Benjamin, would I not say to him: 'No, my friend. For I understand better than you, both Jurith and Glani!' Tell

100

me therefore, Benjamin, that you have tempted me toward a sin, unknowing."

It made Connor think of the stubborness of a woman, or of a priest. It was a quiet assurance which could only be paralleled from a basis of religion or instinct. He knew the danger of pressing too hard upon this instinct or blind faith. He swallowed an oath, and answered, remembering dim lessons out of his childhood:

"Tell me, David, my brother, is there no fire to burn fools? Is there no rod for the shoulders of the proud? Should not such men be taught?"

"And I say to you, Benjamin," said the master of the Garden: "what wrong have these fools done to me with their folly?"

Connor felt that he was being swept beyond his depth. The other went on, changing his voice to gentleness:

"No, no! I have even a kindness for men with such blind faith in their horses. When Jacob comes to me and says privately in my ear: 'David, look at Hira. Is she not far nobler and wiser than Ephraim's horse, Numan?' When he says this to me, do I shake my head and frown and say: 'Risk the clothes on your back and the food you eat to prove what you say.' No, assuredly I do neither of these things, but I put my hand on his shoulder and I say: 'He who has faith shall do great things; and a tender master makes a strong colt.' In this manner I speak to him, knowing that truth is good, but the whole truth is sometimes a fire that purifies, perhaps, but it also destroys. So Jacob goes smiling on his way and gives kind words and fine oats to Hira."

Connor turned the flank of this argument.

"These men are blind. You say that your horses can run a mile in such and such a time, and they shrug their shoulders and answer that they have heard such chatter before—from trainers and stable boys. But you put your horse on a race track and prove what you say, and they pay for knowledge. Once they see the truth they come to value your horses. You open a stud and your breed is crossed with theirs. The blood of Rustir, passing through the blood of Glani, goes among the best horses of the world. A hundred years from now there will be no good horse in the world, of which men do not ask: 'Is the blood of Glani in him? Is he of the line of the Eden Grays?' Consider that, David!"

He found the master of the Garden frowning. He pressed home the point with renewed vigor.

"If you live in this valley, David, what will men know of you?"

"Have you come to take me out of the Garden of Eden?"

"I have come to make your influence pass over the mountains while you stay here. A hundred years from now who will know David of the Garden of Eden? Of the men who used to live here, who remains? Not one! Where do they live now? Inside your head, inside your head, David, and no other place!"

"They live with God," said David hoarsely.

"But here on earth they don't live at all except in your mind. And when you die, they die with you. But if you let me do what I say, a thousand years from today, people will be saying: 'There was a man named David, and he had these gray horses, which were the finest in the world, and he gave their blood to the world.' They'll pick up every detail of your life, and they'll trace back the horses—"

"Do I live for the sake of a horse?" cried David, in a voice unnaturally high.

"No, but because of your horses the world will ask what sort of a man you are. People will follow your example. They'll build a hundred Gardens of Eden. Every one of those valleys will be full of the memories of David and the men who went before him. Then, David, you'll never die!"

It was the highest flight to which Connor's eloquence ever attained. The results were alarming. David spoke, without facing his companion, thoughtfully.

"Benjamin, I have been warned. By sin the gate to the Garden was opened, and perhaps sin has entered in you. For why did the first men withdraw to this valley, led by John, save to live apart, perfect lives? And you, Benjamin, wish to undo all that they accomplished."

"Only the horses," said the gambler. "Who spoke of taking you out of the Garden?"

Still David would not look at him.

"God grant me His light," said the master sadly. "You

have stirred and troubled me. If the horses go, my mind goes with them. Benjamin, you have tempted me. Yet another thing is in my mind. When Matthew came to die he took me beside him and said:

" 'David, it is not well that you should lead a lonely life. Man is made to live, and not to die. Take to yourself a woman, when I am gone, wed her, and have children, so that the spirit of John and Matthew and Luke and Paul shall not die. And do this in your youth, before five years have passed you by.'

"So spoke Matthew, and this is the fifth year. And perhaps the Lord works in you to draw me out, that I may find this woman. Or perhaps it is only a spirit of evil that speaks in you. How shall I judge? For my mind whirls!"

As if to flee from his thoughts, the master of the Garden called on Glani, and the stallion broke into a full gallop. Shakra followed at a pace that took the breath of Connor, but instantly she began to fall behind; before they had reached the lake Glani was out of sight across the bridge.

Full of alarm—full of hope also— Connor reached the house. In the patio he found Zacharias standing with folded arms before a door.

"I must find David at once," he told Zacharias. "Where has he gone?"

"Up," said the servant, and pointed solemnly above him.

"Nonsense!" He added impatiently: "Where shall I find him, Zacharias?"

But again Zacharias waved to the blue sky.

"His body is in this room, but his mind is with Him above the world."

There was something in this that made Connor uneasy as he had never been before.

"You may go into any room save the Room of Silence," continued Zacharias, "but into this room only David and the four before him have been. This is the holy place."

CHAPTER EIGHTEEN

GLANI waited in the patio for the reappearance of the master, and as Connor paced with short, nervous steps on the grass at every turn he caught the flash of the sun on the stallion. Above his selfish greed he had one honest desire: he would have paid with blood to see the great horse face the barrier. That, however, was beyond the reach of his ambition, and therefore the beauty of Glani was always a hopeless torment.

·The quiet in the patio oddly increased his excitement. It was one of those bright, still days when the wind stirs only in soft breaths, bringing a sense of the open sky. Sometimes the breeze picked up a handful of drops from the fountain and showered it with a cool rustling on the grass. Sometimes it flared the tail of Glani; sometimes the shadow of the great eucalyptus which stood west of the house quivered on the turf.

Connor found himself looking minutely at trivial things, and in the meantime David Eden in his room was deciding the fate of the American turf. Even Glani seemed to know, for his glance never stirred from the door through which the master had disappeared. What a horse the big fellow was! He thought of the stallion in the paddock at the track. He heard the thousands swarm and the murmur which comes deep out of a man's throat when he sees a great horse.

The palms of Connor were wet with sweat. He kept rubbing them dry on the hips of his trousers. Rehearsing his talk with David, he saw a thousand flaws, and a thousand openings which he had missed. Then all thought stopped; David had come out into the patio.

He came straight to Connor, smiling, and he said:

"The words were a temptation, but the mind that conceived them was not the mind of a tempter."

Ineffable assurance and good will shone in his face, and Connor cursed him silently.

"I, leaving the valley, might be lost in the torrent. And neither the world nor I should profit. But if I stay here, at least one soul is saved to God."

"Your own?" muttered Connor. But he managed to smile above his rage. "And after you," he concluded, "what of the horses, David?"

"My sons shall have them."

"And if you have no sons?"

"Before my death I shall kill all of the horses. They are not meant for other men than the sons of David."

The gambler drew off his hat and raised his face to the sky, asking mutely if Heaven would permit this crime.

"Yet," said David, "I forgive you."

"You forgive me?" echoed Connor through his teeth.

"Yes, for the fire of the temptation has burned out. Let us forget the world beyond the mountains."

"What is your proof that you are right in staying here?"

"The voice of God."

"You have spoken to Him, perhaps?"

The irony passed harmless by the raised head of David.

"I have spoken to Him," he asserted calmly.

"I see," nodded the gambler. "You keep Him in that room, no doubt?"

"It is true. His spirit is in the Room of Silence."

"You've seen His face?"

A numbness fell on the mind of Connor as he saw his hopes destroyed by the demon of bigotry.

"Only His voice has come to me," said David.

"It speaks to you?"

"Yes."

Connor stared in actual alarm, for this was insanity.

"The four," said David, "spoke to Him always in that room. He is there. And when Matthew died he gave me this assurance—that while the walls of this house stood together God would not desert me or fail to come to me in that room until I love another living thing more than I love God."

"And how, David, do you hear the voice? For while you were there I was in the patio, close by, and yet I heard no whisper of a sound from the room."

"I shall tell you. When I entered the Room of Silence

105

just now your words had set me on fire. My mind was hot with desire of power over other men. I forgot the place you built for me with your promises. And then I knew that it had been a temptation to sin from which the voice was freeing me.

"Could a human voice have spoken more clearly than that voice spoke to my heart? Anxiously I called before my eyes the image of Benjamin to ask for his judgment, but your face remained an unclouded vision and was not dimmed by the will of the Lord as He dims creatures of evil in the Room of Silence. Thereby I knew that you are indeed my brother."

The brain of Connor groped slowly in the rear of these words. He was too stunned by disappointment to think clearly, but vaguely he made out that David has dismissed the argument and was now asking to come for a walk by the lake.

"The lake's well enough," he answered, "but it occurs to me that I've got to get on with my journey."

"You must leave me?"

There was such real anxiety in his voice that Connor softened a little.

"I've got a lot to do," he explained. "I only stopped over to rest my nags, in the first place. Then this other idea came along, but since the voice has rapped it there's nothing for me to do but to get on my way again."

"It is a long trip?"

"Long enough."

"The Garden of Eden is a lonely place."

"You'll have the voice to cheer you up."

"The voice is an awful thing. There is no companionship in it. This thought comes to me. Leave the mule and the horse. Take Shakra. She will carry you swiftly and safely over the mountains and bring you back again. And I shall be happy to know that she is with you while you are away. Then go, brother, if you must, and return in haste."

It was the opening of the gates of heaven to Connor at the very moment when he had surrendered the last hope. He heard David call the servants, heard an order to bring Shakra saddled at once. The canteen was being filled for the journey. Into the incredulous mind of the gambler the truth filtered by degrees, as candlelight probes a room full

106

of treasure, flashing ever and anon into new corners filled with undiscovered riches.

Shakra was his to ride over the mountains. And why stop there? There was no mark on her, and his brand would make her his. She would be safe in an Eastern racing stable before they even dreamed of pursuit. And when her victories on the track had built his fortune he could return her, and raise a breed of peerless horses. A theft? Yes, but so was the stealing of the fire from heaven for the use of mankind.

He would have been glad to leave the Garden of Eden at once, but that was not David's scheme of things. To him a departure into the world beyond the mountains was as a voyage into an unchartered sea. His dignity kept him from asking questions, but it was obvious that he was painfully anxious to learn the necessity of Connor's going.

That night in the patio he held forth at length of the things they would do together when the gambler returned. "The Garden is a book," he explained. "And I must teach you to turn the pages and read in them."

There was little sleep for Connor that night. He lay awake, turning over the possibilities of a last minute failure, and when he finally dropped into a deep, aching slumber it was to be awakened almost at once by the voice of David calling in the patio. He wakened and found it was the pink of the dawn.

"Shakra waits at the gate of the patio. Start early, Benjamin, and thereby you will return soon."

It brought Connor to his feet with a leap. As if he required urging! Through the hasty breakfast he could not retain his joyous laughter until he saw David growing thoughtful. But that breakfast was over, and David's kind solicitations, at length. Shakra was brought to him; his feet were settled into the stirrups, and the dream changed to a sense of the glorious reality. She was his—Shakra!

"A journey of happiness for your sake and a speed for mine, Benjamin."

Connor looked down for the last time into the face of the master of the Garden, half wild and half calm—the face of a savage with the mind of a man behind it. "If he should take my trail!" he thought with horror.

"Good-by!" he called aloud, and in a burst of joy and sudden compunction, "God bless you, David!"

107

"He has blessed me already, for He has given me a friend."

A touch of the rope—for no Eden Gray would endure a bit—whirled Shakra and sent her down the terraces like the wind. The avenue of the eucalyptus trees poured behind them, and out of this, with astonishing suddenness, they reached the gate.

The fire already burned, for the night was hardly past, and Joseph squatted with the thin smoke blowing across his face unheeded. He was grinning with savage hatred and muttering.

Connor knew what profound curse was being called down upon his head, but he had only a careless glance for Joseph. His eye up yonder where the full morning shone on the mountains, his mind was out in the world, at the race track, seeing in prospect beautiful Shakra fleeing away from the finest of the thoroughbreds. And he saw the face of Ruth, as her eyes would light at the sight of Shakra. He could have burst into song.

Connor looking forward, high-headed, threw up his arm with a low shout, and Shakra burst into full gallop down the ravine.

CHAPTER NINETEEN

WHEN Ruth Manning read the note through for the first time she raised her glance to the bearer. The boy was so sun-blackened that the paler skin of the eyelids made his eyes seem supremely large. He was now poised accurately on one foot, rubbing his calloused heel up and down his shin, while he drank in the particulars of the telegraph office. He could hardly be a party to a deception. She looked over the note again, and read:

DEAR MISS MANNING:

I am a couple of miles out of Lukin, in a place to which the bearer of this note will bring you. I am sure you will come, for I am in trouble, out of which you can very easily help me. It is a matter which I cannot confide to any other person in Lukin. I am impatiently expecting you.

BEN CONNOR.

She crumpled the note in her hand thoughtfully, but, on the verge of dropping it in the waste basket, she smoothed it again, and for the third time went over the contents. Then she rose abruptly and confided her place to the lad who idled at the counter.

"The wire's dead," she told him. "Besides, I'll be back in an hour or so."

And she rode off a moment later with the boy. He had a blanket-pad without stirrups, and he kept prodding the sliding elbows of the horse with his bare toes while he chattered at Ruth, for the drum of the sounder had fascinated him and he wanted it explained. She listened to him with a smile of inattention, for she was thinking busily of Connor. Those thoughts made her look down to the dust that puffed up from the feet of the horses and became a light mist behind them; then, raising her head, she saw the blue ravines of the farther mountains and the sun haze about the crests. Connor had always been to her as the ship is to a traveler; the glamor of strange places was about him.

Presently they left the trail, and passing about a hillside, came to an old shack whose unpainted wood had blackened with time.

"There he is," said the boy, and waving his hand to her, turned his pony on the back trail at a gallop.

Connor called to her from the shack and came to meet her, but she had dismounted before he could reach the stirrup. He kept her hand in his for a moment as he greeted her. It surprised him to find how glad he was to see her. He told her so frankly.

"After the mountains and all that," he said cheerfully, "it's like meeting an old chum again to see you. How have things been going?"

This direct friendliness in a young man was something new to the girl. The youths who came in to the dances at Lukin were an embarrassed lot who kept a sulky distance, as though they made it a matter of pride to show that they were able to resist the attraction of a pretty girl. But if she

109

gave them the least encouragement, the merest shadow of a friendly smile, they were at once all eagerness. They would flock around her, sending savage glances at one another, and simpering foolishly at her. They had stock conversation of politeness; they forced out prodigious compliments to an accompaniment of much writhing. Social conversation was a torture to them, and the girl knew it.

Not that she despised them. She understood perfectly well that most of them were fine fellows and strong men. But their talents had been cultivated in roping two-year-olds and bulldogging yearlings. They could encounter the rush of a mad bull far more easily than they could withstand a verbal quip. With the familiarity of years, she knew, they lost both their sullenness and their starched politeness. They became kindly, gentle men with infinite patience, infinite devotion to their "womenfolk." Homelier girls in Lukin had an easier time with them. But in the presence of Ruth Manning, who was a more or less celebrated beauty, they were a hopeless lot. In short, she had all her life been in an amphibious position, of the mountain desert and yet not of the mountain desert. On the one hand she despised the "slick dudes" who now and again drifted into Lukin with marvelous neckties and curiously patterned clothes; on the other hand, something in her revolted at the thought of becoming one of the "womenfolk."

As a matter of fact there are two things which every young girl should have. The first is the presence of a mother, which is the oldest of truisms; the second is the friendship of at least one man of nearly her own age. Ruth had neither. That is the crying hurt of Western life. The men are too busy to bother with women until the need for a wife and a home and children, and all the physical destiny of a man, overwhelms them. When they reach this point there is no selection. The first girl they meet they make love to.

And most of this Ruth understood. She wanted to make some of those lumbering, fearless, strong-handed, gentle-souled men her friends. But she dared not make the approaches. The first kind word or the first winning smile brought forth a volley of tremendous compliments, close on the heels of which followed the heavy artillery of a proposal of marriage. No wonder that she was rejoiced beyond words to meet this frank friendliness in Ben Connor. And what a joy to be able to speak back freely, without putting a guard over eyes and voice!

"Things have gone on just the same—but I've missed you a lot!"

"That's good to hear."

"You see," she explained, "I've been living in Lukin with just half a mind—the rest of it has been living off the wire. And you're about the only interesting thing that's come to me except in the Morse."

And what a happiness to see that there was no stiffening of his glance as he tried to read some profound meaning into her words! He accepted them as they were, with a good-natured laughter that warmed her heart.

"Sit down over here," he went on, spreading a blanket over a chairlike arrangement of two boulders. "You look tired out."

She accepted with a smile, and letting her head go back against the upper edge of the blanket she closed her eyes for a moment and permitted her mind to drift into utter relaxation.

"I *am* tired," she whispered. It was inexpressibly pleasant to lie there with the sense of being guarded by this man. "They never guess how tired I get—never—never! I feel—I feel—as if I were living under the whip all the time."

"Steady up partner." He had picked up that word in the mountains, and he liked it. "Steady, partner. Everybody has to let himself go. You tell me what's wrong. I may not be able to fix anything, but it always helps to let off steam."

She heard him sit down beside her, and for an instant, though her eyes were still closed, she stiffened a little, fearful that he would touch her hand, attempt a caress. Any other man in Lukin would have become familiar long ago. But Connor did not attempt to approach her.

"Turn and turn about," he was saying smoothly. "When I went into your telegraph office the other night my nerves were in a knot. Tell you straight I never knew I *had* real nerves before. I went in ready to curse like a drunk. When I saw you, it straightened me out. By the Lord, it was like a cool wind in my face. You were so steady, Ruth; straight eyes; and it ironed out the wrinkles to hear your voice. I blurted out a lot of stuff. But when I remembered it later on I wasn't ashamed. I knew you'd understand. Besides, I knew that what I'd said would stop with you. Just about one girl in a million who can keep her mouth shut—and each one of 'em is worth her weight in gold. You did me several thousand dollars' worth of good that night. That's honest!"

She allowed her eyes to open, slowly, and looked at him with a misty content. The mountains had already done him good. The sharp sun had flushed him a little and tinted his cheeks and strong chin with tan. He looked more manly, somehow, and stronger in himself. Of course he had flattered her, but the feeling that she had actually helped him so much by merely listening on that other night wakened in her a new self-reverence. She was too prone to look on life as a career of manlike endeavor; it was pleasant to know that a woman could accomplish something even more important by simply sitting still and listening. He was watching her gravely now, even though she permitted herself the luxury of smiling at him.

All at once she cried softly: "Thank Heaven that you're not a fool, Ben Connor!"

"What do you mean by that?"

"I don't think I can tell you." She added hastily: "I'm not trying to be mysterious."

He waved the need of an apology away.

"Tell you what. Never knew a girl yet that was worth her salt who could be understood all the time, or who even understood herself."

She closed her eyes again to ponder this, lazily. She could not arrive at a conclusion, but she did not care. Missing links in this conversation were not vitally important.

"Take it easy, Ruth; we'll talk later on," he said after a time.

She did not look at him as she answered: "Tell me why?"

There was a sort of childlike confiding in all this that troubled Ben Connor. He had seen her with a mind as direct and an enthusiasm as strong as that of a man. This relaxing and softening alarmed him, because it showed him another side of her, a new and vital side. She was very lovely with the shadows of the sombrero brim cutting across the softness of her lips and setting aglow the clear olive tan of her chin and throat. Her hand lay palm upward beside her, very small, very delicate in the making. But what a power was in that hand! He realized with a thrill of not unmixed pleasure that if the girl set herself to the task she could mold him like wax with the gestures of that hand. If into the softness of her voice she allowed a single note of warmth to creep, what would happen in Ben Connor? He left within himself a chord ready to vibrate in answer.

Now he caught himself leaning a little closer to study the purple stain of weariness in her eyelids. Even exhaustion was attractive in her. It showed something new, and newly appealing. Weariness gave merely a new edge to her beauty. What if her eyes, opening slowly now, were to look upon him not with the gentleness of friendship, but with something more—the little shade of difference in a girl's wide eyes that admits a man to her secrets—and traps him in so doing.

Ben Connor drew himself up with a shake of the shoulders. He felt that he must keep careful guard from now on. What a power she was. What a power! If she set herself to the task who could deal with her? What man could keep from her? Then the picture of David jumped into his mind out of nothingness. And on the heels of that picture the inspiration came with a sudden uplifting of the heart, surety, intoxicating insight. He wanted to jump to his feet and shout until the great ravine beneath them echoed. With an effort he remained quiet. But he was thinking rapidly—rapidly. He had intended to use her merely to arrange for shipping Shakra away from Lukin Junction. For he dared not linger about the town where expert horse thieves might see the mare. But now something new, something more came to him. The girl was a power? Why not use her?

What he said was: "Do you know why you close your eyes?"

Still without looking up she answered: "Why?"

"All of these mountains—you see?" She did not see, so he went on to describe them. "There's that big peak opposite us. Looks a hundred yards away, but it's two miles. Comes down in big jags and walks up into the sky

—Lord knows how many thousand feet. And behind it the other ranges stepping off into the horizon with purple in the gorges and mist at the tops. Fine picture, eh? But hard to look at, Ruth. Mighty hard to look at. First thing you know you get to squinting to make out whether that's a cactus on the side of that mountain or a hundred-foot pine tree. Might be either. Can't tell the distance in this air. Well, you begin to squint. That's how the people around here get that long-distance look behind their eyes and the long-distance wrinkles around the corners of their eyes. All the men have those wrinkles. But the women have them, too, after a while. You'll get them after a while, Ruth. Wrinkles around the eyes and wrinkles in the mind to match, eh?"

Her eyes opened at last, slowly, slowly. She smiled at him plaintively.

"Don't I know, Ben? It's a man's country. It isn't made for woman."

"Ah, there you've hit the nail on the head. Exactly! A man's country. Do you know what it does to the women?"

"Tell me."

"Makes 'em like the men. Hardens their hands after a while. Roughens their voices. Takes time, but that's what comes after a while. Understand?"

"Oh, don't I understand!"

And he knew how the fear had haunted her, then, for the first time.

"What does this dry, hot wind do to you in the mountains? What does it do to your skin? Takes the velvet off, after a while; makes it dry and hard. Lord, girl, I'd hate to see the change it's going to make in you!"

All at once she sat up, wide awake.

"What are you trying to do to me, Ben Connor?"

"I'm trying to wake you up."

"I *am* awake. But what can I do?"

"You think you're awake, but you're not. Tell you what a girl needs, a stage—just like an actor. Think they can put on a play with these mountains for a setting? Never in the world. Make the actors look too small. Make everything they say sound too thin.

"Same way with a girl. She needs a setting. A room, a rug, a picture, a comfortable chair, and a dress that goes with it. Shuts out the rest of the world and gives her a chance to make a man focus on her—see her behind the footlights. See?"

"Yes," she whispered.

"Do you know what I've been doing while I watched you just now?"

"Tell me."

He was fighting for a great purpose now, and a quality of earnest emotion crept into his voice. "Around your throat I've been running an edging of yellow old lace. Under your hand that was lying there I put a deep blue velvet; I had your shoulders as white as snow, with a flash to 'em like snow when you turned in the light; I had you proud as a queen, Ruth, with a blur of violets at your breast. I took out the tired look in your face. Instead, I put in happiness."

He stopped and drew a long breath.

"You're pretty now, but you could be—beautiful. Lord, what a flame of beauty you could be, girl!"

Instead of flushing and smiling under the praise, he saw tears well into her eyes and her mouth grow tremulous. She winked the tears away.

"What are you trying to do, Ben? Make everything still harder for me? Don't you see I'm helpless—helpless?"

And instead of rising to a wail her voice sank away at the end in despair.

"Oh, you're trapped well enough," he said. "I'm going to bust the trap! I'm going to give you your setting. I'm going to make you what you ought to be—beautiful!"

She smiled as at any unreal fairy tale.

"How?"

"I can show you better than I can tell you! Come here!" He rose, and she was on her feet in a flash. He led the way to the door of the shack, and as the shadows fell inside, Shakra tossed up her head.

The girl's bewildered joy was as great as if the horse were a present to her.

"Oh, you beauty, you beauty," she cried.

"Watch yourself," he warned. "She's as wild as a mountain lion."

"But she knows a friend!"

Shakra sniffed the outstretched hand, and then with a shake of her head accepted the stranger and looked over Ruth's shoulder at Connor as though for an explanation.

115

Connor himself was smiling and excited; he drew her back and forgot to release her hand, so that they stood like two happy children together. He spoke very softly and rapidly, as though he feared to embarrass the mare.

"Look at the head first—then the bone in the foreleg, then the length above her back—see how she stands! See how she stands! And those black hoofs, hard as iron, I tell you—put the four of 'em in my double hands, almost—ever see such a nick? But she's no six furlong flash! That chest, eh? Run your finger-tips down that shoulder!"

She turned with tears of pleasure in her eyes. "Ben Connor, you've been in the valley of the grays!"

"I have. And do you know what it means to us?"

"To *us?*"

"I said it. I mean it. You're going to share."

"I—"

"Look at the mare again!"

She obeyed.

"Say something, Ruth!"

"I can't say what I feel!"

"Then try to understand this: you're looking at the fastest horse that ever stepped into a race track. You understand? I'm not speaking in comparisons. I'm talking the cold dope! Here's a pony that could have given Salvator twenty pounds, run him sick in six furlongs, and walked away to the finish by herself. Here's a mare that could pick up a hundred and fifty pounds and beat the finest horse that ever faced a barrier with a flyweight jockey in the saddle. You're looking at history, girl! Look again! You're looking at a cold million dollars. You're looking at the blood that's going to change the history of the turf. That's what Shakra means!"

She was trembling with his excitement.

"I see. It's the sure thing you were talking about. The horse that can't be beat—that makes the betting safe?"

But Connor grew gloomy at once.

"What do you mean by sure thing? If I could ever get her safely away from the post in a stake race, yes; sure as anything on earth. But suppose the train is wrecked? Suppose she puts a foot in a hole? Suppose at the post some rotten, cheap-selling plater kicks her and lays her up!"

He passed a trembling hand along the neck of Shakra.

"God, suppose!"

"But you only brought one; nothing else worth while in the valley?"

"Nothing else? I tell you, the place is full of 'em! And there's a stallion as much finer than Shakra as she's finer than that broken-down, low-headed, ewe-necked, straight-shouldered, roach-backed skate you have out yonder!"

"Mr. Connor, that's the best little pony in Lukin! But I know—compared with this—oh, to see her run, just once!"

She sighed, and as her glance fell Connor noted her pallor and her weariness. She looked up again, and the great eyes filled her face with loveliness. Color, too, came into her cheeks and into her parted lips.

"You beauty!" she murmured. "You perfect, perfect beauty!"

Shakra was nervous under the fluttering hands, but in spite of her uneasiness she seemed to enjoy the light-falling touches until the finger-tips trailed across her forehead; then she tossed her head high, and the girl stood beneath, laughing, delighted. Connor found himself smiling in sympathy. The two made a harmonious picture. As harmonious, say, as the strength of Glani and the strength of David Eden. His face grew tense with it when he drew the girl away.

"Would you like to have a horse like that—half a dozen like it?"

The first leap of hope was followed by a wan smile at this cruel mockery.

He went on with brutal tenseness, jabbing the points at her with his raised finger.

"And everything else you've ever wanted: beautiful clothes? Manhattan? A limousine as big as a house. A butler behind your chair and a maid in your dressing room? A picture in the papers every time you turn around? You want 'em?"

"Do I want heaven?"

"How much will you pay?"

He urged it on her, towering over her as he drew close.

"What's it worth? Is it worth a fight?"

"It's worth—everything."

"I'm talking shop. I'm talking business. Will you play partners with me?"

"To the very end."

"The big deaf-mute doesn't own the grays in that valley they call the Gardèn of Eden. They're owned by a white man. They call him David Eden. And David Eden has never been out in the world. It's part of his creed not to. It's part of his creed, however, to go out just once, find a woman for his wife, and bring her back with him. Is that clear?"

"I—"

"You're to go up there. That old gray gelding we saw in Lukin the day of the race. I'll finance you to the sky. Ride it to the gates of the Garden of Eden. Tell the guards that you've got to have another horse because the one you own is old. Insist on seeing David. Smile at 'em; win 'em over. Make them let you see David. And the minute you see him, he's ours! You understand? I don't mean marriage. One smile will knock him stiff. Then play him. Get him to follow you out of the valley. Tell him you have to go back home.. He'll follow you. Once we have him outside you can keep him from going back and you can make him bring out his horses, too. Easy? It's a sure thing! We don't rob him, you see? We simply use his horses. I race them and play them. I split the winnings with you and David. Millions, I tell you; millions. Don't answer. Gimme a chance to talk!"

There was a rickety old box leaning against the wall; he made her sit on it, and dropping upon one knee, he poured out plan, reason, hopes, ambitions in fierce confusion. It ended logically enough. David was under what he considered a divine order to marry, and he would be clay in the hands of the first girl who met him. She would be a fool indeed if she were not able to lead him out of the valley.

"Think it over for one minute before you answer," concluded Connor, and then rose and folded his arms. He controlled his very breathing for fear of breaking in on the dream which he saw forming in her eyes.

Then she shook herself clear of the temptation.

"Ben, it's crooked! I'm to lie to him—live a lie until we have what we want!"

"God A'mighty, girl! Don't you see that we'd be doing

118

the poor fathead a good turn by getting him out of his hermitage and letting him live in the world? A lie? Call it that if you want. Aren't there such things as white lies? If there are, this is one of 'em or I'm not Ben Connor."

His voice softened. "Why, Ruth, you know damned well that I wouldn't put the thing up to you if I didn't figure that in the end it would be the best thing in the world for you? I'm giving you your chance. To save Dave Eden from being a fossil. To earn your own freedom. To get everything you've longed for. Think!"

"I'm trying to think—but I only keep feeling, inside, 'It's wrong! It's wrong! It's wrong!' I'm not a moralizer, but— tell me about David Eden!"

Connor saw his opening.

"Think of a horse that's four years old and never had a bit in his teeth. That's David Eden. The minute you see him you'll want to tame him. But you'll have to go easy. Keep gloves on. He's as proud as a sulky kid. Kind of a chap you can't force a step, but you could coax him over a cliff. Why, he'd be thread for you to wind around your little finger if you worked him right. But it wouldn't be easy. If he had a single suspicion he'd smash everything in a minute, and he's strong enough to tear down a house. Put the temper of a panther in the size of a bear and you get a small idea of David Eden."

He was purposely making the task difficult and he saw that she was excited. His own work with Ruth Manning was as difficult as hers would be with David. The fickle color left her all at once and he found her looking wistfully at him.

She returned neither answer, argument, nor comment. In vain he detailed each step of her way into the Garden and how she could pass the gate. Sometimes he was not even sure that she heard him, as she listened to the silent voice which spoke against him. He had gathered all his energy for a last outburst, he was training his tongue for a convincing storm of eloquence, when Shakra, as though she wearied of all this human chatter, pushed in between them her beautiful head and went slowly toward Ruth with pricking ears, inquisitive, searching for those light, caressing touches.

The voice of Connor became an insidious whisper.

"Look at her, Ruth. Look at her. She's begging you

to come. You can have her. She'll be a present to you. Quick! What's the answer!"

A strange answer! She threw her arms around the shoulder of the beautiful gray, buried her face in the mane, and burst into tears.

For a moment Connor watched her, dismayed, but presently, as one satisfied, he withdrew to the open air and mopped his forehead. It had been hard work, but it had paid. He looked over the distant blue waves of mountains with the eye of possession.

CHAPTER TWENTY

"THE evil at heart, when they wish to take, seem to give," said Abraham, mouthing the words with his withered lips, and he came to one of his prophetic pauses.

The master of the Garden permitted it to the privileged old servant, who added now: "Benjamin is evil at heart."

"He did not ask for the horse," said David, who was plainly arguing against his own conviction.

"Yet he knew." The ancient face of Abraham puckered. "Po' white trash!" he muttered. Now and then one of these quaint phrases would break through his acquired diction, and they always bore home to David a sense of that great world beyond the mountains. Matthew had often described that world, but one of Abraham's odd expressions carried him in a breath into cities filled with men.

"His absence is cheaply bought at the price of one mare," continued the old servant soothingly.

"One mare of Rustir's blood! What is the sin for which the Lord would punish me with the loss of Shakra? And I miss her as I would miss a human face. But Benjamin will return with her. He did not ask for the horse."

"He knew you would offer."

"He will not return?"

"Never!"

"Then I shall go to find him."

"It is forbidden."

Abraham sat down, cross-legged, and watched with impish self-content while David strode back and forth in the patio. A far-off neighing brought him to a halt, and he raised his hand for silence. The neighing was repeated, more clearly, and David laughed for joy.

"A horse coming from the pasture to the paddock," said Abraham, shifting uneasily.

The day was old and the patio was filled with a clear, soft light, preceeding evening.

"It is Shakra, Shakra, Abraham!"

Abraham rose.

"A yearling. It is too high for the voice of a grown mare."

"The distance makes it shrill. Abraham, Abraham, cannot I find her voice among ten all neighing at once?"

"Then beware of Benjamin, for he has returned to take not one but all."

But David smiled at the skinny hand which was raised in warning.

"Say no more," he said solemnly. "I am already to blame for hearkening to words against my brother Benjamin."

Because David could find no ready retort he grew angry.

"Also, think of this. Your eyes and your ears are grown dull, Abraham, and perhaps your mind is misted also."

He had gone to the entrance into the patio and paused there to wait with a lifted head. Abraham followed and attempted to speak again, but the last cruel speech had crushed him. He went out on the terrace, and looking back saw that David had not a glance for him; so Abraham went feebly on.

"I have become as a false prophet," he murmured, "and I am no more regarded."

His life had long been in its evening, and now, at a step, the darkness of old age fell about him. From the margin of the lake he looked up and saw Connor ride to the patio.

David, at the entrance, clasped the hand of his guest while he was still on the horse and helped him to the ground.

"This," he said solemnly, "is a joyful day in my house."

"What's the big news?" inquired the gambler, and added: "Why so happy?"

"Is it not the day of your return? Isaac! Zacharias!"

They came running as he clapped his hands.

"Set out the oldest wine, and there is a haunch of the deer that was killed at the gate. Go! And now, Benjamin, did Shakra carry you well and swiftly?"

"Better than I was ever carried before."

"Then she deserves well of me. Come hither, Shakra, and stand behind me. Truly, Benjamin, my brother, my thoughts have ridden ten times across the mountains and back, wishing for your return!"

Connor was sufficiently keen to know that a main reason for the warmth of his reception was that he had been doubted while he was away, and while they supped in the patio he was even able to guess who had raised the suspicion against him. Word was brought that Abraham lay in his bed seriously ill, but David Eden showed no trace of sympathy.

"Which is the greater crime?" he asked Benjamin a little later. "To poison the food a man eats or the thoughts in his mind?"

"Surely," said the crafty gambler, "the mind is of more inportance than the stomach."

Luckily David bore the main burden of conversation that evening, for the brain of Connor was surcharged with impatient waiting. His great plan, he shrewdly guessed, would give him everything or else ruin him in the Garden of Eden, and the suspense was like an eating pain. Luckily the crisis came on the very next day.

Jacob galloped into the patio, and flung himself from the back of Abra.

David and Connor rose from their chairs under the arcade where they had been watching Joseph setting great stones in place around the border of the fountain pool. The master of the Garden went forward in some anger at this unceremonious interruption. But Jacob came as one of whose news is so important that it overrides all need of conventional approach.

"A woman," he panted. "A women at the gate of the Garden!"

"Why are you here?" said David sternly.

"A woman—"

"Man, woman, child, or beast, the law is the same. They shall not enter the Garden of Eden. Why are you here?"

"And she rides the gray gelding, the son of Yoruba!"

At that moment the white trembling lips of Connor might have told the master much, but he was too angered to take heed of his guest.

"That which has once left the Garden is no longer part of it. For us, the gray gelding does not exist. Why are you here?"

"Because she would not leave the gate. She says that she will see you."

"She is a fool. And because she was so confident, you were weak enough to believe her?"

"I told her that you would not come; that you could not come!"

"You have told her that it is impossible for me to speak with her?" said David, while Connor gradually regained control of himself, summoning all his strength for the crisis.

"I told her all that, but she said nevertheless she would see you."

"For what reason?"

"Because she has money with which to buy another horse like her gelding, which is old."

"Go back and tell her that there is no money price on the heads of my horses. Go! When Ephraim is at the gate there are no such journeyings to me."

"Ephraim is here," said Jacob stoutly, "and he spoke much with her. Nevertheless she said that you would see her."

"For what reason?"

"She said: 'Because.'"

"Because of what?"

"That word was her only answer: 'Because.'"

"This is strange," murmured David, turning to Connor. "Is that one word a reason?

"Go back again," commanded David grimly. "Go back and tell this woman that I shall not come, and that if she comes again she will be driven away by force. And take heed, Jacob, that you do not come to me again on such an errand. The law is fixed. It is as immovable as the rocks in the mountains. You know all this. Be careful hereafter that you remember. Be gone!"

The ruin of his plan in its very inception threatened Ben Connor. If he could once bring David to see the girl he trusted in her beauty and her cleverness to effect the rest. But how lead him to the gate? Moreover, he was angered and his frown boded no good for Jacob. The old servant was turning away, and the gambler hunted his mind desperately for an expedient. Persuasion would never budge this stubborn fellow so used to command. There remained the opposite of persuasion. He determined on an indirect appeal to the pride of the master.

"You are wise, David," he said solemnly. "You are very wise. These creatures are dangerous, and men of sense shun them. Tell your servants to drive her away with blows of a stick so that she will never return."

"No, Jacob," said the master, and the servant returned to hear the command. "Not with sticks. But with words, for flesh of women is tender. This is hard counsel, Benjamin!"

He regarded the gambler with great surprise.

"Their flesh may be tender, but their spirits are strong," said Connor. The opening he had made was too small. At least he had the interest of David, and through that entering wedge he determined to drive with all his might.

"And dangerous," he added gravely.

"Dangerous?" said the master. He raised his head. "Dangerous?"

As if a jackal had dared to howl in the hearing of the lion.

"Ah, David, if you saw her you would understand why I warn you!"

"It would be curious. In what wise does her danger strike?"

"That I cannot say. They have a thousand ways."

The master turned irresolutely toward Jacob.

"You could not send her away with words?"

"David, for one of my words she has ten that flow with pleasant sound like water from a spring, and with little meaning, except that she will not go."

"You are a fool!"

"So I felt when I listened to her."

"There is an old saying, David, my brother," said Connor, "that there is more danger in one pleasant woman

124

than in ten angry men. Drive her from the gate with stones!"

"I fear that you hate women, Benjamin."

"They were the source of evil."

"For which penance was done."

"The penance followed the sin."

"God, who made the mountains, the river and this garden and man, He made woman also. She cannot be all evil. I shall go."

"Then, remember that I have warned you. God, who made man and woman, made fire also."

"And is not fire a blessing?"

He smiled at his triumph and this contest of words.

"You shall go with me, Benjamin."

"I? Never!"

"In what is the danger?"

"If you find none, there is none. For my part I have nothing to do with women."

But David was already whistling to Glani.

"One woman can be no more terrible than one man," he declared to Benjamin. "And I have made Joseph, who is great of body, bend like a blade of grass in the wind."

Farewell, and God keep you!"

"Farewell, Benjamin, my brother, and have no fear."

Connor followed him with his eyes, half-triumphant, half-fearful. What would happen at the gate? He would have given much to see even from a distance the duel between the master and the woman.

At the gate of the patio David turned and waved his hand.

"I shall conquer!"

And then he was gone.

Connor stared down at the grass with a cynical smile until he felt another gaze upon him, and he became aware of the little beast—eyes of Joseph glittering. The giant had paused in his work with the stones.

"What are you thinking of, Joseph?" asked the gambler.

Joseph made an indescribable gesture of hate and fear.

"Of the whip!" he said. "I also opened the gate of the Garden. On whose back will the whip fall this time?"

CHAPTER TWENTY-ONE

NEAR the end of the eucalyptus avenue, and close to the gate, David dismounted and made Jacob do likewise.

"We may come on them by surprise and listen," he said. "A soft step has won great causes."

They went forward cautiously, interchanging sharp glances as though they were stalking some dangerous beast, and so they came within earshot of the gate and sheltered from view of it by the edge of the cliff. David paused and cautioned his companion with a mutely raised hand.

"He lived through the winter," Ephraim was saying. "I took him into my room and cherished him by the warmth of my fire and with rubbing, so that when spring came, and gentler weather, he was still alive—a great leggy colt with a backbone that almost lifted through the skin. Only high bright eyes comforted me and told me that my work was a good work."

David and Jacob interchanged nods of wonder, for Ephraim was telling to this woman the dearest secret of his life.

It was how he had saved the weakling colt, Jumis, and raised him to a beautiful stallion, only to have him die suddenly in the height of his promise. Certainly Ephraim was nearly won over by the woman; it threw David on guard.

"Go back to Abra," he whispered. "Ride on to the gate and tell her boldly to be gone. I shall wait here, and in time of need I shall help you. Make haste. Ephraim grows like wet clay under her fingers. Ah, how wise is Benjamin!"

Jacob obeyed. He stole away and presently shot past at the full gallop of Abra. The stallion came to a sliding halt, and Jacob spoke from his back, which was a grave discourtesy in the Garden of Eden.

"The master will not see you," he said. "The sun is still

high. Return by the way you have come; you get no more from the Garden than its water and its air. He does not sell horses."

For the first time she spoke, and at the sound of her voice David Eden stepped out from the rock; he remembered himself in time and shrank back to shelter.

"He sold this horse."

"It was the will of the men before David that these things should be done, but the Lord knows the mind of David and that his heart bleeds for every gelding that leaves the Garden. See what you have done to him! The marks of the whip and the spur are on his sides. Woe to you if David should see them!"

She cried out at that in such a way that David almost felt she had been struck.

"It was the work of a drunken fool, and not mine."

"Then God have mercy on that man, for if the master should see him, David would have no mercy. I warn you: David is one with a fierce eye and a strong hand. Be gone before he comes and sees the scars on the gray horse."

"Then he is coming?"

"She is quick," thought David, as an embarrassed pause ensued. "Truly, Benjamin was right, and there is danger in these creatures."

"He has many horses," the girl went on, "and I have only this one. Besides, I would pay well for another."

"What price?"

"He should not have asked," muttered David.

"Everything that I have," she was answering, and the low thrill of her voice went through and through the master of the Garden. "I could buy other horses with this money, but not another like my gray. He is more than a horse. He is a companion to me. He understands me when I talk, and I understand him. You see how he stands with his head down? He is not tired, but hungry. When he neighs in a certain way from the corral I know that he is lonely. You see that he comes to me now? That is because he knows I am talking about him, for we are friends. But he is old and he will die, and what shall I do then? It will be like a death in my house!"

Another pause followed.

"You love the horse," said the voice of Ephraim, and it was plain that Jacob was beyond power of speech.

"And I shall pay for another. Hold out your hand."

"I cannot take it."

Nevertheless, it seemed that he obeyed, for presently the girl continued: "After my father died I sold the house. It was pretty well blanketed with a mortgage, but I cleared out this hundred from the wreck. I went to work and saved what I could. Ten dollars every month, for twenty months—you can count for yourself—makes two hundred, and here's the two hundred more in your hand. Three hundred altogether. Do you think it's enough?"

"If there were ten times as much," said Jacob, "it would not be enough. There—take your money. It is not enough. There is no money price on the heads of the master's horses."

But a new light had fallen upon David. Women, as he had heard of them, were idle creatures who lived upon that which men gained with sweaty toil, but this girl, it seemed, was something more. She was strong enough to earn her bread, and something more. Money values were not clear to David Eden, but three hundred dollars sounded a very considerable sum. He determined to risk exposure by glancing around the rock. If she could work like a man, no doubt she was made like a man and not like those useless and decorative creatures of whom Matthew had often spoken to him, with all their graces and voices.

Cautiously he peered and he saw her standing beside the old, broken gray horse. Even old Ephraim seemed a stalwart figure in comparison.

At first he was bewildered, and then he almost laughed aloud. Was it on account of this that Benjamin had warned him, this fragile girl? He stepped boldly from behind the rock.

"There is no more to say," quoth Jacob.

"But I tell you, he himself will come."

"You are right," said David.

At that her eyes turned on him, and David was stopped in the midst of a stride until she shrank back against the horse.

Then he went on, stepping softly, his hand extended in that sign of peace which is as old as mankind.

"Stay in peace," said David, "and have no fear. It is I, David."

He hardly knew his own voice, it was so gentle. A twilight dimness seemed to have fallen upon Jacob and Ephraim, and he was only aware of the girl. Her fear seemed to be half gone already, and she even came a hopeful step toward him.

"I knew from the first that you would come," she said, "and let me buy one horse—you have so many."

"We will talk of that later."

"David," broke in the grave voice of Ephraim, "remember your own law!"

He looked at the girl instead of Ephraim as he answered: "Who am I to make laws? God begins where David leaves off."

And he added: "What is your name?"

"Ruth."

"Come, Ruth," said David, "we will go home together."

She advanced as one in doubt until the shadow of the cliff fell over her. Then she looked back from the throat of the gate and saw Ephraim and Jacob facing her as though they understood there was no purpose in guarding against what might approach the valley from without now that the chief enemy was within. David, in the pause, was directing Jacob to place the girl's saddle on the back of Abra.

"For it is not fitting," he explained, "that you should enter my garden save on one of my horses. And look, here is Glani."

The stallion came at the sound of his name. She had heard of the great horse from Connor, but the reality was far more than the words.

"And this, Glani, is Ruth.

She touched the velvet nose which was stretched inquisitively toward her, and then looked up and found that David was smiling. A moment later they were riding side by side down the avenue of the eucalyptus trees, and through the tall tree-trunks new vistas opened rapidly about her. Every stride of Abra seemed to carry her another step into the life of David.

"I should have called Shakra for you," said David watching her with concern, "but she is ridden by another who has the right to the best in the garden."

"Even Glani?"

"Even Glani, save that he fears to ride my horse, and

therefore he has Shakra. I am sorry, for I wish to see you together. She is like you—beautiful, delicate, and swift."

She urged Abra into a shortened gallop with a touch of her heel, so that the business of managing him gave her a chance to cover her confusion. She could have smiled away a compliment, but the simplicity of David meant something more.

"Peace, Abra!" commanded the master. "Oh, unmannerly colt! It would be other than this if the wise Shakra were beneath your saddle."

"No, I am content with Abra. Let Shakra be for your servant."

"Not servant, but friend—a friend whom Glani chose for me. Consider how fickle our judgments are and how little things persuade us. Abraham is rich in words, but his face is ugly, and I prefer the smooth voice of Zacharias, though he is less wise. I have grieved for this and yet it is hard to change. But a horse is wiser than a fickle-minded man, and when Glani went to the hand of Benjamin without my order, I knew that I had found a friend."

She knew the secret behind that story, and now she looked at David with pity.

"In my house you will meet Benjamin," the master was saying thoughtfully, evidently encountering a grave problem. "I have said that little things make the judgments of men! If a young horse shies once, though he may become a true traveler and a wise head, yet his rider remembers the first jump and is ever uneasy in the saddle."

She nodded, wondering what lay behind the explanation.

"Or if a snake crosses the road before a horse, at that place the horse trembles when he passes again."

"Yes."

She found it strangely pleasant to follow the simple process of his mind.

"It is so with Benjamin. At some time a woman crosses his way like a snake, and because of her he has come to hate all women. And when I started for the gate, even now, he warned me against you."

The clever mind of the gambler opened to her and she smiled at the trick.

"Yes, it is a thing for laughter," said David happily.

"I came with a mind armed for trouble—and I find you, whom I could break between my hands."

He turned, casting out his arms.

"What harm have I received from you?"

They had reached the head of the bridge, and even as David turned a changing gust carried to them a chorus of men's voices. David drew rein.

"There is a death," he said, "in my household."

CHAPTER TWENTY-TWO

THE singing took on body and form as the pitch rose.

"There is a death," repeated David. "Abraham is dead, the oldest and the wisest of my servants. The Lord gave and the Lord has taken away. Glory to His name!"

Ruth was touched to the heart.

"I am sorry," she said simply.

"Let us rejoice, rather, for Abraham is happy. His soul is reborn in a young body. Do you not hear them singing? Let us ride on."

He kept his head high and a stereotyped smile on his lips as the horses sprang into a gallop—that breath-taking gallop which made the spirit of the girl leap; but she saw his breast raise once or twice with a sigh. It was the stoicism of an Indian, she felt, and like an Indian's was the bronze-brown skin and the long hair blowing in the wind. The lake was beside them now, and dense forest beyond opening into pleasant meadows. She was being carried back into a primitive time of which the type was the man beside her. Riding without a saddle his body gave to the swing of the gallop, and she was more conscious than ever of physical strength.

But now the hoofs beat softly on the lawn terraces, and in a moment they had stopped before the house where the death had been. She knew at once. The empty arch into the patio of the servants' house was eloquent, in some manner, of the life that had departed. Before it was the group of singers, all standing quiet, as though their own music had silenced them, or perhaps preparing to sing again. Connor had described the old servant, but she was not prepared for these straight, withered bodies, these bony, masklike faces, and the white heads.

All in an instant they seemed to see her, and a flash of pleasure went from face to face. They stirred, they came toward her with glad murmurs, all except one, the oldest of them all, who remained aloof with his arms folded. But the others pressed close around her, talking excitedly to one another, as though she could not understand what they said. And she would never forget one who took her hand in both of his. The touch of his fingers was cold and as dry as parchment. "Honey child, God bless your pretty face."

Was this the formal talk of which Connor had warned her? A growl from David drove them back from her like leaves before a wind. He had slipped from his horse, and now walked forward.

"It is Abraham?" he asked.

"He is dead and glorious," answered the chorus, and the girl trembled to hear those time-dried relics of humanity speak so cheerily of death.

The master was silent for a moment, then: "Did he leave no message for me?"

In place of answering the group shifted and opened a passage to the one in the rear, who stood with folded arms.

"Elijah, you were with him?"

"I heard his last words."

"And what dying message for David?"

"Death sealed his lips while he had still much to say. To the end he was a man of many words. But first he returned thanks to our Father who breathed life into the clay."

"That was a proper thought, and I see that the words were words of Abraham."

"He gave thanks for a life of quiet ease and wise masters, and he forgave the Lord the length of years he was kept in this world."

"In that," said David gravely, "I seem to hear his voice speaking. Continue."

"He commanded us to sing pleasantly when he was gone."

"I heard the singing on the lake road. It is well."

"Also, he bade us keep the first master in our minds, for John, he said, was the beginning."

At this the face of David clouded a little.

"Continue. What word for David?"

Something that Connor had said about the pride and sulkiness of a child came back to Ruth.

Elijah, after hesitation, went on: "He declared that Glani is too heavy in the forehead."

"Yes, that is Abraham," said the master, smiling tenderly. "He would argue even on the death bed."

"But a cross with Tabari would remedy that defect."

"Perhaps. What more?"

"He blessed you and bade you remember and rejoice that he was gone to his wife and child."

"Ah?" cried David softly. His glance, wandering absently, rested on the girl for a moment, and then came back to Elijah. "His mind went back to that? What further for my ear?"

"I remember nothing more, David."

"Speak!" commanded the master.

The eyes of Elijah roved as though for help.

"Toward the end his voice grew faint and his mind seemed to wander."

"Far rather tremble. Elijah, if you keep back the words he spoke, however sharp they may be. My hand is not light. Remember, and speak."

The fear of Elijah changed to a gloomy pride, and now he not only raised his head, but he even made a step forward and stood in dignity.

"Death took Abraham by the throat, and yet he continued to speak. 'Tell David that four masters cherished Abraham, but David cast him out like a dog and broke his heart, and therefore he dies. Although I bless him, God will hereafter judge him!' "

A shudder went through the entire group, and Ruth herself was uneasy.

"Keep your own thoughts and the words of Abraham well divided," said David solemnly. "I know his mind and its working. Continue, but be warned."

"I am warned, David, but my brother Abraham is dead and my heart weeps for him!"

"God will hereafter judge me," said David harshly. "And what was the further judgment of Abraham, the old man?"

"Even this: 'David has opened the Garden to one and therefore it will be opened to all. The law is broken. The first sin is the hard sin and the others follow easily. It is swift to run downhill. He has brought in one, and another will soon follow.'"

"Elijah," thundered David, "you have wrested his words to fit the thing you see."

"May the dead hand of Abraham strike me down if these were not his words."

"Had he become a prophet?" muttered David. "No, it was maundering of an old man."

"God speaks on the lips of the dying, David."

"You have said enough."

"Wait!"

"You are rash, Elijah."

She could not see the face of David, but the terror and frenzied devotion of Elijah served her as mirror to see the wrath of the master of the Garden.

"David has opened the gate of the Garden. The world sweeps in and shall carry away the life of Eden like a flood. All that four masters have done the fifth shall undo."

The strength of his ecstasy slid from Elijah and he dropped upon his knees with his head weighted toward the earth. The others were frozen in their places. One who had opened his lips to speak, perhaps to intercede for the rash Elijah, remained with his lips parted, a staring mask of fear. In them Ruth saw the rage of David Eden, and she was sickened by what she saw. She had half pitied the simplicity of this man, this gull of the clever Connor. Now she loathed him as a savage barbarian. Even these old men were hardly safe from his furies of temper.

"Arise," said the master at length, and she could feel his battle to control his voice. "You are forgiven, Elijah, because of your courage—yet, beware! As for that old man whose words you repeated, I shall consider him." He turned on his heel, and Ruth saw that his face was iron.

CHAPTER TWENTY-THREE

FROM the gate of the patio Connor, watching all that time in a nightmare of suspense, saw, first of all, the single figure of David come around the trees, David alone and walking. But before that shock passed he saw Glani at the heels of the master, and then, farther back, Ruth!

She had passed the gate and two-thirds of the battle was fought and won. Yet all was not well, as he plainly saw. With long, swift steps David came over the terrace, and finally paused as if his thoughts had stopped him. He turned as Glani passed, and the girl came up to him; his extended arm halted Abra and he stood looking up to the girl and speaking. Only the faint murmur of his voice came unintelligibly to Connor, but he recognized danger in it as clearly as in the hum of bees. Suddenly the girl, answering, put out her hands as if in a gesture of surrender. Another pause—it was only a matter of a second or so, but it was a space for life or death with Connor. In that interval he knew that his scheme was made or ruined. What had the girl said? Perhaps that mighty extended arm holding back Abra had frightened her, and with the wind blowing his long black hair aside, David of Eden was a figure wild enough to alarm her. Perhaps in fear for her life she had exposed the whole plan. If so, it meant broken bones for Connor.

But now David turned again, and this time he was talking by the side of Abra as they came up the hill. He talked with many gestures, and the girl was laughing down to him.

"God bless her!" muttered Connor impulsively. "She's a true-blue one!"

He remembered his part in the nick of time as they came closer, and David helped the girl down from the saddle and brought her forward. The gambler drew himself up and made his face grave with disapproval. Now or never he must prove to David that there was no shadow of a connection between him and the girl. Yet he was by no means easy. There was something forced and stereotyped in the smile of the girl that told him she had been through a crucial test and was still near the breaking point.

David presented them to one another uneasily. He was even a little embarrassed under the accusing eye of Connor.

"I make you known, Ruth," he said, "to my brother Benjamin. He is that man of whom I told you."

"I am happy," said the girl, "to be known to him."

"That much I cannot say," replied the gambler.

He turned upon David with outstretched arm.

"Ah, David, I have warned you!"

"As Abraham warned me against you, Benjamin. And dying men speak truth."

The counter-attack was so shrewd, so unexpected, that the gambler, for the moment, was thrown completely off his guard.

He could only murmur: "You are the judge for yourself, David."

"I am. Do not think that the power is in me. But God loves the Garden and His voice is never far from me. Neither are the spirits of the four who lived here before me and made this place. When there is danger they warn me. When I am in error the voice of God corrects me. And just as I heard the voice against the woman, Ruth, and heed it not."

He seemed to have gathered conviction for himself, much needed conviction, as he spoke. He turned now toward the girl.

"Be not wroth with Benjamin; and bear him no malice."

"I bear him none in the world," she answered truthfully, and held out her hand.

But Connor was still in his rôle. He folded his arms and pointedly disregarded the advance.

"Woman, let there be peace and few words between us. My will is the will of David."

"There speaks my brother!" cried the master of the valley.

"And yet," muttered Connor, "why is she here?"

"She came to buy a horse."

"But they are not sold."

"That is true. Yet she has traveled far and she is in great need of food and drink. Could I turn her away hungry, Benjamin?"

"She could have been fed at the gate. She could surely have rested there."

It was easy to see that David was hardpressed. His eye roved eagerly to Ruth. Then a triumphant explanation sparkled in his eye.

"It is the horse she rides, a gelding from my Garden. His lot in the world has been hard. He is scarred with the spur and the whip. I have determined to take him back, at a price. But who can arrange matters of buying and selling all in a moment? It is a matter for much talk. Therefore she is here."

"I am answered," said Connor, and turning to Ruth he winked broadly.

"It is well," said David, "and I foresee happy days. In the meantime there is a duty before me. Abraham must be laid in his grave and I leave Ruth to your keeping, Benjamin. Bear with her tenderly for my sake."

He stepped to the girl.

"You are not afraid?"

"I am not afraid," she answered.

"My thoughts shall be near you. Farewell."

He had hardly reached the gate of the patio when Joseph, going out after finishing his labor at the fountain, passed between the gambler and the girl. Connor stopped him with a sign.

"The whip hasn't fallen, you see," he said maliciously.

"There is still much time," replied Joseph. "And before the end it will fall. Perhaps on you. Or on that!"

He indicated the girl with his pointing finger; his glance turned savagely from one to the other, and then he went slowly out of the patio and they were alone. She came to Connor at once and even touched his arm in her excitement.

"What did he mean?"

"That's the one I told you about. The one David beat up with the whip. He'd give his eye teeth to get back at me, and he has an idea that there's going to be hell to pay because another person has come into the valley. Bunk! But—what happened down the hill?"

"When he stopped me? Did you see that?"

"My heart stopped the same minute. What was it?"

"He had just heard the last words of Abraham. When he stopped me on the hill his face was terrible. Like a wolf!"

"I know that look in him. How did you buck up under it?"

"I didn't. I felt my blood turn to water and I wanted to run."

"But you stuck it out—I saw! Did he say anything?"

"He said: 'Dying men do not lie. And I have been twice warned. Woman, why are you here?'"

"And you?" gasped Connor. "What did you say?"

"Nothing. My head spun. I looked up the terrace. I wanted to see you, but you weren't in sight. I felt terribly alone and absolutely helpless. If I'd had a gun, I would have reached for it."

"Thank God you didn't!"

"But you don't know what his face was like! I expected him to tear me off the horse and smash me with his hands. All at once I wanted to tell him everything—beg him not to hurt me." Connor groaned.

"I knew it! I knew that was in your head!"

"But I didn't."

"Good girl."

"He said: 'Why are you here? What harm have you come to work in the Garden?'"

"And you alone with him!" gasped Connor.

"That was what did it. I was so helpless that it made me bold. Can you imagine smiling at a time like that?"

"Were you able to?"

"I don't know how. It took every ounce of strength in me. But I made myself smile—straight into his face. Then I put out my hands to him all at once.

"'How could I harm you?' I asked him.

"And then you should have seen his face change and the anger break up like a cloud. I knew I was safe, then, but I was still dizzy—just as if I'd looked over a cliff—you know?"

"And yet you rode up the hill after that laughing down to him! Ruth, you're the gamest sport and the best pal in

138

the world. The finest little act I ever saw on the stage or off. It was Big Time stuff. My hat's off, but—where'd you get the nerve?"

"I was frightened almost to death. Too much frightened for it to show. When I saw you, my strength came back."

"But what do you think of him?"

"He's—simply a savage. What do I think of an Indian?"

"No more than that?"

"Ben, can you pet a tiger after you've seen his claws?" He looked at her with anxiety.

"You're not going to break down later on—feeling as if he's dynamite about to explode all the time?"

"I'm going to play the game through," she said with a sort of fierce happiness. "I've felt like a sneak thief about this. But now it's different. He's more of a wolf than a man. Ben, I saw murder in his face, I swear! And if it isn't wrong to tame wild beasts it isn't wrong to tame him. I'm going to play the game, lead him as far as I can until we get the horses—and then it'll be easy enough to make up by being good the rest of my life."

"Ruth—girl—you've covered the whole ground. And when you have the coin—" He broke off with laughter that was filled with drunken excitement. "But what did you think of my game?"

She did not hear him, and standing with her hands clasped lightly behind her she looked beyond the roof of the house and over the tops of the western mountains, with the sun-haze about them.

"I feel as if I were on top of the world," she said at last. "And I wouldn't have one thing changed. We're playing for big stakes, but we're taking a chance that makes the game worth while. What we win we'll earn—because he's a devil. Isn't it what you'd call a fair bet?"

"The squarest in the world," said Connor stoutly.

CHAPTER TWENTY-FOUR

THEY had no means of knowing when David would return and the ominous shadow of Joseph, lingering near the patio, determined Connor to walk out of any possible earshot. They went down to the lake with the singing of the men on the other side of the hill growing dim as they descended. The cool of the day was beginning, and they walked close to the edge of the water with the brown treetrunks on one side and the green images floating beyond. Peace lay over Eden valley and the bright river that ran through it, but Ben Connor had no mind to dwell on unessentials.

He had found in the girl an ally of unexpected strength. He expected only a difficult tool filled with scruples, drawing back, imperiling his plans with her hesitation. Instead, she was on fire with the plan. He thought well to fan that fire and keep it steadily blazing.

"It's better for David; better for him than it is for us. Look at the poor fool! He's in prison here and doesn't know it. He thinks he's happy, but he's simply kidding himself. In six months I'll have him chatting with millionaires."

"Let a barber do a day's work on him first."

"No. It's just the long-haired nuts like that who get by with the high-steppers. He has a lingo about flowers and trees that'll knock their eyes out. I know the gang. Always on edge for something different—music that sounds like a riot in a junk shop and poetry that reads like a drunken printing-press. Well, David ought to be different enough to suit 'em. I'll boost him, though: 'The Man that Brought Out the Eden Grays!' He'll be headline stuff!"

He laughed so heartily that he did not notice the quick glance of criticism which the girl cast at him.

"I'm not taking anything from him, really," went on Connor. "I'm simply sneaking around behind him so's I

140

can pour his pockets full of the coin. That's all there is to it. Outside of the looks, tell me if there's anything crooked you can see?"

"I don't think there is," she murmured. "I almost hope that there isn't!"

She was so dubious about it that Connor was alarmed. He was fond of Ruth Manning, but she was just "different" enough to baffle him. Usually he divided mankind into three or four categories for the sake of fast thinking. There were the "boobs," the "regular guys," the "high steppers," and the "nuts." Sometimes he came perilously close to including Ruth in the last class—with David Eden. And if he did not do so, it was mainly because she had given such an exhibition of cool courage only a few moments before. He had finished his peroration, now, with a feeling of actual virtue, but the shadow on her face made him change his tactics and his talk.

He confined himself, thereafter, strictly to the future. First he outlined his plans for raising the cash for the big "killing." He told of the men to whom he could go for backing. There were "hard guys" who would take a chance. "Wise ones" who would back his judgment. "Fall guys" who would follow him blindly. For ten percent he would get all the cash he could place. Then it remained to try out the grays in secret, and in public let them go through the paces ridden under wraps and heavily weighted. He described the means of placing the big money before the great race.

And as he talked his figures mounted from tens to hundreds to thousands, until he was speaking in millions. In all of this profit she and David and Connor would share dollar for dollar. At the first corner of the shore they turned she had arrived at a snug apartment in New York. She would have a housekeeper-companion. There would be a cosy living room and a paneled dining room. In the entrance hall of the apartment house, imitation of encrusted marble, no doubt.

But as they came opposite a little wooded island in the lake she had added a maid to the housekeeper. Also, there was now a guest room. Some one from Lukin would be in that room; some one from Lukin would go through the place with her, marveling at her good fortune.

And clothes! They made all the difference. Dressed as

141

she would be dressed, when she came into a room that queer, cold gleam of envy would be in the eyes of the women and the men would sit straighter!

Yet when they reached the place where the shore line turned north and west her imagination, spurred by Connor's talk, was stumbling along dizzy heights. Her apartment occupied a whole floor. Her butler was a miracle of dignity and her chef a genius in the kitchen. On the great table the silver and glass were things of frosted light. Her chauffeur drove a monster automobile with a great purring engine that whipped her about the city with the color blown into her cheeks. In her box at the opera she was allowing the deep, soft luxury of the fur collar to slide down from her throat, while along the boxes, in the galleries, there was a ripple of light as the thousand glasses turned upon her. Then she found that Connor was smiling at her. She flushed, but snapped her fingers.

"This thing is going through," she declared.

"You won't weaken?"

"I'm as cold as steel. Let's go back. He'll probably be in the house by this time."

Time had slipped past her unnoticed, and the lake was violet and gold with the sunset as they turned away; under the trees along the terraces the brilliant wild flowers were dimmed by a blue shadow.

"But I never saw wild flowers like those," she said to Connor.

"Nobody else ever did. But old Matthew, whoever he was, grew 'em and kept crossing 'em until he got those big fellows with all the colors of the rainbow."

"Hurry! We're late!"

"No, David's probably on top of that hill, now; always goes up there to watch the sun rise and the sun set. Can you beat that?"

He chuckled, but a shade had darkened the face of the girl for a moment. Then she lifted her head resolutely.

"I'm not going to try to understand him. The minute you understand a thing you stop being afraid of it; and as soon as I stop being afraid of David Eden I might begin to like him—which is what I don't want."

"What's that?" cried Connor, breaking in on her last words. When Ruth began to think aloud he always stopped listening; it was a maxim of his to never listen when a woman became serious.

"It's that strange giant."

"Joseph!" exclaimed Connor heavily. "Whipping did him no good. He'll need killing one of these days."

But she had already reverted to another thing.

"Do you think he worships the sun?"

"I don't think. Try to figure out a fellow like that and you get to be just as much of a nut as he is. Go on toward the house and I'll follow you in a minute. I want to talk to big Joe."

He turned aside into the trees briskly, and the moment he was out of sight of the girl he called softly: "Joseph!"

He repeated the call after a trifling wait before he saw the big man coming unconcernedly through the trees toward him. Joseph came close before he stopped—very close, as a man will do when he wishes to make another aware of his size, and from this point of vantage, he looked over Connor from head to foot with a glance of lingering and insolent criticism. The gambler was somewhat amused and a little alarmed by that attitude.

"Now, Joseph," he said, "tell me frankly why you're dodging me about the valley. Waiting for a chance to throw stones?"

His smile remained without a reflection on the stolid face of the servant.

"Benjamin," answered the deep, solemn voice, "I know all!"

It made Connor peer into those broad features as into a dim light. Then a moment of reflection assured him that Joseph could not have learned the secret.

"Haneemar, whom you know," continued Joseph, "has told me about you."

"And where," asked Connor, completely at sea, "did you learn of Haneemar?"

"From Abraham. And I know that this is the head of Haneemar."

He brought out in his palm the little watch-charm of carved ivory.

"Of course," nodded Connor, feeling his way. "And what is it that you know from Haneemar?"

"That you are evil, Benjamin, and that you have come

here for evil. You entered by a trick; and you will stay here for evil purposes until the end."

"You follow around to pick up a little dope, eh?" chuckled Connor. "You trail me to find out what I intend to do? Why don't you go to David and warn him?"

"Have I forgotten the whip?" asked Joseph, his nostrils trembling with anger. "But the good Haneemar now gives me power and in the end he will betray you into my hands. That is why I follow you. Wherever you go I follow; I am even able to know what you think! But hearken to me, Benjamin. Take back the head of Haneemar and the bad luck that lives in it. Take it back, and I shall no longer follow you. I shall forget the whip. I shall be ready to do you a service."

He extended the little piece of ivory eagerly, but Connor drew back. His superstitions were under the surface of his mind, but, still, they were there, and the fear which Joseph showed was contagious.

"Why don't you throw it away if you're afraid of it, Joseph?"

"You know as I know," returned Joseph, glowering, "that it cannot be thrown away. It must be given and freely accepted, as I—oh fool—accepted it from you."

There was such a profound conviction in this that Connor was affected in spite of himself. That little trinket had been the entering wedge through which he had worked his way into the Garden and started on the road to fortune. He would rather have cut off his hand, now, than take it back.

"Find some one else to take it," he suggested cheerily, "I don't want the thing."

"Then all that Abraham told me is true!" muttered Joseph, closing his hand over the trinket. "But I shall follow you, Benjamin. When you think you are alone you shall find me by turning your head. Every day by sunrise and every day by the dark I beg Haneemar to put his curse on you. I have done you no wrong, and you have had me shamed."

"And now you're going to have me bewitched, eh?" asked Connor.

"You shall see."

The gambler drew back another pace and through the

shadows he saw the beginning of a smile of animal-cunning on the face of Joseph.

"The devil take you and Haneemar together," he growled. "Remember this, Joseph. I've had you whipped once. The next time I'll have you flayed alive."

Instead of answering, Joseph merely grinned more openly, and the gambler, to forget the ape-face, wheeled and hurried out from the trees. The touch of nightmare dread did not leave him until he rejoined Ruth on the higher terrace.

They found the patio glowing with light, the table near the fountain, and three chairs around it. David came out of the shadow of the arcade to meet them, and he was as uneasy as a boy who had a surprise for grown-ups. He had not even time for a greeting.

"You have not seen your room?" he said to Ruth. "I have made it ready for you. Come!"

He led the way half a pace in front, glancing back at them as though to reprove their slowness, until he reached a door at which he turned and faced her, laughing with excitement. She could hardly believe that this man with his childish gayety was the same whose fury had terrified the servants that same afternoon.

"Close your eyes—close them fast. You will not look until I say?"

She obeyed, setting her teeth to keep from smiling.

"Now come forward—step high for the doorway. So! You are in. Now wait—now open your eyes and look!"

She obeyed again and saw first David standing back with an anxious smile and the gesture of one who reveals, but is not quite sure of its effect. Then she heard a soft, startled exclamation from Connor behind her. Last of all she saw the room.

It was as if the walls had been broken down and a garden let inside—it gave an effect of open air, sunlight and wind. Purple flowers like warm shadows banked the farther corners, and out of them rose a great vine draping the window. It had been torn bodily from the earth, and now the roots were packed with damp moss, yellow-green. It bore in clusters and single flowers and abundant bloom, each blossom as large as the mallow, and a dark gold so rich that Ruth well-nigh listened for the murmur of bees working this mine of pollen. From above, the great flowers hung down against the dull red of the sunset sky; and from below the distant treetops on the terrace pointed up with glimmers of the lake between. There was only the reflected light of the evening, now, but the cuplike blossoms were filled to the brim with a glow of their own.

She looked away.

A dapple deer-skin covered the bed like the shadow under a tree in mid-day, and the yellow of the flowers was repeated dimly on the floor by a great, tawny hide of a mountain-lion. She took up some of the purple flowers, and letting the velvet petals trail over her finger tips, she turned to David with a smile. But what Connor saw, and saw with a thrill of alarm, was that her eyes were filling with tears.

"See!" said David gloomily. "I have done this to make you happy, and now you are sad!"

"Because it is so beautiful."

"Yes," said David slowly. "I think I understand."

But Connor took one of the flowers from her hand. She cried out, but too late to keep him from ripping the blossom to pieces, and now he held up a single petal, long, graceful, red-purple at the broader end and deep yellow at the narrow.

"Think of that a million times bigger," said Connor, "and made out of velvet. That'd be a design for a cloak, eh? Cost about a thousand bucks to imitate this petal, but it'd be worth it to see you in it, eh?"

She looked to David with a smile of apology for Connor, but her hand accepted the petal, and her second smile was for Connor himself.

CHAPTER TWENTY-FIVE

WHEN they went out into the patio again, David had lost a large part of his buoyancy of spirits, as though in some subtle manner Connor had overcast the triumph of the room; he left them with word that the evening meal would soon be ready and hurried off calling orders to Zacharias.

"Why did you do it?" she asked Connor as soon as they were alone.

"Because it made me mad to see a stargazer like that turning your head."

"But didn't you think the room was beautiful?"

"Sure. Like a riot in a florist's shop. But don't let this David take you off guard with his rooms full of flowers and full of silence."

"Silence?"

"Haven't I told you about his Room of Silence? That's one of his queer dodges. That room; you see? When anything bothers him he goes over and sits down in there, because—do you know what he thinks sits with him?"

"Well?"

"God!"

She was between a smile and a gasp.

"Yep, that's David," grinned Connor. "Just plain nut."

"What's inside?"

"I don't know. Maybe flowers."

"Let's find out."

He caught her arm quickly.

"Not in a thousand years!" He changed color at the thought and glanced guiltily around. "That would be the smash of everything. Why, he turned over the whole Garden of Eden to me. I can go anywhere, but not a step inside that room. It's Holy Ground, you see! Maybe it's where he keeps his jack. And I've a hunch that he has a slough of it tucked away somewhere."

She raised her hand as an idea came to her half way through this speech.

"Listen! I have an idea that the clew to all of David's mystery is in that room!"

"Drop that idea, Ruth," he ordered gruffly. "You've seen David on one rampage, but it's nothing to what would happen if you so much as peeked into that place. When the servants pass that door they take off their hats—watch 'em the next time you have a chance. You won't make a slip about that room?"

"No." But she added: "I'd give my soul—for one look!"

Dinner that night under the stars with the whispering of

the fountain beside them was a ceremony which Connor never forgot. The moon rose late and in the meantime the sky was heavy and dark with sheeted patchwork of clouds, with the stars showing here and there. The wind blew in gusts. A wave began with a whisper on the hill, came with a light rushing across the patio, and then diminished quickly among the trees down the terraces. Rough, iron-framed lanterns gave the light and showed the arcade stepping away on either side and growing dim toward the entrance. That uncertain illumination made the crude pillars seem to have only the irregularity of vast antiquity, stable masses of stone. Where the circle of lantern-light overlapped rose the fountain, a pale spray forever dissolving in the upper shadow. Connor himself was more or less used to these things, but he became newly aware of them as the girl sent quick, eager glances here and there.

She had placed a single one of the great yellow blossoms in her hair and it changed her shrewdly. It brought out the delicate coloring of her skin, and to the darkness of her eyes it lent a tint of violet. Plainly she enjoyed the scene with its newness. David, of course, was the spice to everything, and his capitulation was complete; he kept the girl always on an uneasy balance between happiness and laughter. And Connor trembled for fear the mirth would show through. But each change of her expression appeared to delight David more than the last.

Under his deft knife the choicest white meat came away from the breast of a chicken and he heaped it at once on the plate of Ruth. Then he dropped his chin upon his great brown fist and watched with silent delight while she ate. It embarrassed her; but her flush had a tinge of pleasure in it, as Connor very well knew.

"Look!" said David, speaking softly as though Ruth would not hear him. "How pleasant it is, to be three together. When we were two, one talked and the other grew weary—was it not so? But now we are complete. One speaks, one listens, and the other judges. I have been alone. The Garden of Eden has been to me a prison, at many times. And now there is nothing wanting. And why? There were many men before. We were not lacking in numbers. Yet there was an emptiness, and now comes one small creature, as delicate as a colt of three months, this

148

being of smiles and curious glances, this small voice, this woman—and at once the gap is filled. Is it not strange?"

He cast himself back in his chair, as though he wished to throw her into perspective with her surroundings, and all the time he was staring as though she were an image, a picture, and not a thing of flesh and blood. Connor himself was on the verge of a smile, but when he saw the face of Ruth Manning his mirth disappeared in a chill of terror. She was struggling and struggling in vain against a rising tide of laughter, laughter in the face of David Eden and his sensitive pride.

It came, it broke through all bonds, and now it was bubbling from her lips. As one who awaits the falling of a blow, Connor glanced furtively at the host, and again he was startled.

There was not a shade of evil temper in the face of David. He leaned forward, indeed, with a surge of the great shoulders, but it was one who listens to an entrancing music. And when she ceased, abruptly, he sighed.

"Speak to me," he commanded.

She murmured a faint reply.

"Again," said David, half closing his eyes. And Connor nodded a frantic encouragement to her.

"But what shall I say?"

"For the meaning of what you say," said David, "I have no care, but only for the sound. Have you heard dripping in a well, a sound like water filling a bottle and never reaching the top? It keeps you listening for an hour, perhaps, always a soft sound, but always rising toward a climax? Or a drowsy day when the wind hardly moves and the whistling of a bird comes now and then out of the trees, cool and contented? Or you pass a meadow of flowers in the warm sun and hear the ground murmur of the bees, and you think at once of the wax films of the honeycomb, and the clear golden honey? All those things I heard and saw when you spoke."

"Plain nut!" said Connor, framing the words with silent lips.

But though her eyes rested on him, apparently she did not see his face. She looked back at Connor with a wistful little half-smile.

At once David cast out both his hands toward hers.

"Ah, you are strange, new, delightful!" He stopped

149

abruptly. Then: "Does it make you happy to hear me say these things?"

"Why do you ask me that?" she said curiously.

"Because it fills me with unspeakable happiness to say them. If I am silent and only think then I am not so pleased. When I see Glani standing on the hill-top I feel his speed in the slope of his muscles, the flaunt of his tail, the pride of his head; but when I gallop him, and the wind of his galloping strikes my face—ha, that is a joy! So it is speaking with you. When I see you I say within: 'She is beautiful!' But when I speak it aloud your lips tremble a little toward a smile, your eyes darken with pleasure, and then my heart rises into my throat and I wish to speak again and again and again to find new things to say, to say old things in new words. So that I may watch the changes in your face. Do you understand? But now you blush. Is that a sign of anger?"

"It is a sign that no other men have ever talked to me in this manner."

"Then other men are fools. What I say is true. I feel it ring in me, that it is the truth. Benjamin, my brother, is it not so? Ha!"

She was raising the wine-cup; he checked her with his eager, extended hand.

"See, Benjamin, how this mysterious thing is done, this raising of the hand. *We* raise the cup to drink. An ugly thing—let it be done and forgotten. But when *she* lifts the cup it is a thing to be remembered; how her fingers curve and the weight of the cup presses into them, and how her wrist droops."

She lowered the cup hastily and put her hand before her face.

"I see," said Connor dryly.

"Bah!" cried the master of the Garden. "You do not see. But you, Ruth, are you angry? Are you shamed?"

He drew down her hands, frowning with intense anxiety. Her face was crimson.

"No," she said faintly.

"He says that he sees, but he does not see," went on David. "He is blind, this Benjamin of mine. I show him my noblest grove of the eucalyptus trees, each tree as tall as a hill, as proud as a king, as beautiful as a thought that springs up from the earth. I show him these glorious trees.

What does he say? 'You could build a whole town out of that wood!' Bah! Is that seeing? No, he is blind! Such a man would give you hard work to do. But I say to you, Ruth, that to be beautiful is to be wise, and industrious, and good. Surely you are to me like the rising of the sun—my heart leaps up! And you are like the coming of the night making the world beautiful and mysterious. For behind your eyes and behind your words, out of the sound of your voice and your glances, I guess at new things, strange things, hidden things. Treasures which cannot be held in the hands. Should you grow as old as Elijah, withered, meager as a grasshopper, the treasures would still be there. I, who have seen them, can never forget them!"

Once more she covered her eyes with her hand, and David started up from his chair.

"What have I done?" he asked faintly of Connor. He hurried around the table to her. "Look up! How have I harmed you?"

"I am only tired," she said.

"I am a fool! I should have known. Come!" said David.

He drew her from the chair and led her across the lawn, supporting her. At her door: "May sleep be to you like the sound of running water," murmured David.

And when the door was closed he went hastily back to Connor.

CHAPTER TWENTY-SIX

"WHAT have I done? What have I done?" he kept moaning. "She is in pain. I have hurt her."

"Sit down," said Connor, deeply amused.

It had been a curious revelation to him, this open talk of a man who was falling in love. He remembered the way he had proposed to a girl, once. "Say, Betty, don't you think you and me would hit it off pretty well, speaking permanently?"

This flaunting language was wholly ludicrous to Connor. It was book-stuff.

David had obeyed him with childlike docility, and sat now like a pupil about to be corrected by the master.

"That point is this," explained Connor gravely. "You have the wrong idea. As far as I can make out, you like Ruth?"

"It is a weak word. Bah! It is not enough."

"But it's enough to tell her. You see, men outside of the Garden don't talk to a girl the way you do, and it embarrasses her to have you talk about her all the time."

"Is it true?" murmured the penitent David. "Then what should I have said?"

"Well—er—you might have said—that the flower went pretty well in her hair, and let it go at that."

"But it was more, more, more! Benjamin, my brother, these hands of mine picked that very flower. And I see that it has pleased her. She had taken it up and placed it in her hair. It changes her. My flower brings her close to me. It means that we have found a thing which pleases us both. Just as you and I, Benjamin, are drawn together by the love of one horse. So that flower in her hair is a great sign. I dwell upon it. It is like a golden moon rising in a black night. It lights my way to her. Words rush up from my heart, but cannot express what I mean!"

"Let it go! Let it go!" said Connor hastily, brushing his way through this outflow of verbiage, like a man bothered with gnats. "I gather what you mean. But the point is that about nine-tenths of what you think you'd better not say. If you want to talk—well, talk about yourself. That's what I most generally do with a girl. They like to hear a man say what he's done."

"Myself!" said David heavily. "Talk of a dead stump when there is a great tree beside it? Well, I see that I have much to learn."

"You certainly have," said Connor with much meaning. "I'd hate to turn you loose in Manhattan."

"In what?"

"Never mind. But here's another thing. You know that she'll have to leave pretty soon?"

The meaning slowly filtered into David's mind.

"Benjamin," he said slowly, "you are wise in many ways, with horses and with women, it seems. But that

152

is a fool's talk. Let me hear no more of it. Leave me? Why should she leave me?"

Triumph warmed the heart of Connor.

"Because a girl can't ramble off into the mountains and put up in a valley where there are nothing but men. It isn't done."

"Why not?"

"Isn't good form."

"I fail to understand."

"My dear fellow, she'd be compromised for life if it were known that she had lived with us."

David shook his head blankly.

"In one word," said Connor, striving to make his point, "she'd be pointed out by other women and by men. They'd never have anything to do with her. They'd say things that would make her ashamed, hurt her, you know."

Understanding and wrath gathered in David's face.

"To such a man—to such a dog of a man—I would talk with my hands!"

"I think you would," nodded Connor, not a little impressed. "But you might not be around to hear the talk."

"But women surely live with men. There are wives—"

"Ah! Man and wife—all very well!"

"Then it is simple. I marry her and then I keep her here forever."

"Perhaps. But will she marry you?"

"Why not?"

"Well, does she love you?"

"True." He stood up. "I'll ask her."

"For heaven's sake, no! Sit down! You mustn't rush at a woman like this the first day you know her. Give her time. Let me tell you when!"

"Benjamin, my dear brother, you are wise and I am a fool!"

"You'll do in time. Let me coach you, that's all, and you'll come on famously. I can tell you this: that I think she likes you very well already."

"Your words are like a shower of light, a fragrant wind. Benjamin, I am hot with happiness! When may I speak to her?"

"I don't know. She may have guessed something out of what you said to-night." He swallowed a smile. "You might speak to her about this marriage to-morrow."

153

"It will be hard; but I shall wait."

"And then you'll have to go out of the Garden with her to get married."

"Out of the Garden? Never! Why should we?"

"Why, you'll need a minister, you know, to marry you."

"True. Then I shall send for one."

"But he might not want to make this long journey for the sake of one marriage ceremony."

"There are ways, perhaps, of persuading him to come," said David, making a grim gesture.

"No force or you ruin everything."

"I shall be ruled by you, brother. It seems I have little knowledge."

"Go easy always and you'll come out all right. Give her plenty of time. A woman always needs a lot of time to make up her mind, and even then she's generally wrong."

"What do you mean by that?"

"No matter. She'll probably want to go back to her home for a while."

"Leave me?"

"Not necessarily. But you, when a man gets engaged, it's sometimes a couple of years between the time a woman promises to marry him and the day of the ceremony."

"Do they wait so long, and live apart?"

"A thousand miles, maybe."

"Then you men beyond the mountains are made of iron!"

"Do you have to be away from her? Why not go along with her when she goes home?"

"Surely, Benjamin, you know that a law forbids it!"

"You make your own laws in important things like this."

"It cannot be."

And so the matter rested when Connor left his host and went to bed. He had been careful not to press the point. So unbelievably much ground had been covered in the first few hours that he was dizzy with success. It seemed ages since that Ruth had come running to him in the patio in terror of her life. From that moment how much had been done!

Closing his eyes as he lay on his bed, he went back over each incident to see if a false step had been made. As far as he could see, there had not been a single unsound measure undertaken. The first stroke had been the masterpiece. Out of a danger which had threatened instant destruction of their plan she had won complete victory by her facing of David, and when she put her hand in his as a sign of weakness, Connor could see that she had made David her slave.

As the scene came back vividly before his eyes he could not resist an impulse to murmur aloud to the dark: "Brave girl!"

She had grown upon him marvelously in that single half-day. The ability to rise to a great situation was something which he admired above all things in man or woman. It was his own peculiar power—to judge a man or a horse in a glance, and dare to venture a fortune on chance. Indeed, it was hardly a wonder that David Eden or any other man should have fallen in love with her in that one half-day. She was changed beyond recognition from the pale girl who sat at the telegraph key in Lukin and listened to the babble of the world. Now she was out in that world, acting on the stage and proving herself worthy of a rôle.

He rehearsed her acts. And finally he found himself flushing hotly at the memory of her mingled pleasure and shame and embarrassment as David of Eden had poured out his amazing flow of compliments.

At this point Connor sat up suddenly and violently in his bed.

"Steady, Ben!" he cautioned himself. "Watch your step!"

CHAPTER TWENTY-SEVEN

BEN CONNOR awoke the next morning with the sun streaming across the room and sprang out of bed at once, worried. For about dawn noises as a rule began around the house and the singing of the old men farther down the hill. The Garden of Eden awakened at sunrise, and this silence even when the sun was high alarmed the gambler. He dressed hastily, and opening his door, he saw David walking slowly up and down the patio. At the sight of Connor he raised a warning finger.

"Let us keep a guard upon our voices," he murmured, coming to Connor. "I have ordered my servants to move softly and to keep from the house if they may."

"What's happened?"

"She sleeps, Benjamin." He turned toward her door with a smile that the gambler never forgot. "Let her waken rested."

Connor looked at the sky.

"I've come too late for breakfast, even?"

A glance of mild rebuke was turned upon him.

"Surely, Benjamin, we who are strong will not eat before her who is weak?"

"Are you going to starve yourself because she's sleepy?"

"But I have not felt hunger."

He added in a voice of wonder: "Listen!"

Ruth Manning was singing in her room, and Connor turned away to hide his frown. For he was not by any means sure whether the girl sang from the joy she found in this great adventure or because of David Eden. He was still further troubled when she came out to the breakfast table in the patio. He had expected that she would be more or less confused by the presence of David after his queer talk of the night before, but sleep seemed to have wiped everything from her memory. Her first nod, to be sure, was for the gambler, but her smile was for David of Eden. Connor fell into a reverie which was hardly broken through the meal by the deep voice of David or the laughter of Ruth. Their gayety was a barrier, and he was, subtly, left on the outside. David had proposed to the girl a ride through the Garden, and when he went for the horses the gambler decided to make sure of her position. He was too much disturbed to be diplomatic. He went straight to the point.

"I'm sorry this is such a mess for you; but if you can buck up for a while it won't take long to finish the job."

She looked at him without understanding, which was what he least wanted in the world. So he went on: "As a matter of fact, the worst of the job hasn't come. You can do what you want with him right now. But afterward—when you get him out of the valley the hard thing will be to hold him."

"You're angry with poor David. What's he done now?"

"Angry with him? Of course not! I'm a little disgusted, that's all."

"Tell me why in words of one syllable, Ben."

"You're too fine a sort to have understood. And I can't very well explain."

She allowed herself to be puzzled for a moment and then laughed.

"Please don't be mysterious. Tell me frankly."

"Very well. I think you can make David go out of the valley when we go. But once we have him back in a town the trouble will begin. You understand why he's so—fond of you, Ruth?"

"Let's not talk about it."

"Sorry to make you blush. But you see, it isn't because you're so pretty, Ruth, but simply because you're a woman. The first he's ever seen."

All her high coloring departed at once; a pale, sick face looked at Connor.

"Don't say it," murmured the girl. "I thought last night just for a moment—but I couldn't let myself think of it for an instant."

"I understand," said Connor gently. "You took all that highfaluting poetry stuff to be the same thing. But, say, Ruth, I've heard a young buck talk to a young squaw— before he married her. Just about the same line of junk, eh? What makes me sick is that when we get him out in a town he'll lose his head entirely when he sees a room full of girls. We'll simply have to plant a contract on him and —then let him go!"

"Do you think it's only that?" she said again, faintly.

"I leave it to you. Use your reason, and figure it out for yourself. I don't mean that you're in any danger. You know you're not as long as I'm around!"

She thanked him with a wan smile.

"But how can I let him come near me—now?"

"It's a mess. I'm sorry about it. But once the deal goes through I'll make this up to you if it takes me the rest of my life. You believe me?"

"I know you're true blue, Ben! And—I trust you."

He was a little disturbed to find that his pulse was decidedly quickened by that simple speech.

"Besides, I want to thank you for letting me know this. I understand everything about him now?"

In her heart of hearts she was hating David with all her might. For all night long, in her dreams, she had been seeing again the gestures of those strong brown hands, and the flash of his eyes, and hearing the deep tremor of his voice. The newness of this primitive man and his ways and words had been an intoxicant to her; because of his very difference she was a little afraid, and now the warning of Connor chimed in accurately with a premonition of her own. That adulation poured at the feet of Ruth Manning had been a beautiful and marvelous thing; but flung down simply in honor of her sex it became almost an insult. The memory made her shudder. The ideal lover whom she had prefigured in some of her waking dreams had always spoken with ardor—a holy ardor. From this passion of the body she recoiled.

Something of all this Connor read in her face and in her thoughtful silence, and he was profoundly contented. He had at once neutralized all of David's eloquence and fortified his own position. It was both a blow driven home and a counter. Not that he would admit a love for the girl; he had merely progressed as far as jealousy. He told himself that his only interest was in keeping her from an emotion which, once developed, might throw her entirely on the side of David and ruin their joint plans. He had refused to accompany the master of the Garden and the girl on their ride through the valley because, as he told himself, he "couldn't stand seeing another grown man make such an ass of himself" as David did when he was talking with the girl.

He contented himself now with watching her face when David came back to the patio, followed by Glani and the neat-stepping little mare, Tabari. The forced smile with which she met the big man was a personal triumph to the gambler.

"If you can win her under that handicap, David," he said softly to himself, "you deserve her, and everything else you can get."

David helped her into the saddle on Tabari, and himself sprang onto the pad upon Glani's back. They went out side by side.

It was a cool day for that season, and the moment the

158

north wind struck them David shouted softly and sent Glani at a rushing gallop straight into the teeth of the wind. Tabari followed at a pace which Ruth, expert horse-woman though she was, had never dreamed of. For the first time she had that impression of which Ben Connor had spoken to her of the horse pouring itself over the road without strain and without jar of smashing hoofs.

Ruth let Tabari extend herself, until the mare was racing with ears flat against her neck. She had even an impression that Glani, burdened by the great weight of David, was being left behind, but when she glanced to the side she saw that the master half a length back, was keeping a strong pull on the stallion, and Glani went smoothly, easily, with enormous strides, and fretting at the restraint.

She gained two things from that glance. The first was a sense of impatience because the stallion kept up so easily; in the second place, the same wind which drove the long hair of David straight back blew all suspicious thoughts out of her mind. She drew Tabari back to a hand gallop and then to a walk with her eyes dimmed by the wind of the ride and the blood tingling in her cheeks.

"It was like having wings," she cried happily as David let the stallion come up abreast.

"Tabari is sturdy, but she lacks speed," said the dispassionate master. "When she was a foal of six months and was brought to me for judgment. I thought twice, because her legs were short. However, it is well that she was allowed to live and breed."

"Allowed to live?" murmured Ruth Manning.

"To keep the line of the gray horse perfect," said David, "they must be watched with a jealous eye, and those which are weak must not live. The mares are killed and the stallions gelded are sold."

"And can you judge the little colts?"

Her voice was too low for David to catch a sense of pain and anger in it.

"It must be done. It is a duty. Today is the sixth month of Timeh, the daughter of Juri. You shall witness the judging. Elijah is the master."

His face hardened at the name of Elijah, and the girl caught her breath. But before she could speak they broke out of a grove and came in view of a wide meadow across

159

which four yoked cattle drew a harrow, smoothing the plow furrows to an even, black surface.

It carried the girl far back; it was like opening an ancient book of still more ancient tales; the musty smell completes the illusion. The cattle plodding slowly on, seeming to rest at every step, filled in the picture of which the primitive David Eden was the central figure.

"Yokes," she cried. "I've never seen them before!"

"For some work we use the horses, but the jerking of the harrow ruins their shoulders. Besides, we may need the cattle for a new journey."

"A journey? With those?"

"That was how the four came into the Garden. And I am enjoined to have the strong wagons always ready and the ox team always complete in case it becomes necessary to leave this valley and go elsewhere. Of course, that may never be."

CHAPTER TWENTY-EIGHT

HE brought Glani to a halt. They had left the sight of the meadow, though they could still hear the snorting of the oxen at their labor, a distant sound. Here, on one side of the road, the forest tumbled back from a swale of ground across which a tiny stream leaped and flashed with crooked speed, and the ground seemed littered with bright gold, so closely were the yellow wild flowers packed.

"Two days ago," said David, "they were only buds. See them now!"

He slipped from his horse and, stooping, rose again in a moment with his hands full of the yellow blossoms.

"They have a fragrance that makes them seem far away," he said. "See!"

He tossed the flowers at her; the wind caught them and spangled her hair and her clothes with them, and she breathed a rare perfume. David fell to clapping his hands and laughing like a child at the picture she made. She had never liked him so well as she did at this moment. She had never pitied him as she did now; she was not wise enough to shrink from that emotion.

"It was made for you—this place."

And before she could move to defend herself he had raised her strongly, lightly from the saddle, and placed her on the knoll in the thickest of the flowers. He stood back to view his work, nodding his satisfaction, and she, looking up at him, felt the old sense of helplessness sweep over her. Every now and then David Eden overwhelmed her like an inescapable destiny; there was something foredoomed about the valley and about him.

"I knew you would look like this," he was saying. "How do men make a jewel seem more beautiful? They set it in gold! And so with you, Ruth. Your hair against the gold is darker and richer and more like piles and coils of shadow. Your face against the gold is transparent white, with a bloom in it. Your hands are half lost in the softness of that gold. And to think that is a picture you can never see! But I forget."

His face grew dark.

"Here I have stumbled again, and yet I started with strong vows and resolves. My brother Benjamin warned me!"

It shocked her for a reason she could not analyze to hear the big man call Connor his brother. Connor, the gambler, the schemer! And here was David Eden with the green of the trees behind, his feet in the golden wild flowers, and the blue sky behind his head. Brother to Ben Connor?

"And how did he warn you?" she asked.

"That I must not talk to you of yourself, because, he said, it shames you. Is that true?"

"I suppose it is," she murmured. Yet she was a little indignant because Connor had presumed to interfere. She knew he could only have done it to save her from embarrassment, but she rebelled at the thought of Connor as her conversational guardian.

Put a guard over David of Eden, and what would he be? Just like a score of callow youths whom she had known, scattering foolish commonplaces, trying to make their dull eyes tell her flattering things which they had not brains enough to put into words.

"I am sorry," said David, sighing. "It is hard to stand here and see you, and not talk of what I see. When the sun rises the birds sing in the trees; when I see you words come up to my teeth."

He made a grimace. "Well, I'll shut them in. Have I been very wrong in my talk to you?"

"I think you haven't talked to many women," said Ruth. "And—most men do not talk as you do."

"Most men are fools," answered the egoist. "What I say to you is the truth, but if the truth offends you I shall talk of other things."

He threw himself on the ground sullenly. "Of what shall I talk?"

"Of nothing, perhaps. Listen!"

For the great quiet of the valley was falling on her, and the distances over which her eyes reached filled her with the delightful sense of silence. There were deep blue mountains piled against the paler sky; down the slope and through the trees the river was untarnished, solid, silver; in the boughs behind her the wind whispered and then stopped to listen likewise. There was a faint ache in her heart at the thought that she had not known such things all her life. She knew then what gave the face of David of Eden its solemnity. She leaned a little toward him. "Now tell me about yourself. What you have done."

"Of anything but that."

"Why not?"

"No more than I want you to tell me about yourself and what you have done. What you feel, what you think from time to time, I wish to know; I am very happy to know. I fit in those bits of you to the picture I have made."

Once more the egoist was talking!

"But to have you tell me of what you have done—that is not pleasant. I do not wish to know that you have talked to other men and smiled on them. I do not wish to know of a single happy day you spent before you came to the Garden of Eden. But I shall tell you of the four men who are my masters if you wish."

"Tell me of them if you will."

"Very well. John was the beginning. He died before I came. Of the others Matthew was my chief friend. He was very old and thin. His wrist was smaller than yours, almost. His hair was a white mist. In the evening there seemed to be a pale moonshine around his face.

"He was very small and old—so old that sometimes I thought he would dry up or dissolve and disappear. Toward the last, before God called him, Matthew grew weak, and his voice was faint, yet it was never sharp or shaken. Also, until the very end his eyes were young, for his heart was young.

"That was Matthew. He was like you. He liked the silence. 'Listen,' he would say. 'The great stillness is the voice; God is speaking.' Then he would raise one thin finger and we caught our breath and listened.

"Do you see him?"

"I see him, and I wish that I had known him."

"Of the others, Luke was taller than I. He had yellow hair as long and as coarse as the mane of a yellow horse. When he rode around the lake we could hear him coming for a great distance by his singing, for his voice was as strong as the neigh of Glani. I have only to close my eyes, and I can hear that singing of Luke from beside the lake. Ah, he was a huge man! The horses sweated under him.

"His beard was long; it came to the middle of his belly; it had a great blunt square end. Once I angered him. I crept to him when he slept—I was a small boy then—and I trimmed the beard down to a point.

"When Luke wakened he felt the beard and sat for a long time looking at me. I was so afraid that I grew numb, I remember. Then he went to the Room of Silence. When he came out his anger was gone, but he punished me. He took me to the lake and caught me by the heels and swung me around his head. When he loosened his fingers I shot into the air like a light stone. The water flashed under me, and when I struck the surface seemed solid. I thought it was death, for my senses went out, but Luke waded in and dragged me back to the shore. However, his beard remained pointed till he died."

He chuckled at the memory.

"Paul reproved Luke for what he had done. Paul was a big man, also, but he was short, and his bigness lay in his breadth. He had no hair, and he stood under Luke nodding so that the sun flashed back and forth on his bald head. He told Luke that I might have been killed.

" 'Better teach him sober manners now,' said Luke, 'than be a jester to knock at the gate of God.'

"This Paul was wonderfully silent. He was born unhappy and nothing could make him smile. He used to wander through the valley alone in the middle of winter, half dead with cold and eating nothing. In those times, even Luke was not strong enough to make him come home to us.

"I know that for ten days at one time he had gone without speech. For that reason he loved to have Joseph with him, because Joseph understood signs.

"But when silence left him, Paul was great in speech. Luke spoke in a loud voice and Matthew beautifully, but Paul was terrible. He would fall on his knees in an agony and pray to God for salvation for us and for himself. While he kneeled he seemed to grow in size. He filled the room. And his words were like whips. They made me think of all my sins. That is how I remember Paul, kneeling, with his long arms thrown over his head.

"Matthew died in the evening just as the moon rose. He was sitting beside me. He put his hand in mine. After a while I felt that the hand was cold, and when I looked at Matthew his head had fallen.

"Paul died in a drift of snow. We always knew that he had been on his knees praying when the storms struck him and he would not rise until he had finished the prayer.

"Luke bowed his head one day at the table and died without a sound—in spite of all his strength.

"All these men have not really died out of the valley. They are here, like mists; they are faces of thin air. Sometimes when I sit alone at my table, I can almost see a spirit-hand like that of Matthew rise with a shadow-glass of wine.

"But shall I tell you a strange thing? Since you came into the valley, these mist-images of my dead masters grow faint and thinner than ever."

"You will remember me, also, when I have gone?"

"Do not speak of it! But yes, if you should go, every spring, when these yellow flowers blossom, you would return to me and sit as you are sitting now. However you are young, yet there are ways. After Matthew died, for a long time I kept fresh flowers in his room and kept his memory fresh with them. But," he repeated, "you are young. Do not talk of death!"

"Not of death, but of leaving the Garden."

He stared gravely at her, and flushed.

"You are tormenting me as I used to torment my masters when I was a boy. But it is wrong to anger me. Besides I shall not let you go."

"Not *let* me go?"

"Am I a fool?" he asked hotly. "Why should I let you go?"

"You could not keep me."

It brought him to his feet with a start.

"What will free you?"

"Your own honor, David."

His head fell.

"It is true. Yes, it is true. But let us ride on. I no longer am pleased with this place. It is tarnished; there are unhappy thoughts here!"

"What a child he is!" thought the girl, as she climbed into the saddle again. "A selfish, terrible, wonderful child!"

It seemed, after that, that the purpose of David was to show the beauties of the Garden to her until she could not brook the thought of leaving. He told her what grew in each meadow and what could be reaped from it.

He told her what fish were caught in the river and the lake. He talked of the trees. He swung down from Glani, holding with hand and heel, and picked strange flowers and showed them to her.

"What a place for a house!" she said, when, near the north wall, they passed a hill that overlooked the entire length of the valley.

"I shall build you a house there," said David eagerly. "I shall build it of strong rock. Would that make you happy? Very tall, with great rooms."

An impish desire to mock him came to her.

"Do you know what I'm used to? It's a boarding house where I live in a little back bedroom, and they call us to meals with a bell."

The humor of this situation entirely failed to appeal to him.

"I also," he said, "have a bell. And it shall be used to call you to dinner, if you wish."

He was so grave that she did not dare to laugh. But for

some reason that moment of bantering brought the big fellow much closer to her than he had been before. And when she saw him so docile to her wishes, for all his strength and his mastery, the only thing that kept her from opening her heart to him, and despising the game which she and Connor were playing with him, was the warning of the gambler.

"I've heard a young buck talk to a young squaw—before he married her. The same line of junk!"

Connor must be right. He came from the great city.

But before that ride was over she was repeating that warning very much as Odysseus used the flower of Hermes against the arts of Circe. For the Garden of Eden, as they came back to the house after the circuit, seemed to her very much like a little kingdom, and the monarch thereof was inviting her in dumb-show to be the queen of the realm.

CHAPTER TWENTY-NINE

AT the house they were met by one of the servants who had been waiting for David to receive from the master definite orders concerning some woodchopping. For the trees of the garden were like children to David of Eden, and he allowed only the ones he himself designated to be cut for timber or fuel. He left the girl with manifest reluctance.

"For when I leave you of what do you think, and what do you do? I am like the blind."

She felt this speech was peculiar in character. Who but David of Eden could have been jealous of the very thoughts of another? And smiling at this, she went into the patio where Ben Connor was still lounging. Few things had ever been more gratifying to the gambler than the sight of the girl's complacent smile, for he knew that she was judging David.

"What happened?" he asked.

"Nothing worth repeating. But I think you're wrong, Ben. He isn't a barbarian. He's just a child."

"That's another word for the same thing. Ever see anything more brutal than a child? The wildest savage that ever stepped is a saint compared with a ten-year-old boy."

"Perhaps. He acts like ten years. When I mention leaving the valley he flies into a tantrum; he has taken me so much for granted that he has even picked out the site for my house."

"As if you'd ever stay in a place like this!"

He covered his touch of anxiety with loud laughter.

"I don't know," she was saying thoughtfully a moment later. "I like it—a lot."

"Anything seems pretty good after Lukin. But when your auto is buzzing down Broadway—"

She interrupted him with a quick little laugh of excitement.

"But do you really think I can make him leave the valley?"

"Of course I'm sure."

"He says there's a law against it."

"I tell you, Ruth, you're his law now; not whatever piffle is in that Room of Silence."

She looked earnestly at the closed door. Her silence had always bothered the gambler, and this one particularly annoyed him.

"Let's hear your thoughts?" he asked uneasily.

"It's just an idea of mine that inside that room we can find out everything we want to know about David Eden."

"What do we want to know?" growled Connor. "I know everything that's necessary. He's a nut with a gang of the best horses that ever stepped. I'm talking horse, not David Eden. If I have to make the fool rich, it isn't because I want to."

She returned no direct answer, but after a moment: "I wish I knew."

"What?"

She became profoundly serious.

"The point is that: he *may* be something more than a boy or a savage. And if he *is* something more, he's the finest man I've ever laid eyes on. That's why I want to get inside that room. That's why I want to learn the secret

—if there is a secret—the things he believes in, how he happens to be what he is and how—"

Connor had endured her rising warmth of expression as long as he could. Now he exploded.

"You do me one favor," he cried excitedly, more moved than she had ever seen him before. "Let me do your thinking for you when it comes to other men. You take my word about this David Eden. Bah! When I have you fixed up in little old Manhattan you'll forget about him and his mystery inside a week. Will you lay off on the thinking?"

She nodded absently. In reality she was struck by the first similarity she had ever noticed between David of Eden and Connor the gambler: within ten minutes they had both expressed remarkable concern as to what might be her innermost thoughts. She began to feel that Connor himself might have elements of the boy in his make up— the cruel boy which he protested was in David Eden.

She had many reasons for liking Connor. For one thing he had offered her an escape from her old imprisoned life. Again he had flattered her in the most insinuating manner by his complete trust. She knew that there was not one woman in ten thousand to whom he would have confided his great plan, and not one in a million whose ability to execute his scheme he would have trusted.

More than this, before her trip to the Garden he had given her a large sum of money for the purchase of the Indian's gelding; and Ruth Manning had learned to appreciate money. He had not asked for any receipt. His attitude had been such that she had not even been able to mention that subject.

Yet much as she liked Connor there were many things about him which jarred on her. There was a hardness, always working to the surface like rocks on a hard soil. Worst of all, sometimes she felt a degree of uncleanliness about his mind and its working. She would not have recoiled from these things had he been nearer her own age; but in a man well over thirty she felt that these were fixed characteristics.

He was in all respects the antipode of David of Eden. It was easier to be near Connor, but not so exciting. David wore her out, but he also was marvelously stimulating. The dynamic difference was that Connor sometimes inspired her with aversion, and David made her afraid. She was roused out of her brooding by the voice of the gambler saying: "When a woman begins to think, a man begins to swear."

She managed to smile, but these cheap little pat quotations which she had found amusing enough at first now began to grate on her through repetition. Just as Connor tagged and labeled his idea with his aphorism, so she felt that Connor himself was tagged by them. She found him considering her with some anxiety.

"You haven't begun to doubt me, Ruth?" he asked her.

And he put out his hand with a note of appeal. It was a new rôle for him and she at once disliked it. She shook the hand heartily.

"That's a foolish thing to say," she assured him. "But— why does that old man keep sneaking around us?"

It was Zacharias, who for some time had been prowling around the patio trying to find something to do which would justify his presence.

"Do you think David Eden keeps him here as a spy on us?"

This was too much for even Connor's suspicious mind, and he chuckled.

"They all want to hang around and have a look at you— that's the point," he answered. "Speak to him and you'll see him come running."

It needed not even speech; she smiled and nodded at Zacharias, and he came to her at once with a grin of pleasure wrinkling his ancient face. She invited him to sit down.

"I never see you resting," she said.

"David dislikes an idler," said Zacharias, who acknowledged her invitation by dropping his withered hands on the back of the chair, but made no move to sit down.

"But after all these years you have worked for him, I should think he would give you a little house of your own, and nothing to do except take care of yourself."

He listened to her happily, but it was evident from his pause that he had not gathered the meaning of her words.

"You come from the South?" he asked at length.

"My father came from Tennessee."

There was an electric change in the face of the Negro.

"Oh, Lawd, oh, Lawd!" he murmured, his voice changing and thickening a little toward the soft Southern accent. "That's music to old Zacharias!"

"Do you come from Tennessee, Zacharias?"

Again there was a pause as the thoughts of Zacharias fled back to the old days.

"Everything in between is all shadowy like evening, but what I remember most is the little houses on both sides of the road with the gardens behind them, and the babies rolling in the dust and shouting and their mammies coming to the doors to watch them."

"How long ago was that?" she asked, deeply touched.

He grew troubled.

"Many and many a year ago—oh, many a long, weary year, for Zacharias!"

"And you still think of the old days?"

"When the bees come droning in the middle of the day, sometimes I think of them."

He struck his hands lightly together and his misty-bright eyes were plainly looking through sixty years as though they were a day.

"But why did you leave?" asked Ruth tenderly.

Zacharias slowly drew his eyes away from the mists of the past and became aware of the girl's face once more.

"Because my soul was burning in sin. It was burning and burning!"

"But wouldn't you like to go back?"

The head of Zacharias fell and he knitted his fingers.

"Coming to the Garden of Eden was like coming into heaven. There's no way of getting out again without breaking the law. The Garden is just like heaven!"

Connor spoke for the first time.

"Or hell!" he exclaimed.

It caused Ruth Manning to cry out at him softly; Zacharias was mute.

"Why did you say that?" said the girl, growing angry.

"Because I hate to see a bad bargain," said the gambler.

"And it looks to me as if our friend here paid pretty high for anything he gets out of the Garden."

He turned sharply to Zacharias.

"How long have you been working here?"

"Sixty years. Long years!"

"And what have you out of it? What clothes?"

"Enough to wear."

"What food?"

"Enough to eat."

"A house of your own?"

"No."

"Land of your own?"

"No."

"Sixty years and not a penny saved! That's what I call a sharp bargain! What else have you gained?"

"A good bright hope of heaven."

"But are you sure, Zacharias? Are you sure? Isn't it possible that all these five masters of yours may have been mistaken?"

Zacharias could only stare in his horror. Finally he turned away and went silently across the patio.

"Ben," cried the girl softly, "why did you do it. Aside from torturing the poor man, what if this comes to David's ear?"

Connor snapped his finger. His manner was that of one who knows that he has taken a foolish risk and wishes to brazen the matter out.

"It'll never come to the ear of David! Why? Because he'd wring the neck of that old chap if he even guessed that he'd been talking about leaving the valley. And in the meantime I cut away the ground beneath David's feet. He has not standing room, pretty soon. Nothing left to him, by Jove, but his own conceit, and he has tons of that! Well, let him use it and get fat on it!"

She wondered why Connor had come to actually hate the master of the Garden. Sure David of Eden had never harmed the gambler. She remembered something that she had heard long before: that the hatred always lies on the side of injurer and not of the injured.

They heard David's voice, at this point, approaching, and in another moment a small cavalcade entered the patio.

CHAPTER THIRTY

FIRST, a white flash beneath the shadow of the arched way, came a colt at full run, stopping short with four sprawling, braced feet at the sight of the strangers. It was not fear so much as surprise, for now it pricked its ears and advanced a dainty step or two. Ruth cried out with delight at the fawn-like beauty of the delicate creature. The Eden Gray was almost white in the little colt, and with its four dark stockings it seemed, when it ran, to be stepping on thin air. That impression was helped by the comparatively great length of the legs.

Next came the mother, walking, as though she was quite confident that no harm could come to her colt in this home of all good things, but with her fine head held high and her eyes luminous with concern, a little anxious because the youngest had been out of sight for a moment.

And behind them strode David with Elijah at his side.

Ruth could never have recognized Elijah as the statuesque figure which had confronted David on the previous day. He was now bowing and scraping like some withered old man, striving to make a good impression on a creditor to whom a great sum was owing. She remembered then what David had told her earlier in the day about the judging of Timeh, the daughter of Juri. This, then, was the crisis, and here was Elijah striving to conciliate the grim judge. The old man kept up a running fire of talk while David walked slowly around the colt. Ruth wondered why the master of the Garden did not cry out with pleasure at sight of the beautiful creature. Connor had drawn her back a little.

"You see that six months' mare?" he said softly, with a tremor in his voice. "I'd pay ten thousand flat for her the way she stands. Ten thousand—more if it were asked!"

"But David doesn't seem very pleased."

172

"Bah! He's bursting with pleasure. But he won't let on because he doesn't want to flatter old Elijah."

"If he doesn't pass the colt do you know what happens?"

"What?"

"They kill it!"

"I'd a lot rather see them kill a man!" snarled Connor. "But they won't touch *that* colt!"

"I don't know. Look at poor Elijah!"

David, stopping in his circular walk, now stood with his arms folded, gazing intently at Timeh. Elijah was a picture of concern. The whites of his eyes flashed as his glances rolled swiftly from the colt to the master. Once or twice he tried to speak, but seemed too nervous to give voice.

At length: "A true daughter of Juri, O David. And was there ever a more honest mare than Juri? The same head, mark you, deep from the eye to angle of the jaw. And under the head—come hither, Timeh!"

Timeh flaunted her heels at the sun and then came with short, mincing steps.

"At six months," boasted Elijah, "she knows my voice as well as her mother. Stay, Juri!"

The inquisitive mare had followed Timeh, but now, reassured, she dropped her head and began cropping the turf of the patio. Still, from the play of her ears, it was evident that Timeh was not out of the mother's thoughts for an instant.

"Look you, David!" said Elijah. He raised the head of Timeh by putting his hand beneath her chin.

"I can put my whole hand between the angles of her jaw! And see how her ears flick back and forth, like the twitching ears of a cat! Ha, is not that a sign?"

He allowed the head to fall again, but he caught it under his arms and faced David in this manner, throwing out his hand in appeal. Still David spoke not a word.

With a gesture he made Elijah move to one side. Then he stepped to Timeh. She was uneasy at his coming, but under the first touch of his hand Timeh became as still as rock and looked at her mother in a scared and helpless fashion. It seemed that Juri understood a great crisis was at hand; for now she advanced resolutely and with her dainty muzzle she followed with sniffs the hand of David as it moved over the little colt. He seemed to be seeing with his fingertips alone, kneading under the skin in search of vital information. Along the muscles those dexterous fingers ran, and down about the heavy bones of the joints, where they lingered long, seeming to read a story in every crevice.

Never once did he speak, but Ruth felt that she could read words in the brightening, calm, and sudden shadows across his face.

Elijah accompanied the examination with a running-fire of comment.

"There is quality in those hoofs, for you! None of your gray-blue stuff like the hoofs of Tabari, say, but black as night and dense as rock. Aye, David, you may well let your hand linger down that neck. She will step freely, this Timeh of mine, and stride as far as a mountain-lion can leap! Withers high enough. That gives a place for the ligaments to take hold. A good long back, but not too long to carry a weight. She will not be one of your gaunt-bellied horses, either; she will have wind and a bottom for running. She will gallop on the third day of the journey as freely as on the first. And she will carry her tail well out, always, with that big, strong dock."

He paused a moment, for David was moving his hands over the hindlegs and lingering long at the hocks. And the face of Elijah grew convulsed with anxiety.

"Is there anything wrong with those legs?" murmured Ruth to Connor.

"Not a thing that I see. Maybe the stifles are too straight. I think they might angle out a bit more. But that's nothing serious. Besides, it may be the way Timeh is standing. What's the matter?"

She was clinging to his arm, white-faced.

"If that colt has to die I—I'll want to kill David Eden!"

"Hush, Ruth! And don't let him see your face!"

David moved back from Timeh and again folded his arms.

"The body of the horse is one thing," ran on Elijah uneasily, "and the spirit is another. Have you not told us, David, that a curious colt makes a wise horse? That is Timeh! Where will you guess that I found her when I went to bring her to you even now? She had climbed up the face of the cliff, far up a crevice where a man would not dare to go. I dared not even cry out to her for fear she would fall if she turned her head. To have climbed so high was almost impossible, but how would she come down when there was no room for her to turn?

"I was dizzy and sick with grief. But Timeh saw me, and down she came, without turning. She lifted her hoofs and put them down as a cat lifts and puts down wet paws. And in a moment she was safe on the meadow and frisking around me. Juri had been so worried that she made Timeh stop running and nosed her all over to make sure that she was unhurt by that climb. But tell me: will not a colt that risks its life to climb for a tuft of grass, run till its heart breaks for the master in later years?"

For the first time David spoke.

"Is she so wise a colt?" he said.

"Wise?" cried Elijah, his eye shining with joy at the opening which he had made. "I talk to her as I talk to a man. She is as full of tricks as a dog. Look, now!"

He leaned over and pretended to pick at the grass, whereat Timeh stole up behind him and drew out a handkerchief from his hip pocket. Off she raced and came back in a flashing circle to face Elijah with the cloth fluttering in her teeth.

"So!" cried Elijah, taking the handkerchief again and looking eagerly at the master of the Garden. "Was there ever a colt like my Timeh?"

"The back legs," said David slowly.

Elijah had been preparing himself to speak again, with a smile. He was arrested in the midst of a gesture and his face altered like a man at the banquet at the news of a death.

"The hind legs, David," he echoed hollowly. "But what of them? They are a small part of the whole! And they are not wrong. They are not very wrong, oh my master!"

"The hocks are sprung in and turned a little."

"A very little. Only the eye of David could see it and know that it is wrong!"

"A small flaw makes the stone break. At a rotten knothole the great tree snaps in the storm. And a small sin may undermine a good man. The hind legs are wrong, Elijah."

"To be sure. In a colt. Many things seem wrong in a colt, but in the grown horse they disappear!"

"This fault will not disappear. It is the set of the joint and that can never be changed. It can only grow worse."

Elijah, staring straight ahead, was searching his brain, but that brain was numbed by the calamity which had befallen him. He could only stroke the lovely head of the little colt and pray for help.

"Yesterday," he said at length in a trembling voice, "Elijah, as a fool, spoke words which angered his master. Back on my head I call them now. David, do not judge Timeh with a wrathful heart.

"Let the sins of Elijah fall on the head of Elijah, but let Timeh go unpunished for my faults."

"You grow old, Elijah, and you forget. The judgment of David is never colored by his own likes and dislikes, his own wishes and prejudice. He sees the right, and therefore his judgments are true."

"Aye, David, but truth is not merciful, and blessed above all things is mercy. When you see Timeh, think of Elijah. How he has watched over the colt, and loved it, and played with it, and taught it, by the hours, the proper manners for a colt and a mare of the Garden of Eden."

"That is true. It is a well-mannered colt."

Elijah caught at a new straw of hope.

"Also, in the field, if two colts race home for water and Timeh is one, she reaches the water first—always. She comes to me like a child. In the morning she slips out of the paddock, and coming to my window, she puts in her head and calls me with a whinny as soft as the voice of a man. Then I arise and go out to her and to Juri."

Ruth was weeping openly, her hand closed hard on the arm of Connor; and she felt the muscles along that arm contract. She almost loved the gambler for his rage at the inexorable David.

"Consider Juri, also," said Elijah. "Seven times—I numbered them on my fingers and remembered—seven times when the horses were brought before you in the morning, you have called to Juri and mounted her for the morning ride—that was before Glani was raised to his full strength. And always the master has said:

" 'Stout-hearted Juri! She pours out her strength for her rider as a generous host pours out his wine!' "

David frowned, but plainly he was touched.

"Juri!" he called, and when the noble mare came to him, he laid his hand on her mane.

"Who has spoken of Juri? Surely I am not judging her

this day. It was Matthew who judged her when she was a foal of six months."

"And it was Matthew," added Elijah hastily, "who loved her above all horses!"

"Ah!" muttered David, deeply moved.

"Consider the heart of Juri," went on Elijah, timidly following this new thread of argument. "When the mares neigh and the colts come running, there will be none to gallop to her side. When she goes out in the morning there will be no daughter to gallop around and around her, tossing her head and her heels. And when she comes home at night there will be no tired foal leaning against her side for weariness."

"Peace, Elijah! You speak against the law."

In spite of himself, the glance of Elijah turned slowly and sullenly until it rested upon Ruth Manning. David followed the direction of that look and he understood. There stood the living evidence that he had broken the law of the Garden at least once. He flushed darkly.

"The colt's gone," said Connor in a savagely-controlled murmur to the girl. "That devil has made up his mind. His pride is up now!"

Elijah, too, seemed to realize that he had thrown away his last chance.

He could only stretch out his hands with the tears streaming down his wrinkled face and repeat in his broken voice: "Mercy, David, mercy for Timeh and Juri and Elijah!"

But the face of David was iron.

"Look at Juri," he commanded. "She is flawless, strong, sound of hoof and heart and limb. And that is because her sire and her mother before her were well seen to. No narrow forehead has ever been allowed to come into the breed of the Eden Grays. I have heard Paul condemn a colt because the very ears were too long and flabby and the carriage of the horse dull. The weak and the faulty have been gelded and sent from the Garden or else killed. And therefore Juri to-day is stout and noble, and Glani has a spirit of fire. It is not easy to do. But if I find a sin in my own nature, do I not tear it out at a price of pain? And shall I spare a colt when I do not spare myself? A law is a law and a fault is a fault. Timeh must die!"

The extended arms of Elijah fell. Connor felt Ruth surge

forward from beside him, but he checked her strongly.

"No use!" he said. "You could change a very devil more easily than you can change David now! He's too proud to change his mind."

"Oh," sobbed the girl softly, "I hate him! I hate him!"

"Let Timeh live until the morning," said David in the same calm voice. "Let Juri be spared this night of grief and uneasiness. If it is done in the morning she will be less anxious until the dark comes, and by that time the edge of her sorrow shall be dulled."

"Whose hand," asked Elijah faintly—"whose hand must strike the blow?"

"Yesterday," said David, "you spoke to me a great deal of the laws of the Garden and their breaking. Do you not know that law which says that he from whose household the faulty mare foal has come must destroy it? You know that law. Then let it not be said that Elijah, who so loves the law, has shirked his lawful burden!"

At this final blow poor Elijah lifted his face.

"Lord God!" he said, "give me strength. It is more than I can bear!"

"Go!" commanded the master of the Garden.

Elijah turned slowly away. As if to show the way, Timeh galloped before him.

CHAPTER THIRTY-ONE

DAVID watched them go, and while his back was turned a fierce, soft dialogue passed between Ruth Manning and Ben Connor.

"Are you a man?" she asked him, through her set teeth. "Are you going to let that beautiful little thing die?"

"I'd rather see the cold-hearted fool die in place of Timeh. But what can we do? Nothing. Just smile in his face."

"I hate him!" she exclaimed.

"If you hate him, then use him. Will you?"

"If I can make him follow me, tease him to come, make him think I love him, I'll do it. I'd do anything to torture him."

"I told you he was a savage."

"You were right, Ben. A fiend—not a man! Oh, thank Heavens that I see through him."

Anger gave her color and banished her tears. And when David turned he found what seemed a picture of pleasure. It was infinitely grateful to him. If he had searched and studied for the words he could not have found anything to embitter her more than his first speech.

"And what do you think of the justice of David?" he asked, coming to them.

She could not speak; luckily Connor stepped in and filled the gap of awkward silence.

"A very fine thing to have done, Brother David," he said. "Do you know what I thought of when I heard you talk?"

"Of what?" said David, composing his face to receive the compliment. At that Ruth turned suddenly away, for she dared not trust her eyes, and the hatred which burned in them.

"I thought of the old story of Abraham and Isaac. You were offering up something as dear to you as a child, almost, to the law of the Garden of Eden."

"It is true," said David complacently. "But when the flesh is diseased it must be burned away."

He called to Ruth: "And you, Ruth?"

This childish seeking after compliments made her smile, and naturally he misjudged the smile.

"I think with Benjamin," she said softly.

"Yet my ways in the Garden must seem strange to you," went on David, expanding in the warmth of his own sense of virtue. "But you will grow accustomed to them, I know."

The opening was patent. She was beginning to nod her acquiescence when Connor, in alarm, tapped on the table, once and again in swift telegraphy: "No! No!"

The faint smile went out on her face.

"No," she said to David.

The master of the Garden turned a glance of impatience and suspicion upon the gambler, but Connor carefully made his face a blank. He continued to drum idly on the edge of the table, and the idle drumming was spelling to the girl's quick ear: "Out!"

"You cannot stay?" murmured David.

She drank in his stunned expression. It was like music to her.

"Would you," she said, "be happy away from the Garden, and the horses and your servants? No more am I happy away from my home."

"You are not happy with us?" muttered David. "You are not happy?"

"Could you be away from the Garden?"

"But that is different. The Garden was made by four wise men."

"By five wise men," said the girl. "For you are the fifth."

He was so blind that he did not perceive the irony.

"And therefore," he said, "the Garden is all that the heart should desire. John and Matthew and Luke and Paul made it to fill that purpose."

"But how do you know they succeeded? You have not seen the world beyond the mountains."

"It is full of deceit, hard hearts, cruelty, and cunning."

"It is full of my dear friends, David!"

She thought of the colt and the mare and Elijah; and it became suddenly easy to lure to deceive this implacable judge of others. She touched the arm of the master lightly with her finger tips and smiled.

"Come with me, and see my world!"

"The law which the four made for me—I must not leave!"

"Was it wrong to let me enter?"

"You have made me happy," he argued slowly. "You have made me happier than I was before. And surely I could not have been made happy by that which is wrong. No, it was right to bring you into the valley. The moment I looked at you I knew that it was right."

"Then, will it be wrong to go out with me? You need not stay! But see what lies beyond the mountains before you judge it!"

He shook his head.

"Are you afraid? It will not harm you."

He flushed at that. And then began to walk up and down across the patio. She saw Connor white with anxiety, but about Connor and his affairs she had little concern at this moment. She felt only a cruel pleasure in her control over this man, half savage and half child. Now he stopped abruptly before her.

"If the world, after I see it, still displeases me, when I return, will you come with me, Ruth? Will you come back to the Garden of Eden?"

In the distance Ben Connor was gesturing desperately to make her say yes. But she could not resist a pause—a pause in which torment showed on the face of David. And then, deliberately, she made her eyes soften—made her lips smile.

"Yes, David, I will come back!"

He leaned a little toward her, then straightened with a shudder and crossed the patio to the Room of Silence. Behind that door he disappeared, and left Connor and the girl alone. The gambler threw down his arms as if abandoning a burden.

"Why in the name of God did you let him leave you?" he groaned. "Why? Why? Why?"

"He's going to come," asserted Ruth.

"Never in a thousand years. The fool will talk to his dummy god in yonder and come out with one of his iced looks and talk about 'judgment'! Bah!"

"He'll come."

"What makes you think so?"

"Because—I know."

"You should have waited—to-morrow you could have done it, maybe, but to-day is too soon."

"Listen to me, Ben. I know him. I know his childish, greedy mind. He wants me just as much as he wants his own way. It's partly because I'm new to him, being a woman. It's chiefly because I'm the first thing he's ever met that won't do what he wants. He's going to try to stay with me until he bends me." She flushed with angry excitement.

"It's playing with fire, Ruth. I know you're clever, but—"

"You don't know how clever, but I'm beginning to guess what I can do. I've lost all feeling about that cruel barbarian, Ben. That poor little harmless, pretty colt—oh, I want to make David Eden burn for that! And I can do it. I'm going to wind him around my finger. I've thought of ways while I stood looking at him just now. I know how I can smile at him, and use my eyes, and woo him on, and pretend to be just about to yield and come back with him—then grow cold the next minute and give him his work to do over again. I'm going to make him crawl on his knees in the dust. I'm going to make a fool of him before people. I'm going to make his sign over his horses to us to keep them out of his vicious power. And I can do it—I hate him so that I know I can make him really love me. Oh, I know he doesn't really love me now. I know you're right about him. He simply wants me as he'd want another horse. I'll change him. I'll break him. When he's broken I'm going to laugh in his face—and tell him—to remember Timeh!"

"Ruth!" gasped Connor.

He looked guiltily around, and when he was sure no one was within reach of her voice, he glanced back with admiration.

"By the Lord, Ruth, who'd ever have guessed at all this fire in you? Why, you're a wonder. And I think you can do it. If you can only get him out of the infernal Garden. That's the sticking point! We make or break in the next ten minutes!"

But he had hardly finished speaking before David of Eden came out of the Room of Silence, and with the first glance at his face they knew that the victory was theirs. David of Eden would come with them into the world!

"I have heard the Voice," he said, "and it is just and proper for me to go. In the morning, Ruth, we shall start!"

CHAPTER THIRTY-TWO

NIGHT came as a blessing to Ruth, for the scenes of the early day had exhausted her. At the very moment when David succumbed to her domination, her own strength began to fail. As for Connor, it was another story. The great dream which had come to him in far away Lukin, when he watched the little gray gelding win the horse race, was now verging toward a reality. The concrete accomplishment was at hand. Once in the world it was easy to see that David would become clay, molded by the touch of clever Ruth Manning, and then—it would be simply a matter of collecting the millions as they rolled in.

But Ruth was tired. Only one thing sustained her, and that was the burning eagerness to humble this proud and selfish David of Eden. When she thought how many times she had been on the verge of open admiration and sympathy with the man, she trembled and grew cold. But through the fate of poor little Timeh, she thanked Heaven that her eyes had been opened.

She went to her room shortly after dinner, and she slept heavily until the first grayness of the morning. Once awake, in spite of the early hour, she could not sleep again, so she dressed and went into the patio. Connor was already there, pacing restlessly. He had been up all night, he told her, turning over possibilities.

"It seems as though everything has worked out too much according to schedule," he said. "There'll be a break. Something will happen and smash everything!"

"Nothing will happen," she assured him calmly.

He took her hand in his hot fingers.

"Partner"—he began, and then stopped as though he feared to let himself go on.

"Where is he?" she asked.

"On his mountain, waiting for the sun, I guess. He told the servants a while ago that he was leaving to-day. Great excitement. They're all chattering about it down in the servants' house."

"Is no one here?"

"Not a soul, I guess."

"Then—we're going into that Room of Silence!"

"Take that chance now? Never in the world! Why, Ruth, if he saw us in there, or guessed we'd been there, he'd probably murder us both. You know how gentle he is when he gets well started?"

"But how will he know? No one is here, and David won't be back from the mountain for a long time if he waits for the sun."

"Just stop thinking about it, Ruth."

"I'll never stop as long as I live, unless I see it. I've dreamed steadily about that room all night."

"Go alone, then, and I'll stay here."

She went resolutely across the patio, and Connor, following with an exclamation, caught her arm roughly at the door.

"You aren't serious?"

"Deadly serious!"

The glitter of her dark eyes convinced him more than words.

"Then we'll go together. But make it short!"

They swept the patio with conscience-stricken glances, and then opened the door. As they did so, the ugly face of Joseph appeared at the entrance to the patio, looked and hastily was withdrawn.

"This is like a woman," muttered Connor, as they closed the door with guilty softness behind them. "Risk her life for a secret that isn't worth a tinker's damn!"

For the room was almost empty, and what was in it was the simplest of the simple. There was a roughly made table in the center. Five chairs stood about it. On the table was a book, and the seven articles made up the entire furnishings. Connor was surprised to see tears in the eyes of Ruth.

"Don't you see?" she murmured in reply to his exclamation. "The four chairs for the four dead men when David sits in his own place?"

"Well, what of that?"

"What's in the book?"

"Are you going to wait to see that"

"Open the door a little, Ben, and then we can hear if any one comes near."

He obeyed and came back, grumbling. "We can hear every one except David. That step of his wouldn't break eggs."

He found the girl already poring over the first page of the old book, on which there was writing in a delicate hand.

She read aloud. "The story of the Garden of Eden, who made it and why it was made. Told without error by Matthew."

"Hot stuff!" chuckled Connor. "We got a little time

184

before the sun comes up. But it's getting red in the east. Let's hear some more."

There was nothing imposing about the book. It was a ledger with a half-leather binding such as storekeepers use for accounts. Time had yellowed the edges of the paper and the ink was dulled. She read:

"In the beginning there was a man whose name was John."

"Sounds like the start of the Bible," grinned Connor. "Shoot ahead and let's get at the real dope."

"Hush!"

Without raising her eyes, she brushed aside the hand of Connor which had fallen on the side of the ledger. Her own took its place, ready to turn the page.

"In the beginning there was a man whose name was John. The Lord looked upon John and saw his sins. He struck John therefor. First He took two daughters from John, but still the man was blind and did not read the writing of his Maker. And God struck down the eldest son of John, and John sorrowed, but did not understand. Thereat, all in a day, the Lord took from John his wife and his lands and his goods, which were many and rich.

"Then John looked about him, and lo! he was alone.

"In the streets his friends forgot him and saw not his passing. The sound of his own football was lonely in his house, and he was left alone with his sins.

"So he knew that it was the hand of God which struck him, and he heard a voice which said in the night to him: 'O John, ye who have been too much with the world must leave it and go into the wilderness.

"Then the heart of John smote him and he prayed God to send him not out alone, and God relented and told him to go forth and take with him three simple men.

"So John on the next morning called to his Negro, a slave who was all that remained in his hands.

" 'Abraham,' he said, 'you who were a slave are free.'

"Then he went into the road and walked all the day until his feet bled. He rested by the side of the road and one came who kneeled before him and washed his feet, and John saw that it was Abraham. And Abraham said: 'I was born into your service and I can only die out of it.'

"They went on together until they came to three robbers

fighting with one strong man, and John helped this man and drove away the robbers.

"Then the tall man began to laugh. 'They would have robbed me because I was once rich,' he said, 'but another thief had already plundered me, and they have gotten only broken heads for their industry.' Then John was sorry for the fortune that was stolen.

"'Not I,' said the tall man, 'but I am sorry for the brother I lost with the money.' Then he told them how his own brother had cheated him. 'But,' he said, 'there is only one way to beat the devil, and that is to laugh at him.'

"Now John saw this was a good man, so he opened his heart to Luke, which was the name of him who had been robbed. Then Luke fell in with the two and went on with them.

"They came to a city filled with plague so that the dead were buried by the dying and the dog howled over his master in the street; the son fled from the father and the mother left her child. They found one man who tended the sick out of charity and the labor was too great for even his broad shoulders. He had a broad, ugly face, but in his eye was a clear fire.

"'Brother, what is your name?' said John, and the man answered that he was called Paul, and begged them for the sweet mercy of Christ to aid him in his labors.

"But John said: 'Rise, Paul, and follow me.'

"And Paul said: 'How can I follow the living when the dying call to me?'

"But John said: 'Nevertheless, leave them, for these are carrion, but your soul in which is life eternal is worth all these and far more.'

"Then Paul felt the power of John and followed him and took, also, his gray horses which were unlike others, and of his servants those who would follow him for love, and in wagons he put much wealth.

"So they all rode on as a mighty caravan until they came, at the side of the road, to a youth lying in the meadow with his hands behind his head whistling, and a bird hovering above him repeated the same note. They spoke to him and he told them that he was an outcast because he would not labor.

"'The world is too pleasant to work in,' he said, and whistled again, and the bird above him made answer.

"Then John said: 'Here is a soul worth all of ours. Rise, brother, and come with us.'

"So Matthew rose and followed him, and he was the third and last man to join John, who was the beginning.

"Then they came to a valley set about with walls and with a pleasant river running through it, and here they entered and called it the Garden of Eden because in it men should be pure of heart once more. And they built their houses with labor and lived in quiet and the horses multiplied and the Garden blossomed under their hands."

Here Ruth marked her place with her finger while she wiped her eyes.

"Do you mean to say this babble is getting you?" growled Ben Connor.

"Please!" she whispered. "Don't you see that it's beautiful?"

And she returned to the book.

CHAPTER THIRTY-THREE

"THEN John sickened and said: 'Bring me into the room of silence.' So they brought him to the place where they sat each day to converse with God in the holy stillness and hear His voice.

"Then John said: 'I am about to depart from among you, and before my going I put this command on you that you find in the world a male infant too young to know its father or mother, or without father and mother living. Rear that child to manhood in the valley, for even as I depart so will you all do, and the Garden of Eden will be left tenantless.'

"So when John was dead Matthew went forth and found a male child and brought him to the valley and the two said: 'Where was the child found and what is its name?' And Matthew said: 'It was found in the place to which God led me and its name hereafter shall be David.'

"So peace was on the valley, and David grew tall and

strong. Then Luke died, and Paul died in a drift of snow and Matthew grew very old and wrote these words for the eye of David."

The smooth running, finely made letters come to an end, the narrative was taken up in fresher ink and in a bold, heavy hand of large characters.

"One day Matthew called for David and said: 'My hands are cold, whereby I know I am about to die. As I lay last night with death for a bedfellow thoughts came to me, which are these: We have been brother and father and son to one another. But do not grieve that I am gone. I inherit a place of peace, but you shall come to torment unless you find a woman in the world and bring her here to bear children to you and be your wife.'

"Then David groaned in his heart and he said: 'How shall I know her when I find her?'

"And Matthew said: 'By her simplicity.'

"And David said: 'There may be many who are simple.'

"And Matthew said: 'I have never known such a woman. But when you see her your heart will rise up and claim her. Therefore, within five years, before you are grown too old, go out and find this woman and wed her.'

"And on that day Matthew died, and a great anguish came to David. The days passed heavily. And for five years he has waited."

There was another interval of blank paper, and then the pen had been taken up anew, hurriedly, and driven with such force and haste that it tore the paper-surface.

"The woman is here!"

Her fingers stiffened about the edges of the book. Raising her head, she looked out through the little window and saw the tree tops down the hillside brightening against the red of the dawn. But Connor could not see her face. He only noted the place at which she had stopped, and now he began to laugh.

"Can you beat that? That poor dub!"

She turned to him, slowly, a face so full of mute anguish that the gambler stopped his laughter to gape at her. Was she taking this seriously? Was this the Bluebeard's chamber which was to ruin all his work

Not that he perceived what was going on in her mind, but her expression made him aware, all at once, of the morning-quiet. Far down the valley a horse neighed and a bird swooping past the window cast in on them one thrilling phrase of music. And Connor saw the girl change under his very eye. She was looking straight at him without seeing his face and into whatever distance her glance went he felt that he could not follow her. Here at the very threshold of success the old ledger was proving a more dangerous enemy than David himself. Connor fumbled for words, the Open Sesame which would let in the common sense of the everyday world upon the girl. But the very fear of that crisis kept him dumb. He glanced from the pale hand on the ledger to her face, and it seemed to him that beauty had fallen upon her out of the book.

"The woman is here! God has sent her!"

At that she cried out faintly, her voice trembling with self-scorn: "God has sent me—me!"

"The heart of David stood up and beat in his throat when he saw her," went on the rough, strong writing. "She passed the gate. Every step she took was into the soul of David. As I went beside her the trees grew taller and the sky was more blue.

"She has passed the gate. She is here. She is mine!

"What am I that she should be mine? God has sent her to show me that my strength is clumsy. I have no words to fit her. When I look into her eyes I see her soul; my vision leaps from star to star, a great distance, and I am filled with humility. O Father in Heaven, having led her to my hand, teach me to give her happiness, to pour her spirit full of content."

She closed the book reverently and pressed her hands against her face. He heard her murmuring: "What have I done? God forgive me!"

Connor grew angry. It was no time for trifling.

He touched her arm: "Come on out of this, Ruth. If you're going to get religion, try it later."

At that she flung away and faced him, and what he saw was a revelation of angry scorn.

"Don't touch me," she stammered at him. "You cheat! Is that the barbarian you were telling me about? Is that the cruel, selfish fool you tried to make me think was David of Eden?"

His own weapons were turning against him, but he retained his self-control.

"I won't listen to you, Ruth. It's this hush-stuff that's

got you. It's this infernal room. It makes you feel that the fathead has actually got the dope from God."

"How do you know that God hasn't come to him here? At least, he's had the courage and the faith to believe it. What faith have we? I know your heaven, Ben Connor. It's paved with dollar bills. And mine, too. We've come sneaking in here like cowardly thieves. Oh, I hate myself, I loathe myself. I've stolen his heart, and what have I to give him in exchange? I'm not even worthy to love him! Barbarian? He's so far greater and finer than we are that we aren't worthy to look in his face!"

"By the Lord!" groaned Connor. "Are you double-crossing me?"

"Could I do anything better? Who tempted me like a devil and brought me here? Who taught me to play the miserable game with David? You, you, you!"

Perspiration was streaming down the white face of Connor.

"Try to give me a chance and listen one minute, Ruth. But for God's sake don't fly off the handle and smash everything when we're next door to winning. Maybe I've done wrong. I don't see how. I've tried to give this David a chance to be happy the way any other man would want to be happy. Now you turn on me because he's written some high-flying chatter in a book!"

"Because I thought he was a selfish sham, and now I see that he's real. He's humbled himself to me—to me! I'm not worthy to touch his feet! And you—"

"Maybe I'm rotten. I don't say I'm all I should be, but half of what I've done has been for you. The minute I saw you at the key in Lukin I knew I wanted you. I've gone on wanting you ever since. It's the first time in my life—but I love you, Ruth. Give me one more chance. Put this thing through and I'll turn over the rest of my life to fixing you up so's you'll be happy."

She watched him for a moment incredulously; then she broke into hysterical laughter.

"If you loved me could you have made me do what I've done? Love? You? But I know what real love is. It's written into that book. I've heard him talk. I'm full of his voice, of his face.

"It's the only fine thing about me. For the rest, we're

shams, both of us—cheats—crooked—small, sneaking cheats!"

She stopped with a cry of alarm; the door behind her stood open and in the entrance was David of Eden. In the background was the ugly, grinning face of Joseph. This was his revenge.

Connor made one desperate effort to smile, but the effort failed wretchedly. Neither of them could look at David; they could only steal glances at one another and see their guilt.

"David, my brother—" began the gambler heavily.

But the voice of the master broke in: "Oh, Abraham, Abraham, would to God that I had listened!"

He stood to one side, and made a sweeping gesture.

"Come out, and bring the woman."

They shrank past him and stood blinking in the light of the newly risen sun. Joseph was hugging himself with the cold and his mute delight. The master closed the door and faced them again.

"Even in the Room of Silence!" he said slowly. "Was it not enough to bring sin into the Garden? But you have carried it even into the holy place!"

Connor found his tongue. The fallen head of Ruth told him that there was no help to be looked for from her, and the crisis forced him into a certain boisterous glibness of speech.

"Sin, Brother David? What sin? To be sure, Ruth was too curious. She went into the Room of Silence, but as soon as I knew she was there I went to fetch her, when—"

He had even cast out one arm in a gesture of easy persuasion, and now it was caught at the wrist in a grip that burned through the flesh to the bones. Another hand clutched his coat at the throat. He was lifted and flung back against the wall by a strength like that of a madman, or a wild animal. One convulsive effort showed him his helplessness, and he cried out more in horror than fear. Another cry answered him, and Ruth strove to press in between, tearing futilely at the arms of David.

A moment later Connor was miraculously freed. He found David a long pace away and Ruth before him, her arms flung out to give him shelter while she faced the master of the garden.

"He is saved," said David, "and you are free. Your love

has ransomed him. What price has he paid to win you so that you will even risk death for him?"

"Oh, David," sobbed the girl, "don't you see I only came between you to keep you from murder? Because he isn't worth it!"

But the master of the Garden was laughing in a way that made Connor look about for a weapon and shrink because he found none; only the greedy eyes of Joseph, close by. David had come again close to the girl; he even took both her hands in one of his and slipped his arm about her. To Connor his self-control now seemed more terrible than one outbreak of murdering passion.

"Still lies?" said David. "Still lies to me? Beautiful Ruth —never more beautiful than now, even when you lied to me with your eyes and your smiles and your promises! The man is nothing. He came like a snake to me, and his life is worth no more than the life of a snake. Let him live, let him die; it is no matter. But you, Ruth! I am not even angered. I see you already from a great distance, a beautiful, evil thing that has been so close to me. For you have been closer to me than you are now that my arm is around you, touching you for the last time, holding your warmth and your tender body, keeping both your hands, which are smaller and softer than the hands of a child. But mighty hands, nevertheless.

"They have held the heart of David, and they have almost thrown his soul into eternal hellfire. Yet you have been closer to me than you are now. You have been in my heart of hearts. And I take you from it sadly—with regret, for the sin of loving you has been sweet."

She had been sobbing softly all this time, but now she mastered herself long enough to draw back a little, taking his hands with a desperate eagerness, as though they gave her a hold upon his mind.

"Give me one minute to speak out what I have to say. Will you give me one half minute, David?"

His glance rose past her, higher, until it was fixed on the east, and as he stood there with his head far back Connor guessed for the first time at the struggle which was going on within him. The girl pressed closer to him, drawing his hands down as though she would make him stoop to her.

"Look at me, David!"

"I see your face clearly."

"Still, look at me for the one last time."

"I dare not, Ruth!"

"But will you believe me?"

"I shall try. But I am glad to hear your voice, for the last time."

"I've come to you like a cheat, David, and I've tried to win you in order to steal the horses away, but I've stayed long enough to see the truth.

"If everything in the valley were offered me—the horses and the men—and everything outside of the valley, without you, I'd throw them away. I don't want them. Oh, if prayers could make you believe, you'd believe me now; because I'm praying to you, David.

"You love me, David. I can feel you trembling, and I love you more than I ever dreamed it was possible to love. Let me come back to you. I don't want the world or anything that's in it. I only want you. David—I only want you! Will you believe me?

And Connor saw David of Eden sway with the violence of his struggle.

But he murmured at length, as one in wonder:

"How you are rooted in me, Ruth! How you are wound. into my life, so that it is like tearing out my heart to part from you. But the God of the Garden and John and Matthew has given me strength." He stepped back from her.

"You are free to go, but if you return the doom against you is death like that of any wild beast that steals down the cliffs to kill in my fields. Begone, and let me see your face no more. Joseph, take them to the gate."

And he turned him back with a slowness which made his resolution the more unmistakable.

CHAPTER THIRTY-FOUR

IT was, unquestionably, a tempting of Providence, but Connor was almost past caring. Far off he heard the neighing of an Eden Gray; Ruth, with her bowed head and face covered in her hands, was before him, sobbing; and all that he had come so near to winning and yet had lost rushed upon the mind of the gambler. He hardly cared now whether he lived or died. He called to the master of the Garden, and David whirled on him with the livid face. Connor walked into the reach of the lion.

"I've made my play," he said through his teeth, "and I don't holler because I've lost the big stakes. Now I'm going to give you something to show that I'm not a piker—some free advice, Dave!"

"O man of many lies," said David. "Peace! For when I hear you there is a great will come on me to take you by the throat and hear your life go out with a rattle."

"A minute ago," said Connor coolly enough, "I was scared, and I admit it, but I'm past that stage. I've lost too much to care, and now you're going to hear me out to the last damned word!"

"God of Paul and Matthew," said David, his voice broken with rage, "let temptation be far from me!"

"You can take it standing or sitting," said Connor, "and be damned to you!"

The blind fury sent David a long step nearer, but he checked himself even as one hand rose toward Connor.

"It is the will of God that you live to be punished hereafter."

"No matter about the future. I'm chattering in the present. I'm going to come clean, not because I'm afraid of you, but because I'm going to clear up the girl. Abraham had the cold dope, well enough. I came to crook you out of a horse, Dave, my boy, and I did it. But after I'd got away with the goods I tried to play hog, and I came back for the rest of the horses."

He paused; but David showed no emotion.

"You take the punishment very well," admitted Connor. "There's a touch of sporting blood in you, but the trouble is that the good in you has never had a fair chance to come to the top. I came back, and I brought Ruth with me.

"I'll tell you about her. She's meant to be an honest-to-God woman—the kind that keeps men clean—she's meant for the big-time stuff. And where did I find her? In a jay town punching a telegraph key. It was all wrong.

"She was made to spend a hundred thousand a year.

194

Everything that money buys means a lot to her. I saw that right away. I like her. I did more than like her. I loved her. That makes you flinch under the whip, does it? I don't say I'm worthy of her, but I'm as near to her as you are.

"I admit I played a rotten part. I went to this girl, all starved the way she was for the velvet touch. I laid my proposition before her. She was to come up here and bamboozle you. She was to knock your eyes out and get you clear of the valley with the horses. Then I was going to run those horses on the tracks and make a barrel of coin for all of us.

"You'd think she'd take on a scheme like that right away; but she didn't. She fought to keep from going crooked until I showed her it was as much to your advantage as it was to ours. Then she decided to come, and she came. I worked my stall and she worked hers, and she got into the valley.

"But this voice of yours in the Room of Silence—why didn't it put you wise to my game? Well, David, I'll tell you why. The voice is the bunk. It's your own thoughts. It's your own hunches. The god you've been worshiping up here is yourself, and in the end you're going to pay hell for doing it.

"Well, here's the girl in the Garden, and everything going smooth. We have you, and she's about to take you out and show you how to be happy in the world. But then she has to go into your secret room. That's the woman of it. You blame her? Why, you infernal blockhead, you've been making love to her like God almighty speaking out of a cloud of fire! How could she hear your line of chatter without wanting to find out the secrets that made you the nut you are?

"Well, we went in, and we found out. We found out what? Enough to make the girl see that you're 'noble,' as she calls it. Enough to make me see that you're a simp. You've been chasing bubbles all your life. You're all wrong from the first.

"Those first four birds who started the Garden, who were they? There was John, a rich fellow who'd hit the high spots, had his life messed up, and was ready to quit. He'd lived enough. Then there was Luke, a gent who'd been double-crossed and was sore at the world on general principles.

"Paul would have been a full-sized saint in the old days. He was never meant to live the way other men have to live. And finally there's a guy who lies in the grass and whistles to a bird—Matthew. A poet—and all poets are nuts.

"Well, all those fellows were tired of the world—fed up with it. Boil them down, and they come to this: they thought more about the welfare of their souls than they did about the world. Was that square? It wasn't! They left the mothers and fathers, the brothers and sisters, the friends, everything that had brought them into the world and raised 'em. They go off to take care of themselves.

"That wasn't bad enough for 'em—they had to go out and pluck you and bring you up with the same rotten hunches. Davie, my boy, d'you think a man is made to live by himself?

"You haven't got fed up with the world; you're no retired high liver; you haven't had a chance to get double-crossed more than once; you're not a crazy poet; and you're a hell of a long ways from being a martyr.

"I'll tell you what you are. You're a certain number of pounds of husky muscle and bone going to waste up here in the mountains. You've been alone so much that you've got to thinking that your own hunches come from God, and that'd spoil any man.

"Live alone? Bah! You've had more happiness since Ruth came into this valley than you've ever had before or you'll ever have again.

"Right now you're breaking your heart to take her in your arms and tell her to stop crying, but your pride won't let you.

"You tried to make yourself a mystery with your room of silence and all that bunk. But no woman can stand a mystery. They all got to read their husband's letters. You try to bluff her with a lot of fancy words and partly scare her. It's fear that sent the four men up here in the first place—fear of the world.

"And they've lived by fear. They scared a lot of poor unfortunate men into coming with them for the sake of their souls, they said. And they kept them here the same way. And they've kept you here by telling you that you'd be damned if you went over the mountains.

"And you still keep them here the same way. Do you think they stay because they love you? Give them a chance and see if they won't pack up and beat it for their old homes.

"Now, show me that you're a man and not a fatheaded bluff. Be a man and admit that what you call the Voice is just your pride. Be a man and take that girl in your arms and tell her you love her. I've made a mess of things; I've ruined her life, and I want to see you give her a chance to be happy.

"Because she's not the kind to love more than one man if she lives to be a thousand. Now, David Eden, step out and give yourself a chance!"

It had been a gallant last stand on the part of Connor. But he was beaten before he finished, and he knew it.

"Are you done?" said David.

"I'm through, fast enough. It's up to you!"

"Joseph, take the man and this woman out of the Garden of Eden."

The last thing that Connor ever saw of David Eden was his back as he closed the door of the Room of Silence upon himself. The gambler went to Ruth. She was dry-eyed by this time, and there was a peculiar blankness in her expression that went to his heart.

Secretly he had hoped that his harangue to David would also be a harangue to the girl and make her see through the master of the Garden; but that hope disappeared at once.

He stayed a little behind her when they were conducted out of the patio by the grinning Joseph. He helped her gently to her horse, the old gray gelding, and when he was in place on his own horse, with the mule pack behind him, they started for the gate.

She had not spoken since they started. At the gate she moved as if to turn and look back, but controlled the impulse and bowed her head once more. Joseph came beside the gambler and stretched out his great palm. In the center of it was the little ivory ape's head which had brought Connor his entrance into the valley and had won the hatred of the big Negro, and had, eventually, ruined all his plans.

"It was given freely," grinned Joseph, "and it is freely returned."

"Very well."

Connor took it and hurled it out of sight along the

197

boulders beyond the gate. The last thing that he saw of the Garden of Eden and its men was that broad grin of Joseph, and then he hurried his horse to overtake Ruth, whose gelding had been plodding steadily along the ravine.

He attempted for the first time to speak to her.

"Only a quitter tries to make up for the harm he's done by apologizing. But I've got to tell you the one thing in my life I most regret. It isn't tricking David of Eden, but it's doing what I've done to you. Will you believe me when I say that I'd give a lot to undo what I've done?"

She only raised her hand to check him and ventured a faint smile of reassurance. It was the smile that hurt Connor to the quick.

They left the ravine. They toiled slowly up the difficult trail, and even when they had reached such an altitude that the floor of the valley of the Garden was unrolling behind them the girl never once moved to look back.

"So," thought Connor," she'll go through the rest of her life with her head down, watching the ground in front of her. And this is my work."

He was not a sentimentalist, but a lump was forming in his throat when, at the very crest of the mountain, the girl turned suddenly in her saddle and stopped the gray.

"Only makes it worse to stay here," muttered Connor. "Come on, Ruth."

But she seemed not to hear him, and there was something in her smile that kept him from speaking again.

CHAPTER THIRTY-FIVE

THE Room of silence had become to David Eden a chamber of horror. The four chairs around him, which had hitherto seemed filled with the ghosts of the four first masters of the Garden, were now empty to his imagination. In this place where he had so often found unfailing consolation, unfailing counsel, he was now burdened by the squat, heavy walls, and the low ceiling. It was like a prison to him.

For all his certainty was gone. "You've made yourself your God," the gambler had said. "Fear made the Garden of Eden, fear keeps the men in it. Do you think the others stay for love of you?"

Benjamin had proved a sinner, no doubt, but there had been a ring of conviction in his words that remained in the mind of David. How could he tell that the man was not right? Certainly, now that he had once doubted the wisdom of that silent Voice, the mystery was gone. The room was empty; the holiness had departed from the Garden of Eden with the departing of Ruth.

He found himself avoiding the thought of her, for whenever her image rose before him it was torture.

He dared not even inquire into the depression which weighed down his spirits, for he knew that the loss of the girl was the secret of it all.

One thing at least was certain: the strong, calming voice which he had so often heard in the Room of Silence, no longer dwelt there, and with that in mind he rose and went into the patio.

In a corner, screened by a climbing vine, hung a large bell which had only been rung four times in the history of the Garden of Eden, and each time it was for the death of the master. David tore the green away and struck the bell. The brazen voice crowded the patio and pealed far away, and presently the men came. They came in wild-eyed haste, and when they saw David alive before them they stared at him as if at a ghost.

"As it was in the beginning," said David when the circle had been formed and hushed, "death follows sin. Sin has come into the Garden of Eden and the voice of God has died out of it. Therefore the thing for which you have lived here so long is gone. If for love of David, you wish to stay, remain; but if your hearts go back to your old homes, return to them. The wagons and the oxen are yours. All the furnishings of the houses are yours. There is also a large store of money in my chest which Elijah shall divide justly among you. And on your journey Elijah shall lead you, if you go forth, for he is a just man and fit to lead others. Do not answer now, but return to your house and speak to one another. Afterward, send one man.

If you stay in the Garden he shall tell me. If you depart I shall bid you farewell through him. Begone!"

They went out soft-footed, as though the master of the Garden had turned into an animal liable to spring on them from behind.

He began to pace up and down the patio, after a time, rather impatiently. No doubt the foolish old men were holding forth at great length. They were appointing the spokesman, and they were framing the speech which he would make to David telling of their devotion to him, whether the spirit was gone or remained. They would remain; and Benjamin's prophecy had been that of a spiteful fool. Yet even if they stayed, how empty the valley would be—how hollow of all pleasure!

It was at this point in his thoughts that he heard a sound of singing down the hillside from the house of the servants —first a single, thin, trembling voice to which others were added until the song was heartened and grew full and strong. It was a song which David had never heard before. It rang and swung with a peculiarly happy rhythm, growing shriller as the old men seemed to gather their enthusiasm. The words, sung in a thick dialect, were stranger to David than the tune, but as nearly as he could make out the song ran as follows:

"Oh, Jo, come back from the cold and the stars
For the cows they has come to the pasture bars,
And the little game chicken's beginning to crow:
Come back to us, Jo; come back to us, Jo!

"He was walkin' in the gyarden in the cool o' the day
When He seen my baby Jo in the clover blossoms play.

"He was walkin' in the gyarden an' the dew was on His feet
When He seen my baby Jo so little an' sweet.

"They was flowers in the gyarden, roses, an' such,
But the roses an' the pansies, they didn't count for much.

"An' He left the clover blossoms fo' the bees the next day
An' the roses an' the pansies, but He took Jo away.

"Oh, Jo, come back from the cold and the stars

For the cows they has come to the pasture bars,
And the little game chicken has started to crow:
Come back to us, Jo; come back to us, Jo!"

He knew their voices and he knew their songs, but never
had David heard his servants sing as they sang this song.
Their hymns were strong and pleasant to the ear, but in
this old tune there was a melody and a lilt that brought a
lump in his throat. And there was a heart to their singing,
so that he almost saw them swaying their shoulders to
the melody.

It was the writing on the wall for David.

Out of that song he built a picture for their old lives,
the hot sunshine, the dust, and all the things which Matthew had told him of the slaves and their ways before the
time of the making of the Garden.

He waited, then, either for their messenger or for
another song; but he neither saw the one nor heard the
other for a considerable time. An angry pride sustained
him in the meantime, in the face of a life alone in the
Garden. Far off, he heard the neigh of the grays in the
meadow near the gate, and then the clarion clear answer
of Glani near the house. He was grateful for that sound.
All men, it seemed, were traitors to him. Let them go.
He would remain contented with the Eden Grays. They
would come and go with him like human companions.
Better the noble head of Glani near him than the treacher-
ous cunning of Benjamin! He accepted his fate, then, not
with calm resignation, but with fierce anger against Connor, who had brought this ruin on him, and against the
men who were preparing to desert him.

He could hear plainly the creaking of the great wains
as the oxen were yoked to them and they were dragged
into position to receive the burdens of the property they
were to take with them into the outer world. And, in the
meantime, he paced through the patio in one of those
silent passions which eat at the heart of a man.

He was not aware of the entrance of Elijah. When he
saw him, Elijah had fallen on his knees near the entrance
to the patio, and every line of his time-dried body expressed the terror of the bearer of bad tidings. David
looked at him for a moment in silent rage.

"Do you think, Elijah," he said at last, "that I shall be

so grieved to know that you and the others will leave me and the Garden of Eden? No, no! For I shall be happier alone. Therefore, speak and be done!"

"Timeh—" began the old man faintly.

"You have done that last duty, then, Elijah? Timeh is no longer alive?"

"The day is still new, David. Twice I went to Timeh, but each time when I was about to lead her away, the neighing of Juri troubled me and my heart failed."

"But the third time you remembered my order?"

"But the third time—there was no third time. When the bell sounded we gathered. Even the watchers by the gates—Jacob and Isaac—came and the gate was left unguarded—Timeh was in the pasture near the gate with Juri—and—"

"They are gone! They have passed through the gate! Call Zacharias and Joseph. Let them mount and follow and bring Juri back with the foal!"

"Oh, David, my master—"

"What is it now, Elijah, old stammerer? Of all my servants none has cost me so much pain; to none shall I say farewell with so little regret. What is it now? Why do you not rise and call them as I bid you? Do you think you are free before you pass the gates?"

"David, there are no horses to follow Juri!"

"What!"

"The God of John and Paul give me strength to tell and give you strength to hear me in patience! When you had spoken, and the servants went back to speak of the strange things you had said, some of them spoke of the old days before they heard the call and followed to the Garden, and then a song was raised beginning with Zacharias—"

"Zacharias!" echoed David softly and fiercely. "Him whom I have favored above the others!"

"But while the others sang, I heard a neighing near the gate and I remembered your order and your judgment of Timeh, and I went sorrowfully to fulfill your will. But near the gate I saw the meadow empty of the horses, and while I stood wondering, I heard a chorus of neighing beyond the gate. There was a great answer just behind me, and I turned and saw Glani racing at full speed. I called to him, but he did not hear and went on, straight through the pillars of the gate, and disappeared in the ravine beyond. Then I ran to the gate and looked out, but the horses were gone from sight—they have left the Garden—they are free—"

"And happy!" said David in a terrible voice. "They, too, have only been held by fear and never by love. Let them go. Let all go which is kept here by fear. Why should I care? I am enough by myself. When all is gone and I am alone the Voice shall return and be my companion. It is well. Let every living thing depart. David is enough unto himself. Go, Elijah! And yet pause before you go!"

He went into his room and came out bearing the heavy chest of money, which he carried to the gate.

"Go to your brothers and bid them come for the money. It will make them rich enough in the world beyond the mountains, but to me there is need of no money. Silence and peace is my wish. Go, and let me hear their voices no more, let me not see one face. Ingrates, fools, and traitors! Let them find their old places; I have no regret. Begone!"

And Elijah, as one under the shadow of a raised whip, skulked from the patio and was gone.

CHAPTER THIRTY-SIX

THE last quiet began for David. He had heard the sounds of departure. He had heard the rumble of the oxwains begin and go slowly toward the gate with never the sound of a human voice, and he pictured, with a grim satisfaction, the downcast faces and the frightened, guilty glances, as his servants fled, conscious that they were betraying their master. It filled him with a sort of sulky content which was more painful than sorrow. But before the sound of the wagons died out the wind blew back from the gate of the Garden a thin, joyous chorus of singing voices. They were leaving him with songs!

He was incredulous for a time. He felt, first, a great regret that he had let them go. Then, in an overwhelming wave of righteousness, he determined to dismiss them from his mind. They were gone; but worse still, the horses were gone, and the valley around him was empty! He remembered the dying prophecy of Abraham, now, as the stern Elijah had repeated it. He had let the world into the Garden, and the tide of the world's life, receding, would take all the life of the Garden away beyond the mountains among other men.

The feeling that Connor had been right beset him: that the four first masters had been wrong, and that they had raised David in error. Yet his pride still upheld him.

That day he went resolutely about the routine. He was not hungry, but when the time came he went into the big kitchen and prepared food. It was a place of much noise. The great copper kettles chimed and murmured whenever he touched them, and they spoke to him of the servants who were gone. Half of his bitterness had already left him and he could remember those days in his childhood when Abraham had told him tales, and Zacharias had taught him how to ride at the price of many a tumble from the lofty back of the gentle old mare. Yet he set the food on the table in the patio and ate it with steady resolution. Then he returned to the big kitchen and cleansed the dishes.

It was the late afternoon, now, the time when the sunlight becomes yellow and loses its heat, and the heavy blue shadow sloped across the patio. A quiet time. Now and again he found that he was tense with waiting for sounds in the wind of the servants returning for the night from the fields, and the shrill whinny of the colts coming back from the pastures to the paddocks. But he remembered what had happened and made himself relax.

There was a great dread before him. Finally he realized that it was the coming of the night, and he went into the Room of Silence for the last time to find consolation. The book of Matthew had always been a means of bringing the consolation and counsel of the Voice, but when he opened the book he could only think of the girl, as she must have leaned above it. How had she read? With a smile of mockery or with tears? He closed the book; but still she was with him. It seemed that when he turned in the chair he must find her waiting behind him and he found himself growing tense with expectation, his heart beating rapidly.

Out of the Room of Silence he fled as if a curse lived in it, and without following any conscious direction, he went to the room of Ruth.

The fragrance had left the wild flowers, and the great golden blossoms at the window hung thin and limp, the bell lips hanging close together, the color faded to a dim yellow. The green things must be taken away before they molded. He raised his hand to tear down the transplanted vine, but his fingers fell away from it. To remove it was to destroy the last trace of her. She had seen these flowers; on account of them she had smiled at him with tears of happiness in her eyes. The skin of the mountain lion on the floor was still rumpled where her foot had fallen, and he could see the indistinct outline where the heel of her shoe had pressed.

He avoided that place when he stepped back, and turning, he saw her bed. The dappled deerskin lay crumpled back where her hand had tossed it as she rose that morning, and in the blankets was the distinct outline of her body. He knew where her body had pressed, and there was the hollow made by her head in the pillow.

Something snapped in the heart of David. The sustaining pride which had kept his head high all day slipped from him like the strength of the runner when he crosses the mark. David fell upon his knees and buried his face where her head had lain, and his arms curved as though around her body. Connor had been right. He had made himself his god, and this was the punishment. The mildness of a new humility came to him in the agony of his grief. He found that he could pray, not the proud prayers of the old days when David talked as an equal to the voice, but that most ancient prayer of sinners:

"O Lord, I believe. Help Thou mine unbelief!"

And the moment the whisper had passed his lips there was a blessed relief from pain. There was a sound at the window, and turning to it, he saw the head and the arched neck of Glani against the red of the sunset—Glani looking at him with pricked ears. He went to the stallion, incredulous, with steps as short as a child which is afraid, and at his coming Glani whinnied softly. At that the last of David's pride fell from him. He cast his arms around the neck of the stallion and wept with deep sobs that tore his throat, and under the grip of his arms he felt the stallion trembling. He was calmer, at length, and he climbed through the window and stood beside Glani under the brilliant sunset sky.

"And the others, O Glani," he said. "Have they returned likewise? Timeh shall live. I, who have judged others so often, have been myself judged and found wanting. Timeh shall live. What am I that I should speak of the life or the death of so much as the last bird in the trees? But have they all returned, all my horses"

He whistled that call which every gray knew as a rallying sound, a call that would bring them at a dead gallop with answering neighs. But when the thin sound of the whistle died out there was no reply. Only Glani had moved away and was looking back to David as if he bid the master follow.

"Is it so, Glani?" said the master. "They have not come back, but you have returned to lead me to them? The woman, the man, the servants, and the horses. But we shall leave the valley, walking together. Let the horses go, and the man and the woman and the servants; but we shall go forth together and find the world beyond the mountains."

And with his hand tangled in the mane of the stallion, he walked down the road, away from the hill, the house, the lake. He would not look back, for the house on the hill seemed to him a tomb, the monument of the four dead men who had made this little kingdom.

By the time he reached the gate the Garden of Eden was awash with the shadows of the evening, but the higher mountaintops before him were still rosy with the sunset. He paused at the gate and looked out on them, and when he turned to Glani again, he saw a figure crouched against the base of the rock wall. It was Ruth, weeping, her head fallen into her hands with weariness. Above her stood Glani, his head turned to the master in almost human inquiry. The deep cry of David wakened her. The gentle hands of David raised her to her feet.

"You have not come to drive me away again?"

"To drive you from the Garden? Look back. It is black. It is full of death, and the world and our life is before us. I have been a king in the Garden. It is better to be a man among men. All the Garden was mine. Now my hands are

206

empty. I bring you nothing, Ruth. Is it enough? Ah, my dear, you are weeping!"

"With happiness. My heart is breaking with happiness, David."

He tipped up her face and held it between his hands. Whatever he saw in the darkness that was gathering it was enough to make him sigh. Then he raised her to the back of Glani, and the stallion, which had never borne a weight except that of David, stood like a stone. So David went up the valley holding the hand of Ruth and looking up to her with laughter in his eyes, and she, with one hand pressed against her breast, laughed back to him, and the great stallion went with his head turned to watch them.

"How wonderful are the ways of God!" said David. "Through a thief he has taught me wisdom; through a horse he has taught me faith; and you, oh, my love, are the key with which he has unlocked my heart!"

And they began to climb the mountain.